AF093430

A DAY FOR DEAD SAINTS

RYAN KIRK

OLIVERHEBERBOOKS

All rights reserved.

No part of this publication may be sold, copied, distributed, reproduced or transmitted in any form or by any means, mechanical or digital, including photocopying and recording or by any information storage and retrieval system without the prior written permission of both the publisher, Oliver Heber Books and the author, Ryan Kirk, except in the case of brief quotations embodied in critical articles and reviews.

NO AI TRAINING: Without in any way limiting the author's [and publisher's] exclusive rights under copyright, any use of this publication to "train" generative artificial intelligence (AI) technologies and/or large language models to generate text, or any other medium, is expressly prohibited. The author reserves all rights to license uses of this work for the training and development of any generative AI and/or large language models.

PUBLISHER'S NOTE: This is a work of fiction. Names, characters, places, and incidents either are the product of the author's imagination or are used fictitiously. Any resemblance to actual persons, living or dead, business establishments, events, or locales is entirely coincidental.

A Day for Dead Saints Copyright 2026 © Ryan Kirk

Cover design by JV Arts

Published by Oliver-Heber Books

0 9 8 7 6 5 4 3 2 1

CHAPTER 1
REUNION

My prayer for you, young ones, is that you'll never have to wipe the blood of vengeance from your hands.

—FROM *THE LOST WISDOM OF BRENNOR*

Veynar thought about murder as he swept his broom lightly across the stone walkway leading to the halgard.

High Keeper Maeryn's warning echoed in his thoughts. *Slow down! You're not racing anyone, so there's no need to murder the creatures who learned to call this place home in our absence.*

He brushed aside an anthill built between two stones and watched the ants scurry to safety as their home was destroyed. With a gentle hand on the broom, he swept them into the long grass bordering the walkway. Two ants tried to return, searching for a home they'd lost for good, and again he brushed them away.

Maeryn always spoke with clarity and purpose. If she said

"murder," it was with the intent to pass along a teaching, but what lesson was he supposed to take from her word choice?

Murder carried with it the stench of dishonor, of dark deeds done out of sight. Why use it to describe the death of ants and spiders if he swept too vigorously?

No matter how long he considered the matter, he found no answer.

The sound of fabric brushing against itself brought his gaze up in time to see an acorn speeding straight for his nose. His hand, quick as a snake's tongue as it tasted the air, snatched the acorn before it struck true.

An exaggerated groan came from behind a nearby silver maple. "I didn't think you'd react in time."

A tall young man stepped from behind the tree and swept curly black hair away from his eyes. Long legs closed the distance between them in a few unhurried steps. Dark loose-fitting robes hung off Malric's lanky frame, concealing enough sharpened steel to arm a small garrison.

"The Keepers still demand we complete our physical training. I haven't gone that soft," Veynar said.

"Care to spar sometime and prove it?"

His friend was nothing if not consistent. In a clan of hunters, warriors, and trackers, the Keepers stood apart. They carried the clan's history, knowledge, and traditions, the candle of wisdom burning bright against the ever-encroaching dark. Malric recognized the need for the Keepers, but he wished loudly and often that his friend carried steel more often than paper.

Malric stepped onto the section of the stone path Veynar had just finished sweeping. A spider scurried in front of him. He squished it with his toe, then wiped his boot clean against the stone, leaving a smear of dead spider.

"You know full well he's not allowed to spar until his

apprenticeship is complete," came a third voice, whose owner followed the path of the walkway as she approached.

Coriselle had braided her long hair in an intricate pattern, her appearance revealing her plans for the day. She wore a set of vivid blue robes that she'd only worn once before, at her older sister's wedding. Her gentle gaze settled on Veynar, and she smiled, warming him to the core. He returned the smile as heat rushed to his cheeks.

"I still can't believe that my closest friend, the man I'd have by my side no matter the danger, chose the white robes." Malric put the back of his hand to his forehead and pretended to swoon like some woman from the cities. "My heart is shattered into a thousand pieces."

Cori's eyes rolled up in her head. She told Veynar, "I was surprised to hear you elected to remain at the halgard. Most everyone is visiting Brenwick today to catch the beginning of the Harvest Festival."

It wasn't that he didn't want to go. The Harvest Festival was an annual tradition for Caelen's Clan, a time when they handed off their duties at the border of the Broken Lands to other clans and journeyed west to Brenwick. It was the only time of the year where they could truly be at ease. They feasted and met with old friends, and when they returned to the border, it was laden with the fruits of the harvest. Ever since he'd been a child, the Harvest Festival had been the best time of the year.

Veynar fumbled for an explanation, but Malric saved him from having to answer. He threw his arm over Cori's shoulder. She shrugged it off immediately, but it didn't make Veynar want to hit Malric any less. The glint in Malric's eyes told Veynar his old friend was well aware of the effects of his actions. With a sardonic grin, he said, "Cori and I are joining a group heading in today. Want us to visit your sister for you?"

Cori elbowed Malric in the side. "Ignore him. We came to invite you, too, if you're interested."

Veynar gripped his broom tighter. "I appreciate the offer, but I'll stay here. I'll join you some other day."

Cori tilted her head, as though a slightly different perspective would shed some light on her friend's refusal. She studied him for a moment, then shrugged. She reached into her robes and pulled out a sealed letter. "This came for you in today's mail from Brenwick."

Veynar took the letter, recognizing Lirael's handwriting at a glance. He wouldn't have thought it possible, but her time in the House of Brennor had improved her already beautiful calligraphy. He tucked it into his white robes without opening it. "Thank you."

"You're sure you don't want to join us?" Malric asked. "I promise a day of entertainment you're not likely to forget. I've already made some new friends in town."

Veynar grinned. Malric could be as abrasive as a whetstone, but a day in his company was never without excitement. "Hearing that only makes me want to stay well away. Cori, you're a braver person than I am."

She laughed. "I'm sure Malric will be on his best behavior."

Malric's grin revealed Cori's hope to be empty, but she knew well enough what trouble she courted by accompanying him into Brenwick for a day. It was her choice to make, though Veynar wished she would stay behind and go for a walk with him after his chores were done.

After a long farewell, the two left Veynar alone with his broom. The moment they disappeared from sight, he reached into his pocket and pulled out the letter from his sister. He broke the seal and devoured the words within like a starving man set before a feast.

Autumn leaves crunched beneath Veynar's feet as he hurried through the forest between Brenwick and Caelen's Rest. Had the ground not been coated with the vivid reds and oranges of fallen maple leaves he would have tried to silence his steps, but only a wandering spirit could have slipped between the trees without a sound, and so he gave up on his hope of surprising his sister.

He was also late.

His right hand reached into the pocket of his robes, and his fingertips brushed against the note tucked within, reassuring him that this was real and not a dream. When she'd left, she'd promised to hold him in her thoughts, to keep the memory of their family close.

He hoped her time in the House of Brennor hadn't made her change her mind.

Almost ten months had passed since Veynar had heard from Lirael, and ten remained before he would have expected to. That she'd risked reaching out to him was evidence enough of —something—though he couldn't guess what. If trouble, she would have reached out to their parents instead of him. More likely, she was lonely, desperate for a familiar face after being surrounded by strangers who shared little in common with a former Keeper.

His left hand brushed against the treasure held in the other pocket, a collection of candies he'd quickly run to the outskirts of Brenwick to buy with what little money he possessed. Sisters in training weren't allowed sweets, which had made Lirael's decision to join them that much more surprising. If her time in the House of Brennor had doused the fire in her spirit, the candies would help rekindle it.

The House of Brennor was, in many ways, a mirrored reflection of Caelen's Keepers, though one that looked beyond the obvious differences. The House of Brennor kept the lore and wisdom of its god, just as the Keepers did. Only they served on a scale Caelen's handful of Keepers could only imagine. In the legends of Brennor, he'd been a builder whose masterwork was the foundations of the city of Brenwick. The House he built had attracted scholars and their books from across the land, making it a destination for all who sought to dive deep into the mysteries of the world, including his sister.

The Sisters who inherited the wisdom of the House did more than just study, though. They were active in the administration of the city, from the Head Sister who sat at the side of the King to the apprentices lending their services to neighborhoods in need. The Sisters and the city sometimes felt as though they were one and the same.

Veynar reached their tree before the sun fell below the tall spires of the Brenwick's castles and looked up. Lirael's slight frame wasn't among the branches. It was unlike her to be late for anything, but he couldn't guess what obstacles she'd had to overcome to escape the Sisters' clutches. His family believed he was still at the halgard and wouldn't suspect he'd left for a bit, and so he leaned back against the tree and waited.

Their tree was a wide, old maple whose leaves turned a vibrant red as the season's first frosts approached. They'd chosen it as children because its limbs had always been spaced in such a way that they could run up the trunk, grab its lowest-hanging limbs, then climb to the highest reaches of the tree. In those days, hours had passed like minutes, and each had found a favorite perch that suited them well. Veynar had lost track of the number of sunsets he'd watched from its upper boughs. The clan didn't spend much time at Caelen's Rest, but every time they visited, Veynar and Lirael had returned to the tree.

He hadn't been here since Lirael had left. They'd spent their last evening together at the tree, a tradition they hadn't completed as often as they'd gotten older and assumed more responsibilities within the clan. That sunset had been bittersweet, and Veynar had sensed it would be among the last times they climbed the maple's limbs together. With each passing year, they surrendered a bit more of their childhood to the unceasing demands of adulthood.

After Lirael had left, there'd been no point in returning to the tree. It had been theirs, not his. He'd embarked upon his first Watch, and now he apprenticed under the Keepers.

He reached into his pocket and ran the edge of his thumb around Lirael's note. The calligraphy inside had been neat but hurried, and he wondered again what had caused her to break the isolation of her training to reach out to him.

The soft crunch of leaves on the other side of the tree almost made him jump out of his boots. It was too loud to be one of the chipmunks in the area, but he could have sworn he was alone. He leaned over and looked around the tree. Someone was sitting there, legs sticking straight out.

"Lirael?" he asked as he pushed off the tree and stepped around it.

His older sister sat on the other side of the maple, her back propped up in a hollow between two roots that snaked deep into the soil. She stared ahead, unblinking.

Blood bubbled from her throat. Her eyes shifted slowly, rising to the sky, the first sign that she was still alive.

The sight froze Veynar faster than a mid-winter blizzard.

Her lips parted, but no sound came out, and Veynar's shock shattered like ice struck by a pickaxe. He dropped to his knees and reached for his sister, but he couldn't convince himself to touch her, a deep and irrational part of his spirit warning him that if he did, this would be real and there'd be no returning to the life he'd once known.

He tried to ask what had happened, but the words tripped over one another as they left his lips, and all that escaped was an incomprehensible, blubbering mess.

Her eyes completed their long journey, resting on his face. Her lips moved again, but all he heard was the pounding of his heart. The wound on her neck, thin as a sheet of paper and wide as his thumb, bubbled once more, then stilled. Her eyes were open, but the light had fled.

"Lirael, no!"

He grabbed her shoulders and shook. Her head bobbed limply and fell forward, almost striking him in the nose. He yelped and pushed her away, toward their tree. Her back struck the gnarled bark hard, and for a moment, he feared she would tip forward, but she remained upright.

Veynar scrambled back until he was a few feet away. Leaves crunched and snapped beneath him.

"Lirael?"

As if he called to her, she would come back from whatever halls her spirit had entered, as if death could be reversed with a word alone.

The trembling started in his arms and spread through his gut and down his legs. He clutched his knees tight to his chest, but he couldn't stop the tremors. His teeth chattered.

He had to let the wardens know. Quickly, so they could search the area for clues and hunt down the killer. Only he trembled too much to stand, too much to even call for help, though he was deep enough in the woods it was unlikely any would hear him.

Veynar released his legs and tried to stand. They betrayed him and gave out, sending him face first into the dried leaves surrounding the maple.

Exhaustion ambushed him. He wanted nothing more in the

world than to sleep, to dream this all away. His eyes started to close.

No.

The wardens. He needed to reach the wardens and tell them what had happened.

Summoning all the strength in his body, he pushed himself carefully to his feet, willing his legs to support him. A single step tired him to the point of surrender, his foot landing as heavy as an anvil. The crunch of leaves rang in his ears, and he covered them with his hands to dull the sound.

His eyes closed against his will, but he took another halting step forward.

He could take no more.

His body toppled forward. He waited for the pain of impact, but someone caught him in strong arms and lowered him to the ground like a parent putting an infant down to sleep.

His last thought before darkness took him was that he hadn't heard the crunch of leaves.

CHAPTER 2
OF GRIEF AND MADNESS

Mourn not for those whose spirits no longer dance among you, children, for those that have served me well dine by my side forevermore.

— FROM *THE BOOK OF BRENNOR*

Veynar woke from an endless nightmare. He sat straight up and twisted to take in his unfamiliar surroundings. Four bare walls gave him little clue where he'd woken up. His eyes landed on a familiar pack, still filled with clothes and supplies. He wore his white robes, rumpled from a full night of sleep but otherwise clean. Early morning light streamed through a window cracked open. Sounds of familiar clan activity trickled through the crack and snuck into his ears.

Neighbors greeted one another. A gruff voice muttered to himself about rising prices as he walked past the window. Two children chased one another between the houses.

His heart slowed. He knew this place and knew this bed, for

it was his. Or, at least, it was the bed he used when the clan camped at Caelen's Rest. He hadn't yet adjusted to the thick walls and warm bed, or to living with his parents again after living in his own tent for so many months, and he hoped the clan would leave before he did, before the comforts of living near Brenwick softened his spirit.

Lirael!

His heart raced as though he'd just sparred against Malric all afternoon. He closed his eyes and watched her die again. He threw off his covers and started for the door. His legs wobbled and gave out, and he crashed back down on the bed, the wooden slats groaning under the abuse.

A deep breath steadied shaky nerves, but the world twisted around him as though he were drunk. Blinking cleared the worst of the dancing visions, but he didn't trust his legs or his balance. He held his head in his hands and tried to remember what had happened after Lirael had died.

No matter how deeply he pillaged his memories, he came up empty-handed. He'd watched her die, and then nothing.

Except, no. He'd been caught.

Or had he? His memories betrayed him, fled like frightened prey as he tried to pin them in place. They flashed like a white-tail deer as it sprinted away, then vanished in a forest of darkness his sight couldn't penetrate.

He tried again to stand, and this time remained upright on unsteady legs. Strength returned to his limbs, but slowly.

How had he ended up at home?

The smell of sizzling venison wafted under his door and made his mouth water. He stumbled toward the door, confidence and strength returning with every step. When he put his hand on the doorknob, there was a knock, not on his bedroom door, but out front.

Footsteps glided softly across the kitchen, and the front

door opened. "Good morning," his father said, a trace of worry in his voice.

Veynar didn't recognize the voice that answered. A woman, likely older than his father, but he couldn't guess beyond that. "Good morning, may we come in?"

Father hesitated, an event so unusual Veynar almost went for the short swords propped against the wall next to his pack. "Certainly. Please come in and make yourselves comfortable."

Veynar's hand floated toward the hilts of his swords. They were weapons specific to the clan, to be used when the fighting was too close for bows. Longer than a dagger, but shorter than the more traditional swords the wardens in Brenwick carried.

Two pairs of additional footsteps followed Father into the kitchen. No chairs scraped against the floor, so the visitors hadn't taken a seat.

The woman spoke again. "I appreciate your generosity, but we won't stay long. Is your son home?"

"Veynar? Yes, he's home, and I heard him wake up a few moments ago. He'll be out shortly. Is he in some kind of trouble? He's normally respectful, but his temper can get the best of him sometimes, and his friends aren't always helpful."

Veynar bristled, though Father's words were true enough. Malric got them into more trouble in a week than Veynar would have found on his own in a decade, and that was doubly true in the days around the Harvest Festival.

Confident his legs wouldn't betray him again, Veynar opened the door and stepped through. He stopped when he saw their visitors.

The older woman wore the uniform of a Sister of Brennor. The insignia on her shoulders certainly meant something, but Veynar knew so little about Lirael's order that he couldn't say what. Standing behind her, though, was one of Brenwick's wardens. He wore gray robes and carried a pair of swords, one long and one short. A few days' worth of stubble grew across his face, but his sharp eyes glittered as he stared at Veynar. Muscular arms were crossed over his chest, and he leaned against a wall as though he were its sole lawful owner.

Veynar looked away, then remembered he'd meant to look for a warden last night.

Before he could speak up, the Sister said, "I'm glad you're all here. There's no easy way to say this, and I'm sorry, but I've come to inform you that your daughter, Lirael, passed away yesterday. I'm certain her spirit is feasting with Brennor as we speak, but I'm terribly sorry for your loss. She was a remarkable woman, and the world is a darker place for her passing."

Both Mother and Father had been born and raised among the clans, and their muted reactions were typical of those who'd grown up learning how to hide their emotions, how to stay calm no matter what dangers and surprises life threw at them. Father paled and gripped the edge of a table for support. Mother sank deeper into her chair, her gaze distant, searching for a daughter she'd never embrace again.

"You mean she was murdered," Veynar said.

The Sister's eyes went wide, and her lips formed a little circle of surprise. The warden, though, likely had spent at least some time among the clans during training, and so had learned to keep his face as still as a mountain lake on a breezeless summer day.

Father looked up sharply, as if he meant to hit Veynar for speaking out of line. Mother hadn't heard a word he'd said.

The Sister shook her head vigorously, as though she could dislodge the suggestion from her memories. "No! I'm sorry, Veynar, if I wasn't clear. She'd been sick the last few days, possibly from working too hard. She was among the best of us and drove herself to the point of breaking in her efforts to serve those who needed aid in Brenwick. Our best healers cared for her, but her condition deteriorated rapidly. Lirael passed away peacefully yesterday afternoon in prayer."

Veynar pressed his hands to his eyes. She couldn't have died yesterday afternoon, for he'd seen her yesterday at dusk. Nothing the Sister said could be true.

Veynar ignored his father's glare. "She was killed," he insisted, "a stab wound to her throat. I was there when she died!"

"Veynar!" his father barked, but Veynar's attention focused on the Sister only, searching for any sign of deceit.

The Sister shook her head again, confusion written across every line of her face, as lost as Veynar felt. "That's not possible, young man. She was attended in prayer by many of our novices. Her passing was witnessed."

"I saw her last night in the park! She had written me a letter to meet her, and I'd brought candies."

Veynar reached into his pockets. He was still wearing yesterday's clothes. His right hand searched for the letter, but his pocket was empty. His left hand searched the left pocket for the candies, but they were gone, too.

The Sister waited for him to produce his evidence, but when he found none, she pressed her palms together and bowed. "I'm sorry, Veynar. Death is never easy, and harder yet when the deceased is so close to us. Grief plays tricks on the mind."

"Then why did you bring a warden if she wasn't murdered?"

"Veynar!" Father shouted louder as the Sister paled.

The warden dipped his head toward Veynar. "I came to protect her as she visited Caelen's Rest. It's not safe with all you clanners here."

"Liar!" Veynar shouted. His hands tightened into fists, and if he'd had so much as his belt knife, he'd have shown the warden just how dangerous Caelen's Rest could be.

"VEYNAR!" Father thundered, face red with grief and fury.

Veynar swallowed hard but pressed his lips together.

Father bowed deeply toward the warden, far deeper than a warrior of his stature should have ever bowed to another. "I apologize for my son. Grief has made him disrespectful."

It was all Veynar could do to keep silent. He seethed, his breath through his nose loud enough for all to hear, closer to a panting bull than an honored Keeper of their clan's legacies.

Father held the bow, and Veynar realized he would continue to do so until Veynar apologized.

Fists clenched tight at his sides, Veynar stiffly bowed. "Apologies, warden."

"Apology accepted. You've got some manners, kid. I'll give you that."

Father rose from his bow, which allowed Veynar to as well. He danced on the edge of trouble there'd be no escape from, but he had to know. "Sister, would it be possible to see her before she's cremated? I'd...I'd like to say goodbye."

Father said nothing about the request, and the Sister said, "Of course. If you come this afternoon, we'll be finished preparing the body. We'd be honored to have you join us at her cremation, too."

The Sisters had sent Lirael's body to the Hall of the Dead for the cleaning and ritual preparation common among the citizens of the cities. Such efforts were wasted on a body whose only future was to be burned to ash, but the ways of the cities and the ways of the clans had diverged generations ago, and when Lirael joined the Sisters, she gave up the ways of her birth for the new ways, the better ways.

It was one foolishness among many. Walking Brenwick's streets was every bit as pleasant as sticking needles in his arm.

He wore the white robes of a clan Keeper, for he owned nothing that would show his sister more respect, but as a consequence, his passage through the streets earned him stares and harsh whispers.

"There's one of them Keepers," said an older woman to a young girl who appeared to be a grandchild. "They say spirits possess their bodies and give them the gift of speaking with the dead."

The girl made a sign to ward off evil, and Veynar pretended he hadn't heard. The misunderstandings between the clans and the cities ran deep, and would only run deeper if he responded in anger.

The legends said that before the Breaking, all people had been one, though Veynar had never been able to imagine such a world. Regardless of the truth of that legend, the gods had parted ways after the Breaking. Caelen, along with the other gods of hunting and war, had made their way toward the borders while Brennor and others turned their attentions toward building cities. If there ever had been unity, it was a memory of a distant past. The clans were shaped by the border and their duties, while Brennor's people were shaped by trade, discovery, and wealth.

Caelen's clan had at least kept relations with Brennor and the city that grew up in his name. Other hunting clans, such as Eiran's, had cut themselves off completely, claiming that trade and relations with the cities only served to weaken their people.

Perhaps Eiran's clan had the right of it. Veynar had no friends in Brenwick he looked forward to seeing, and despite his clan's attempts at openness and friendliness, Brenwick's citizens still believed a Keeper spoke with the dead.

If I could, I'd know what happened to my sister.

Father walked beside him, stiff-legged, as though he was an old man with a bad back and not one of the clan's most feared sword instructors, a man with more Watches under his belt than almost anyone else.

They reached the long, narrow building that served as Brenwick's Hall of the Dead. Walls of stone protected the recently deceased from the sea-swept rains that frequented the city, and stone statues of Brennor stood at every corner of the stout building to protect against evil spirits.

Veynar imagined he was supposed to be awed by the sight, but the cold stone was dead to his senses. He stared at the nearest statue as they passed, daring Brennor to speak, to answer the question of what Lirael had suffered.

The silent stone had no answers, but the warden from earlier waited near the entrance for them. At Veynar's glare, he held up his hands. "Just keeping the peace, kid. So long as you follow the rules, you won't even know I'm here. The Head Sister is waiting inside."

When Father remained silent, Veynar asked, "Why?"

"Because she liked your sister. Don't know if it would be fair to call the two of them close, but they had a lot of respect for one another. The Sister who brought the news of Lirael's death reported back to her, and word is that it got under her skin. She's been looking into the matter."

"And?"

The warden shrugged. "I'm sorry, kid, but your sister died in prayer yesterday. I've been following the Sister around all day, and there's no doubt of it. Not even a question."

Except I saw her die.

Veynar sensed no deceit in the warden, though he searched the warrior's face for it. Either he was a skilled liar or he believed the falsehoods he spread.

The warden said, "Follow me. It is our custom to remain quiet within the Hall of the Dead, and I'd ask that you honor our traditions. If you become disruptive, I'll remove you, by force if necessary, but I'd prefer not to fight here. This is a sacred place."

Veynar sensed the difference the moment he passed underneath the arched doorway of the hall. The air was heavy with incense and the sweet smell of decay. As his eyes adjusted to the darkness, he saw bones.

Thousands of bones.

All were clean, as though they'd been left in the wilderness for years, enduring predation and the never-ending heat of the sun as it passed overhead. They had been stacked into walls and columns. Like a mason choosing the perfect stones to build his wall, the builders of the hall had chosen bones small and large to fit together and create walls much taller than the height of a man. No mortar held the bones in place, but if Veynar pulled, none would easily slip free.

He stood and stared, mouth agape.

His clan could never create something like this. Not only did it require more bones than the clan could produce in a decade, but because the planning, preparation, and building of this hall must have taken years.

It also required hundreds, if not thousands, of people willing to gift their bones to Brennor. The clans didn't have the time or the foresight to build such a monument. Their lives didn't allow it. Lirael had chosen well, at least in this regard. She must have loved this place, must have sensed the power within it.

Veynar did, and he'd never been as sensitive as her. The silent stone outside protected the bones and the devotion they represented. Each bone was an offering, a sacrifice to Brennor, and all of them together made Veynar feel as though his head had been dunked in cold water. Every sense was sharpened. He stood on the edge of deeper waters, but didn't know how to reach the depths. Lirael might have, though. She would have learned during her apprenticeship.

Father's tug on the hem of his robes returned his focus to more mundane matters. The warden had walked a third of the way down the hall before realizing he was no longer accompanied, and he watched Veynar through narrowed eyes. Veynar looked around one more time and followed.

Tables with legs of bone and surfaces of stone ran down each of the long sides of the hall. Most were empty, but a few held bodies cared for by the Sisters.

An older woman with steel-gray hair stood beside a table at the end of the hall, cloaked in shadows. Her head was bowed until the warden came over and gently placed his hand on her elbow. When she looked up, she looked like she hadn't slept for a week. And yet, there was a strength within her that reminded Veynar of his High Keeper, Maeryn. A determination the world wouldn't be able to break. Something about her presence made Veynar's stomach turn, though that very well might have been their proximity to the covered corpse. Though shrouded, Veynar knew full well they stood next to Lirael's body. The warden introduced the older woman as the Head Sister of Brennor.

The Head Sister bowed to them. "I'm very sorry for your loss. She was well-loved." She gently pulled the shroud down, then stepped away to give the men a moment alone with Lirael.

Veynar stared for the last time upon the face of his sister, as still as the statues of Brennor outside. There was no wound on her throat, no scar, no stitches. No hint of a stain of blood.

His body trembled as his vision blurred.

He saw her climbing their tree as a little girl, exhorting him ever higher. Heard her laughing as he recounted his and Malric's latest adventure. Watched her help Mother butcher an enormous antlered deer that had been brought to the camp that afternoon.

One memory swam vividly through his tears. The sight of her perched on a rock overlooking a lake, the wind blowing her hair across her face. She wasn't meditating, wasn't scouting the movement of herds. She was just sitting, enjoying the quiet grandeur of the wilderness. He didn't think they'd said anything to one another that day. They'd simply sat together for an afternoon in silence.

That had been the afternoon when he decided that perhaps being a Keeper wasn't the failure he'd thought. That had been the afternoon that had given him hope when he had little left.

He blinked and wiped away his tears, and for the briefest of moments, he thought he saw the wound on her throat. He blinked again and leaned closer, but no, he must have imagined it. Her skin was pale and untouched.

He prayed to Caelen, asking that he keep his sister's spirit warm and sheltered until he could see her again. He kissed her gently on the forehead, memorized his last look of her, then turned and left Brennor's Hall of the Dead.

VEYNAR WAITED on a stone bench outside, oblivious to the rest of the world. He didn't stir until he felt a familiar hand on his shoulder. He looked up to see his father beside him. Veynar stood.

"They asked if her bones could join with those of other honored Sisters in the Hall of the Dead. I gave them permission."

Veynar's fists clenched. She'd been Caelen's before she was Brennor's. He swallowed his anger, recognizing it quickly enough. He only feared that if her bones joined the Hall of the Dead, he might never see her again once his own spirit passed through the veil between worlds.

She'd chosen Brennor, though. Father had done nothing but obey her wishes.

He forced himself to nod, and Father's posture relaxed.

"Did you see what you needed?" Father asked.

"You don't believe me either, do you?" He didn't know why he had asked. He already knew the answer.

Father looked away. The hero of Baelin's Pass, and he couldn't meet the eyes of his son. "You came home yesterday after you finished your chores at the halgard. You said you were tired and didn't feel well and went to your room, and you were home when dusk fell, asleep in your room."

Veynar blinked, at a loss for words. He'd been at their tree. He'd bought candies. Hadn't he? He rummaged through his memories, only to find them fragmented and filled with shadows. "Why didn't you say anything earlier?"

"It didn't seem wise. Your temper was already running hot, and we feared telling you would unbalance you further."

Veynar pressed his face into his hands. He shuddered and then regained control. "I don't know what's happening."

Father reached out and placed a reassuring hand on Veynar's shoulder. "Neither do I. Tomorrow morning you should speak to Maeryn. The mind of a Keeper is beyond my understanding, but I'm sure she'll guide you well."

It was good advice, and Veynar said he'd take it.

He plunged his hands deep into the pockets of his robe as they left the city, then frowned. At the very bottom of his pockets, his fingers scratched against something. He grasped a bit between his fingers and pulled. He rubbed it between thumb and forefinger, recognizing it instantly.

It was the crumbled remains of a leaf. A red maple, to be precise.

CHAPTER 3
WHAT REMAINS

Leave nothing but silence in your wake. Take only what was meant for you.

— FROM *THE SAYINGS OF CAELEN*
(APOCRYPHAL)

Veynar trudged up the stone path that led to the halgard, oblivious to the chirping of the songbirds as they sang their farewells to autumn, the crunch of leaves under his boots, or the reconstruction a colony of ants attempted upon the ruins of their earlier hill. His memories of finding Lirael in the woods faded faster now, a nightmare dissipating under the light of day and the passage of time. He grasped for them, but the more he struggled, the slipperier they became.

Veynar had watched her body burn the night before, her corpse an offering in death as her last months had been in life. He kept waiting for that memory to suffer the same degradation, but it burned as bright as the pyre had. Mother and Father had been there, and Malric and Cori had come, too, a kindness he hadn't properly thanked them for yet.

First, though, Maeryn, and if the gods willed it, answers.

He stopped outside the halgard and instinctively compared it with Brenwick's Hall of the Dead. He found it wanting.

No stone or bone protected the mysteries within, for the buildings of the clan weren't designed to withstand the ravages of time. Logs from the nearby forest formed the eight walls, joined roughly and packed with clay. The thatched roof needed to be replaced, maybe not on this visit, but certainly by the next. The stone walkway would last longer than the halgard, but even it would soon be overgrown if it wasn't maintained.

He'd often found solace within those walls, but they seemed a poor substitute for the majesty of Brennor's halls.

As was customary when the clan visited Caelen's Rest, the wooden door that protected the halgard in their absence had been removed and replaced with hanging furs. Veynar reached to pull them aside, but they moved before he could touch them, and another Keeper stepped out. He stood half a head taller than Veynar, and his long hair was starting to turn gray, but he moved like a hunter even here, outside the halgard.

Veynar bowed, and Gavrin smoothly stepped to the side and returned the gesture. "I heard about Lirael. I'm sorry."

Veynar's throat tightened at the sound of her name. "Thank you."

He expected Gavrin to move on, but the other Keeper lingered, as though looking for the right words to express his sympathy. In the end, he said, "I know it doesn't feel like it now, but Caelen's watching over you. I can sense it."

From anyone else, except perhaps High Keeper Maeryn, the words would have rung hollow, the sort of phrase well-meaning friends uttered when they didn't know what else to say in the face of unspeakable grief. But like Maeryn, Gavrin didn't let meaningless words pass his lips, and if there was a Keeper who could sense Caelen's will, it was him. He'd been one of the clan's greatest warriors before becoming a Keeper, and there still wasn't anyone in the camp who could beat him with a sword, not even Father. Gavrin supervised the Keeper's physical training, and none of them could keep the pace he set, though many of them were more than a decade younger.

His words settled deep in Veynar's chest, slowing his heart and calming the storm of his thoughts. Veynar bowed again, holding the honor a moment longer to express his thanks. When he rose, Gavrin was holding the furs aside for him.

Veynar hurried through and thanked the Keeper once again. Gavrin nodded, then let the furs settle back into place, casting the halgard into relative darkness. Once Veynar's eyes adjusted to the darkness, he took a seat on the cushion across from the High Keeper.

"I too am sorry for your loss," Maeryn said.

"Thank you, High Keeper." At her inviting gesture, he launched into his story, the words tumbling out of him like boulders in a rockslide. By the time he finished, his throat was dry, and he was certain she would decide he had fallen into madness.

There was a long silence, which to Veynar's ears was filled with doubt. It lasted long enough that he began to shift on the cushion. Perhaps it had been a mistake to come here.

"A troubling story," she finally said.

"You believe me?"

"Veynar, I've known you since you were a child, and though you've adopted a fair amount of Malric's deviousness, I know how close you and Lirael were. How much she meant to you. No, you wouldn't lie about her."

"But I'm no longer sure I even saw what I think I saw."

"Nor should you. I sense the strands of the gods knotting up around you, but I don't yet know the best way forward. I can't give you the answers you seek yet, but you have my word that I'll think deeply on this matter."

"What can I do to help?"

Maeryn shook her head, silver hair flashing in the crack of sunlight that snuck through a gap in the furs. "For now, nothing. The answers will be beyond your skill as a Keeper to seek. Continue your training. Mourn the loss of your sister, for her spirit burned brightly."

It wasn't an answer, but she'd believed him. It was the most he'd been offered yet.

"You're sure there's nothing I can do?"

The look she gave him was ominous. "Train, Veynar, and prepare. I know not what the gods intend, but you're going to want every skill you can acquire for what I fear is coming."

"You don't really believe her, do you?" Malric asked.

Cori shot the lanky warrior a glare, but he pretended not to notice.

"I'm being serious. She didn't promise to find any answers. She only told you that she would try to help you find a way forward. You know how careful she is with her words. If she meant to find you answers, she would have said so."

When Veynar didn't immediately answer, Malric rolled his eyes. "Gods, you don't believe me, do you?" He raised his voice so the entire street could hear. "Help! I've been abducted by fools!"

He coughed as Cori drove her fist into his side. "Show some respect."

"I've tried! I understand the elders still look to the Keepers for knowledge, and if you put me to torture, I'll eventually admit that it's important for the clan to draw wisdom from its past, but once you try to convince me the gods are real and care about us, no. That's where we're done. You've all served a Watch, same as me, and you know perfectly well that if gods ever existed, they've long since abandoned us."

Cori had no answer to that, and Veynar didn't expect her to answer, because he knew that if she was pressed, she would agree. The age of the gods, if it had ever existed at all, was so far in the past it was no better than a distant dream. She respected the traditions of the clan more than Malric, but that was as far as her belief went.

"I'm not asking you to believe in the gods," Veynar admitted, silencing Malric's next diatribe. "But I am asking you to believe in Maeryn. If she didn't promise answers, it's because she is unsure she could keep her promise. A way forward is all she could give her word to keep."

Malric had no sharp retort to that. As much as he might disagree with the Keepers, he'd say nothing against Maeryn, who'd earned the clan's respect time and again over the years. His silence lasted for two long blocks, but in the end, silence was one enemy he'd never learned how to defeat. "What *do* you think happened? Because everything you've told us makes no sense."

Veynar dug his hands deep into the pockets of his robes, which he still hadn't washed. His fingers brushed against the small fragments of the leaves crumpled at the very bottom, a reminder he wasn't as mad as he feared. "I think I saw something true," he said.

Malric's expected rebuttal didn't come, and Veynar glanced curiously at his friend. The dark-robed warrior shrugged. "You've always had some strange ideas, but if you tell me Lirael was murdered, I'll believe you."

"Agreed," Cori added.

Their belief in him filled a void in his heart he hadn't realized was there, and he looked down at his boots, grateful beyond words. "Thanks."

Cori nudged him with her shoulder. "We're here."

Veynar looked up and saw Cori was right. The House of Brennor rose before them, a monument to both a god and humanity's ability to build. Tall spires rose from each corner of the enormous structure, an edifice of wood and stone that rose higher than the tallest trees Veynar had ever climbed. Ornate carvings decorated every exposed surface, and Veynar could have spent a lifetime studying and deciphering the scenes depicted across the building.

If he knew his sister, she'd felt the same.

"Incredible," Cori whispered, wrapping her arms around one of his. He nodded.

Malric belched. "Seems like a waste of effort."

Two of the three friends admired the building for a moment longer before Veynar led them in.

Four guards stood at the gate of the outer wall, each wearing the two swords popular with Brenwick's warriors. They wore tunics made of a fabric so thin Veynar wondered if they ripped in the wind and pants that didn't look like they'd ever been introduced to mud or dirt. The guards eyed the new arrivals with disdain. One of the four stepped forward and glared at them. "What are *you* doing here?"

Cori's hand on Malric's wrist prevented a fight, and Veynar said, "I'm Apprentice Lirael's brother. I was told I could come for her effects."

The guard's eyes narrowed. "So, you're the one tying the Head Sister into knots. You're not welcome here."

Veynar stood perfectly still and calmly met the guard's gaze. Both of them knew full well the guard had no authority to stop them. The guard spat at Veynar's feet and stood aside.

"Just make it quick, and then return to the woods and stay there."

Veynar dipped his head, and Cori dragged a glaring Malric past the laughing guards.

On the other side of the gate, they discovered a garden that brought Veynar to a stop. The same power that had permeated the Hall of the Dead was present here too, though it possessed a distinct quality. Even the life here was ordered. Wild roses climbed trellises, but were trimmed whenever they threatened to scratch visitors wandering the stone paths. Beds of lavender and sage grew in neat rows, and foxgloves stood at measured intervals, their purple bells nodding in unison whenever a breeze snuck through the garden.

It lacked the casual disorder of a meadow of wildflowers, but it captivated Veynar's attention all the same.

Lirael's decision to join the Sisters had always haunted him, had forced him to question his own beliefs. He'd chased after her for as long as he could remember, but her decision to leave the clan was one he couldn't follow. The more he experienced of the House of Brennor, the better he felt he understood her choice.

They made their way slowly through the garden and at the entrance to the House proper were greeted by a smiling young woman. "How can I help you today?"

Veynar stepped forward. "I'm apprentice Lirael's younger brother, here to collect her effects."

The young woman's smile fell from her face. "I'm sorry for your loss. Let me summon someone to take you to your sister's rooms."

Another woman, about Lirael's age, came around the corner. "There's no need, Em. I can show them."

The woman at the desk bowed in deference. "Of course. Thank you."

The newcomer seemed different from most of the other Sisters-in-training they passed, sharper-edged, in a way. She wasn't clan, but she was more disciplined than most. She addressed them with respect and introduced herself as Avelin.

"Did you know Lirael?" Veynar asked as she guided them.

Avelin tucked some hair that had escaped its braid behind her ear. She thought for a moment, then said, "I did, yes. We'd grown close these last few months."

She held something back, but Veynar chose not to press her. As they walked, Avelin tapped her fingers together and often looked over her shoulder, as though expecting to find someone following them. After several twists and turns, she stopped outside a closed door. She produced a key from beneath her robes and unlocked it. "This was where she lived."

Veynar's hand clenched into a fist. His sister had given up the wide-open skies of her youth for this?

The room was cozy enough, he supposed. A lamp hung on the wall and another sat on a small writing desk. The bed, nicer than the ones in Caelen's Rest and far nicer than the furs they slept on near the border, was in one corner, a trunk at its foot. A small bookshelf sat next to the bed, and the writing desk was in the corner opposite. Veynar wasn't sure all three of them would fit in the room at the same time.

Veynar fixed Malric with a look, then glanced meaningfully at Avelin. It seemed clear there was more she wanted to say, and if anyone could pry it out of her, it was his friend. Malric grinned and nodded as he caught Veynar's meaning.

The hardened clan warrior transformed before Veynar's eyes. Malric's smile softened. No longer the grin of a predator on the hunt, it reflected a deep inner joy, a child-like pleasure in life and all its mysteries. He didn't slouch, exactly, but his lanky frame seemed to shrink so he didn't tower so high over the shorter Sister. He approached Avelin, and Veynar guided Cori into his sister's room.

Though the walls were dead stone, Veynar swore he sensed the lingering presence of his sister. He could easily imagine her here, sitting at the writing desk and absorbed in her studies. She loved nothing more than understanding, and in the House of Brennor, she'd likely found a treasure greater than any the clans could offer.

Cori opened Lirael's trunk and found it nearly empty. "There won't be much to bring back."

There wouldn't be. "She always walked lightly, no matter where she went."

Veynar went first to the books sitting on the small bookshelf. All were stamped as the property of the House of Brennor, which didn't surprise Veynar. Lirael wouldn't have been able to afford much in the way of books, for money was one of Brennor's creations, an idea that had little use among the clans.

He let his eyes drift from title to title, but he saw nothing that shed any light on Lirael's death. She'd been interested in a wide range of topics, the same as she'd always been.

Cori began working her way through the writing desk while Veynar finished running his fingers along the book spines. "This is strange," she said.

Veynar tore himself away from the books. "What is?"

Cori swept her hand across the desk. "There's nothing here. A pile of blank paper, but there's not a single note or letter here. Your sister was always surrounded by her notes and half-finished letters."

Veynar frowned and lifted the surface of the desk, revealing the storage space beneath. As Cori had observed, there was nothing but blank paper and unused ink. He let the surface of the desk fall back down and looked around the room. He got on hands and knees and looked beneath the bed.

The search took only a moment. It wasn't as though there were many places for the papers to be.

"What do you make of it?" Cori asked.

"I don't know." Veynar looked around the room again, but it mocked his search with its cleanliness. He shrugged. "I suppose we should gather her belongings and carry them back with us."

"Do you think she hid her papers someplace?"

"Where, though? If they're not here, they could be anywhere."

They made one last search of the room, seeking any hidden storage spaces. They ended without success. Gathering Lirael's belongings took only a moment, and once Veynar's pack was half-filled with the culmination of all she'd left behind, they left the room.

Malric had his arm around Avelin, and she leaned toward him, staring at him as though he were some sort of hero of legend. Veynar resisted the urge to shake his head.

Malric whispered something into Avelin's ear, and her face turned red before she nodded. He stood and dipped into an elegant bow.

Veynar asked Avelin, "Has anybody else been in my sister's room since she died?"

The words caught in his throat, but he forced them out.

Avelin thought for a moment, then shook her head. "There shouldn't have been. The door was locked, and only a few people would have had another key, mostly older Sisters. No one who would have had any reason to visit."

Her answer was meant to reassure, but her eyes darted up and down the hallway again.

Malric inclined his head slightly, which Veynar took as a sign to leave well enough alone. He forced a smile onto his face. "Thank you, Avelin, for everything."

It wasn't until they were out of the House of Brennor and

out of sight of the guards at the gates that they spoke of what they'd learned. Malric listened to Cori and Veynar, then said, "I wasn't so sure of your ideas before, but something smells like dead fish in that House. Your sister was always surrounded by notes, and Avelin knows something that she's scared to say."

"Maybe we need to speak to her again," Veynar suggested.

Malric grinned. "Luckily for you, I'm a step ahead. Unlike you two, who were on hands and knees searching for scraps of paper, I was using my time in a more valuable manner. It turns out I have a date for tonight with one lovely Sister."

Veynar rolled his eyes.

Malric's grin faded. "Don't be like that. I think she knows more than she's been saying and wants to let us know. She only needed an excuse to escape the Sisters for a night."

Veynar hoped it was true, because otherwise, he didn't have a clue how to find out what had happened to Lirael. Foolish as it seemed, it appeared he had no choice but to trust Malric. He only hoped the trust wasn't misplaced.

CHAPTER 4
A DATE FOR MALRIC

Let love bloom wherever your steps may lead, for it is love, in the end, that will give your life meaning.

— FROM *THE BOOK OF BRENNOR*

Veynar stared at the pair of short swords sitting on his bed. They were beautiful weapons, gifted to him by his father on the eve of his first patrol. He'd only drawn them once in combat, but he maintained them with the same devotion he served the halgard, and so they shone in the last light of the sun coming through the window.

He looked up at the knock on the front door of his family's house. Visitors had been stopping by since daybreak as word of Lirael's death spread. Her swords, twins of his own, which she'd left behind when she joined the House of Brennor, had been placed on top of her former Keeper's robes and left on a mantle. Visitors came, bowed deeply to the weapons and Lirael's memory, then sat with his parents, sharing in their grief.

He'd been glad to run to Brenwick earlier in the day to

escape the mourners that made him feel like an invader in his own home. It was hard enough to share the house with his parents after growing used to his own tent, but he couldn't bring himself to share in his parent's grief.

For grief could only come after vengeance.

He forgot the visitor as soon as the door opened, cocooned as he was in his small room with his dark thoughts. He jumped when another knock sounded, this time at the door to his room. Cori entered without waiting for permission. She took in his dark clothing, the weapons on his bed, and the surprise on his face. Her expression darkened as she pointed at the blades.

"Think you'll need those tonight?"

"Probably not, but I'd like to be prepared."

He expected a verbal lashing, but Cori surprised him with a question. "What will you do if you find Lirael was killed, and you find her killer?"

Veynar picked up the short swords from the bed and slid them smoothly into the sheaths already tied to his hips. Though he hadn't been part of the Watch for months, his blades found the sheaths without hesitation. "Then I'll deliver justice."

Cori didn't seem so convinced. "Will you?"

In the blink of an eye, he was back on that mountainside far to the east, staring at the face of his enemy as the sword came down to separate his head from his shoulders. He shoved the memory aside. Yes, he'd learned something about himself that night, but it didn't apply here. Not when someone had killed his sister. "I will."

He'd thought she'd be proud of him, but her expression remained carefully guarded, a sure sign she didn't want him witnessing her true beliefs. She studied him a moment longer, then said, "Malric wants to leave earlier than we'd planned. He's hoping to rope you into some fun before we meet with Avelin."

Veynar checked to ensure his swords were secure, then nodded. "We shouldn't keep him waiting, then."

Night in Brenwick was *wrong*. The falling of the sun was supposed to mark a time of rest for those who had labored through the day, and a time of silent vigilance for those who fought to keep the sleepers safe. Animals driven to shade by the heat of the day came out at night to hunt and sing, and the stars told their silent stories as they spun overhead.

Brenwick's streets, lit by lamps, acted as though the difference between light and dark was meaningless, dishonoring the simple and natural rhythms of life in the wilderness. Vendors and merchants shouted as loudly as they had when the three friends had visited during the afternoon. Amidst the noise and chaos, it was those who acted most outrageously that drew the most attention, and thus the greatest number of the notes that passed as money here.

The sights and sounds made Veynar dizzy, as though he'd stepped into a room of crooked mirrors where nothing was as it should be. Citizens jostled and pushed against one another without concern for their neighbors, and children cried when parents denied them the toys and sweets they craved.

There was no honor here, and worst of all, no one cared about its absence. Children laughed with delight as jugglers twirled dull knives in the air. Drunken men called after passing women, and women picked at plates of food as though they feared an ambush might spring from their potatoes.

"Why do we fight to defend this?" Veynar growled.

Malric, whose grin hadn't faltered since the moment they'd stepped into Brenwick, laughed out loud. "Because this, my friend, is fun! You should try it sometime. But be careful! You might even like it." He disappeared into the crowd, though Veynar was certain they would see him again, probably sooner than they wished.

Cori took his hand and pointed to a quiet corner of the market. A man and a woman, who appeared to be about their age, were sitting at a table sharing a small meal. They leaned close as they talked, smiling like love-struck fools at whatever the other said.

Without a word, she pointed to a stand that was handing out bread and soup, run by the Sisters of the House of Brennor. The portions were no more than a clan warrior would have eaten on the trail, and the fare simple compared to much of what the market served, but no money traded hands, and the Sisters who served the meals beamed with quiet contentment.

"Look closer," Cori said, "and don't let your preconceptions blind you."

He dipped his head toward her in thanks. She was right, of course, and unspoken between them was the understanding the city in the throes of the Harvest Festival was different than the city as it would otherwise be found. Farmers and warriors from all over visited, enjoying the week-long festivities before the cold of winter forced most indoors.

He and Cori walked slowly. He asked, "Do you like it in Brenwick? Have you ever considered leaving the clan and staying?"

The corner of her mouth turned up in a smile. "There have been long days on Watch when I've considered it. Those days when it's raining, and the mud is in your boots and in your eyes and there's no escaping the water, not even when you set up your tent. Those are the days I long for stone streets, thick walls, and decadent food."

They walked a while longer, his fingers lightly intertwined with hers. "But no, the cities aren't for me. There's a part of me that feels like it's missing here, and besides, the people I care for would never consider leaving the clan."

She gave him a meaningful look, and he squeezed her hand. "That's an excellent answer."

Malric rejoined them, flushed from exertion and his grin somehow wider than before. "It's about time."

They made their way through the market, and Malric guided them to one of the many city squares. He claimed the square was called "the lover's square," and Veynar begrudgingly admitted the name fit. The buildings that surrounded the square were more ornate than most, and though there were plenty of benches, most were filled with young couples. Cori and Veynar found a reasonably quiet alley where they could watch the meeting without drawing attention to themselves.

"Do you think she'll know anything?" Cori asked.

"I want to believe she will, but given how confusing everything surrounding Lirael is, I'm not sure."

He searched the crowd for a sign of Avelin, but she hadn't arrived in the square yet. He wasn't sure how hard it was to leave the House of Brennor, or whether Malric deserved to be as confident in his charm as he was.

The square Malric and Avelin had chosen for their rendezvous wasn't as close to the center of Brenwick as the House of Brennor was, but the buildings still towered higher than trees, constructions of stone and wood that loomed over the square like blocky protectors. Most of the windows on the upper levels were lit. Even those wise enough to stay indoors at night remained awake long past the hour decent folk were in bed.

Veynar shook his head, remembering Cori's wisdom. It was too easy to see all that he despised in Brenwick, and it tore his attention away from where it belonged.

Cori nudged him and tilted her chin toward one of the

major thoroughfares leading toward the square. Avelin approached, though she didn't wear the uniform of a Sister. She glanced furtively around, then looked behind her for a good long while. She either knew she was being followed or was anxious about the possibility.

Malric spotted her a moment later. He brushed his hands against his robes and shifted from one foot to the other.

"I think he's nervous," Cori said, no doubt already imagining the ways in which she would torment him later.

"I am, too," Veynar said.

And he was, far more than he should be. He stood up straighter and brought his attention back to his body. A small den of snakes had made its way into his belly, writhing around his core and unable to settle. Instead of pushing the sensation aside or covering it up, he kept his attention on it, waiting patiently to understand why his nerves threatened to betray him.

It wasn't the meeting between Malric and Avelin. His hopes were too thin to believe a random girl from the House of Brennor would possess the secrets that would unlock the mystery surrounding Lirael's death. He couldn't summon the nerves he felt from the slim hope he held.

There was something more, something his body recognized that hadn't risen to the level of his conscious awareness yet. His eyes darted around the square but found nothing suspicious to latch onto. Avelin reached the edge of the square, found Malric, and started toward him.

Above, on the rooftops surrounding the square, a shadow moved, barely discernible against the starless night sky. He squinted and wondered if it was real or imagined. Instinct drove him toward Avelin, and he broke from the shadows of the alley as Cori whispered curses after him.

Another glimpse, he thought, of the shadow above, but

when he blinked, it was gone. Cori reached for his arm to pull him back into the alley, but he slid out of reach and wove through the scattered crowd to reach Avelin. Cori swore again and followed.

The Sister didn't notice them approaching from the alley. She'd had eyes for no one and nothing except Malric. Not affection, though. More the look of a woman who was searching for rescue and saw in Malric the hope of safety. Veynar was only five paces away and closing fast, and still she didn't notice him.

A second shadow detached from the building but didn't disappear when Veynar stared at it. It fell, gathering speed as it dropped toward Avelin.

Veynar's body sprinted before he fully understood the danger. He flung himself through an opening between two passersby and leaped at Avelin. He wrapped his arms around her waist and tackled her. His momentum carried the pair of them several paces, and they landed hard against the stone. He'd tried to twist to absorb most of the impact, but he'd only been partially successful. She cried out as soft flesh met unforgiving cobblestone.

A statue from the nearby roof struck the ground where Avelin had stood an instant before. The crack of breaking stone split the air and caused Veynar's ears to ring. Echoes of the destruction reverberated between the surrounding buildings, filling the square. Fragments of shattered stonework, sharp as blades, went spinning through the crowd. At least two larger pieces cut Veynar through his robes.

Citizens close to the impact screamed and scattered, some clutching wounds, while those near the opposite edge of the square stared on in wide-eyed wonder.

Malric was by their side as the crowd shifted around them. He had knives in his hands, kept close to his body so they wouldn't draw attention. "You hurt?"

Veynar stood and brushed himself off. "A few cuts, plenty of bruises. Nothing that needs immediate attention."

Malric put his hand on Avelin's shoulder and gently turned her more onto her side. "How hurt are you?"

Her face was pale, and her body trembled. Words were beyond her, but she shook her head, which Veynar took to mean she was unharmed.

Malric said, "I'm going to help you to your feet. Let me know if anything hurts."

He reached his arms around and under her and lifted her to her feet. She wasn't much help, but she didn't resist, either. Once she was standing with Malric's help, he turned again to Veynar. "What just happened?"

"Something in the square felt wrong. I thought I saw shadows on the rooftops, and then the stone was falling."

"H-H-Help me," Avelin said through trembling lips.

"What can we do?" Malric asked, always the considerate hero when the situation demanded it.

She pressed her lips together, then took a deeper, steadying breath and stood tall, fighting against her fear. "I-I think they don't want me talking to you. Please, if you can keep me safe, I'll tell you everything I know." She looked straight at Veynar. "I'll tell you what I think happened to your sister."

CHAPTER 5
LIGHTNING UNDER THE FULL MOON

Remember, children, that no matter how much you think you know, the world will always be full of mystery.

— FROM *THE BOOK OF BRENNOR*

Malric held tightly to Avelin's arm, keeping her upright as her balance faltered. His eyes searched the rooftops for any sign of Veynar's shadow, any sign the danger Avelin feared was more than her imagining. Veynar and Cori joined the hunt. If an enemy prowled the shadows above, their combined efforts couldn't fail to bring it to light.

No further masonry followed the shattered stone already scattered across the square, and citizens slowly returned to the distractions, conversations, and entertainment that had consumed them before. Avelin's near-death was reduced to a mere story, an anecdote to be told to friends the next morning. A momentary disruption quickly forgotten.

Though not for Avelin. Her body trembled like that of a hare dragged from its den. Her teeth chattered as the last of her blood drained from her face and her weight sagged against Malric's grip. He guided her close, wrapping his other arm around her and holding her tight.

"Please—help," Avelin said, and Malric nodded, squeezing her once before releasing her. He gently lifted her chin with his hand until she looked into his eyes, and her posture straightened as she unconsciously mirrored his strength and conviction.

"You have my word as a blooded warrior of Caelen's clan. We'll keep you safe," Malric said.

She wrapped her arms around him. "Thank you."

Malric looked to his friends, and Veynar nodded his approval. One could say whatever they wanted about his friend, and most of it would be true, but once Malric's word was given, Veynar trusted it every bit as much as Maeryn's.

"We should get her someplace safer," Cori suggested.

The buildings surrounding the square loomed ever closer, and Malric was quick to agree. They started east instinctively, toward their camp and away from the House of Brennor. Malric guided Avelin on his left arm while Veynar and Cori spread out, Cori in the lead and Veynar watching behind. They slipped through the streets like salmon swimming upstream, against the gentle current of humanity that pushed toward the center of Brenwick.

The buildings and homes shrank as they left the House of Brennor farther behind, and the streets quieted. It was too early for any to be empty, but they were open enough no enemy could use the cover of a crowd to follow their flight.

Avelin's ankle twisted roughly, and she cried out as she hopped on one foot. Malric caught her before she fell and guided her to the side of the street while she cursed her foolishness. They found a bench around the next corner where she could stretch her ankle as Malric probed it with gentle thumbs.

"It doesn't feel like anything's broken. Can you put weight on it?"

Avelin hissed as she tried. "Maybe in a bit. I'll need help."

"You'll have it," Malric assured her.

While Avelin stretched her ankle, Veynar searched the streets for signs of pursuit. A few passersby had looked over sympathetically, but when they saw Avelin was well cared for, they paid the young apprentice and her friends no more mind.

"Veynar," Avelin said.

He turned from his study of the streets to look at her. She stared at him as though he were a clan elder sitting in judgment, and she the young warrior guilty of negligence on patrol. But why should he sit in judgment of her? They'd only met for the first time this afternoon, and then only briefly.

"I'm sorry, Veynar. I'm afraid that I might have gotten your sister killed, but I swear, it was never my intent!"

Before Veynar could respond, she clutched at her head and groaned. Malric leaned in closer. "Avelin?"

The apprentice Sister pressed her palms to her ears, shutting out the world as she wrestled with whatever agonies tormented her. Unable to help, the three friends could do nothing but watch on and keep an eye on the streets. In time she straightened, and she apologized again.

Veynar wanted to shake her, to force her to share all she knew, but he held onto the last shreds of his patience. She was no enemy holding tightly to secrets, and she was in pain, and she'd tell all soon enough.

Avelin's weak voice forced them to all lean in. "I'm worried. It's like I have two memories living side by side in my head. In the one I remember most clearly, Lirael took ill and passed quickly. In another..." her voice trailed off and she shook her head. "In another, I got her killed."

The parallels to Veynar's experience were too obvious to ignore.

"How?" Veynar asked.

Avelin groaned. "It shouldn't be so hard to remember. I asked her to carry something for me, like a messenger. She was never supposed to get hurt. No one was."

Veynar squatted beside her. "Avelin, you need to remember. What happened?"

She frowned and squinted, as though her memory was a vague shape in the distance. "I...I took something from the mysteries."

"The mysteries?" Veynar asked.

Avelin looked away, these memories coming easier. "I don't know much about them. Most don't. But there is more to the House of Brennor than most people see. There are teachings that only a few are permitted. Lirael and I were both beginning our induction into the mysteries. Except...I took something, and I gave it to her to deliver because the Head Sister had given her permission to leave, to see you. I wrote them a note to tell them where to meet her."

"What did you take? What did she have?"

Avelin shook her head. "I don't remember. It was important, but not worth anyone's life. At least, I didn't think so."

She stared hard at Veynar. "Please forgive me. I never meant to get her hurt. It should have been me."

How could he not take pity? "I don't need to forgive you for something you didn't intend. Just tell me, who killed her?"

Tears streamed down her cheeks and she punched the bench she was sitting on. "Why can't I remember?"

Veynar's insides twisted, and he checked the streets and rooftops once again. But no, it was only his reaction to hearing about his sister's final days. To getting so close to the truth and yet be stuck so far away.

Despite watching Lirael's body burn, he couldn't bring himself to believe she was dead. She'd always been by his side growing up, and even after she joined the House of Brennor, he thought of her often, diving deep into her studies, just the way Avelin described. How could a person who'd been there, both in person and in his thoughts, for so many days, suddenly not be there anymore? It was like the sun not rising one morning.

"We should get her back to Caelen's Rest quickly," Malric said. "She needs Maeryn's attention, and perhaps the Keeper has some way of restoring her lost memories."

Veynar wasn't sure that was true, but any hope was better than none.

"Can you stand if we help you?" Cori asked.

Avelin put her foot down, grimaced, but nodded. "I won't be able to relax until I'm in your camp. I've had this feeling, ever since your sister died, that they're after me, too."

Malric and Cori helped her to her feet, and it was decided that Malric could support enough of her weight on his own. Cori once again took the lead, and Veynar followed, always keeping an eye on the streets behind them. It didn't take them long to leave the cobblestones of the city center behind and return to the packed dirt of the city's outskirts. The homes and shops were entirely framed with the oak and pine that grew abundantly in the forests beyond. Though they lacked the stonework that defined the heart of the city, the care the builders put into the houses was seen in the decorative carving and the joints that seemed to melt into one another.

Avelin died in the space between Veynar's breaths. He glanced over his shoulder to ensure they weren't being followed, then turned back. A shroud of darkness fell on top of Avelin from the nearby rooftops, mist and shredded fabric and raven's feathers, the only sharp and definable feature the glint of silver reflected in the moonlight. A silver blade flashed and plunged into her skull, slicing through the bone as easy as an axe through an overripe grape. She crumpled under the weight and the blow, but the unnatural darkness prevented Veynar from witnessing the moment she struck the ground. She thumped to the ground, somehow both hollow and heavy, the sound of a body as it lost its spirit.

Malric's swords flashed before Veynar had time to gasp. They sought the heart of shadow but struck nothing. Veynar's eyes narrowed as he reached for his own swords, but what was he supposed to attack? A blade in the dark had to be carried by a hand, but Veynar saw neither hand nor arm.

Malric suffered the same challenge, but he cut anyway, undeterred by the small complication of not having a target to strike at. Darkness shifted, swirled, and danced without a sound, mocking Malric's inability to cut it. A sword thrust from the darkness, long and straight, a sword one of Brennor's guardsman might carry. Malric's swords intercepted the blow, but the force of the cut sent him flying backward, barely keeping his feet.

One of Cori's throwing knives passed through the patch of darkness, punching a hole in what should have been the shadow's chest. The knife flew through unopposed and whistled past Veynar's head and the handle thunked against a wall behind him.

The darkness misted toward Cori, covering the distance in the blink of an eye. Veynar meant to shout, but the warning stuck in his throat and he watched as Cori cowered under the mysterious assault. She scrambled back, a single sword in hand, eyes sharp for any blades that struck from the darkness.

She barely deflected the cut, and the force of it sent her skipping backward. Feet skidded in the dirt of the street before they found purchase, but not in time to block the shadow's second attack.

Malric rushed the shadow, preventing it from landing a killing blow on his friend. Swords crossed, and again Malric was forced back. He was among the best of Caelen's warriors, but against this shadow he was as outmatched as a child against a master sword.

The roots tying Veynar to the ground broke as he watched his friends fighting for their lives. He sprinted forward, but he was too slow and the clash of blades too fast. He threw one of his two swords, and he'd never dared toss such a valuable weapon. His aim was true, and even if the spin was wrong, a blow from the hilt of the blade should have at least distracted the assassin for a crucial moment.

The mis-thrown blade spun through the place the assassin should have been without slowing. It stuck harmlessly in the wall of a small house. Malric lost ground faster now, his parries carrying grunts of desperation. He had but moments left, and Veynar couldn't reach him.

A white-hot bolt of light flashed from one of the nearby rooftops. Veynar would have called it lightning, but the sky was perfectly clear and lightning didn't come from rooftops. The light flashed through the air, burning a line between the rooftop and the assassin.

The shadows and feathers were already retreating, respecting the bolt of light in the way it should have respected Malric and Cori's blades. The bolt struck the street and vanished. No thunder accompanied the light, and Veynar caught sight of something embedded in the street. He glanced again, and it was gone.

The assassin slowed as the darkness that surrounded it approached Veynar. His stomach churned as it came close, and he settled into a fighting stance with his one remaining sword. He cursed his decision to throw the first. Against the longer blade the assassin wielded, he had little chance of defending well.

A second bolt of light came from the same rooftop, and again the assassin, gifted with preternatural instincts, avoided it. The bolt of light struck close to Veynar's feet, and though his eyes were blinded for the briefest of moments, he swore he saw an arrow with red fletching. He blinked, and it was gone, an illusion like so much of what he'd seen the past few days.

The assassin hesitated, but when Malric recovered his wits and charged, it decided it had enough. Feather, shadow, and mist roiled and condensed, shrinking until it was all a violently spinning ball of darkness. It vanished, leaving Malric, Cori, and Veynar alone in an empty street with the body of a dead Sister-in-training, who'd only wanted them to save her.

CHAPTER 6
LIES BETWEEN FRIENDS

May the truth be ever on your tongue. For I say to you, it is better to cut a lying tongue out and never speak again than to let a lie pass over your lips.

— FROM *THE SAYINGS OF CAELEN*

Malric pulled Veynar's embedded sword from the building before rejoining his friend. He crossed the street slowly, as though dragging a great burden. His gaze was locked on Avelin's corpse, sprawled upon the hard-packed dirt like she'd only tripped and hadn't yet gotten back up. Only her glassy, unblinking stare and the pool of blood spreading around her head gave lie to the impression.

Veynar's pulse thundered in his ears, and the air tasted bitter on his tongue. He remembered this feeling all too well, the way fear leeched the life and warmth from his limbs, the way it poisoned his thoughts and prevented him from thinking calmly. He hated it then, on the borders of civilization and barbarity, hated it enough to leave the honored ranks of clan warriors, and he hated it now even more.

His thoughts repeated, recalling not Avelin's terrible and sudden death, but in those last moments when he'd thought the assassin would turn that deadly blade on him. He'd had his sword in hand, but would he have fought, or frozen like he had on that day?

The same question danced behind Malric's eyes, unspoken but still a wall that stood between them. Veynar's oldest friend fixed him with a hard stare, and Veynar looked away, for he had no answer. Malric grunted and handed the sword hilt-first to Veynar. "It's a beautiful weapon. Would be a shame for you to lose it."

Beneath his words, the same question once again. Did Veynar deserve such a weapon?

They both wanted the answer to be yes, but the truth remained stubbornly elusive. Veynar accepted the weapon with a bow. "Thank you."

Cori cleared her throat and reminded them that more important questions demanded their immediate attention. She crouched next to Avelin's cooling corpse. "I've never seen a strike like that," she said. "Or a warrior like that. If not for her, I'd say we imagined it all."

Malric growled. "I was standing right next to her and had no idea she was in danger. Veynar?"

He frowned and said, "Before the strike I had the same feeling I did before the stone fell in the square, like I was sick to my stomach." His eyes fell. "I thought it was because of what she was telling us. I saw nothing."

Malric and Cori shared a look Veynar couldn't decipher. "What?" he asked.

Neither answered immediately, until Malric swore under his breath. "Cori cares for you too much to say it, but *how*? How could you sense both attacks when we couldn't, and *why didn't you warn us*?"

Veynar started to reply, but they already knew the answer, and he was in no mood to condemn himself further. He hadn't thought to warn them. That was the naked truth. He should have and didn't. He couldn't blame fear, though he wished he could. His foolishness had denied his friends warning. He hung his head, but Malric wouldn't let the matter drop so easily.

"I gave my word!" he whispered. "Now she's dead because of you, and I'm a liar."

"Malric," Cori cautioned.

Malric snarled and turned on his heel. "We need to leave. It won't be long before somebody comes down this street and finds the body." He left Avelin's corpse behind without a second glance.

Cori tugged on Veynar's arm. "He's right. It's best if we leave. There's nothing we could say that would help the wardens, and it's every bit as likely they'd arrest us for the murder."

Veynar let himself be pulled away. Avelin was dead, and if not by his hands, by both his actions and inaction. If the wardens or witnesses found them by the body, there'd be no limit to their trouble. Too many of Brenwick's citizens already viewed the clan as barbaric killers, barely fit to walk their streets. They probably wouldn't even bother with a trial as they rushed the three of them toward a scaffold. He didn't tear his eyes from the Sister-in-training's corpse until Cori pulled him around a corner and the body disappeared from view.

They walked quickly. Not so fast that they would draw attention, but they passed through the outskirts of the town and into the fields beyond in short order. No one pursued them now, but Veynar feared their rapid departure wouldn't be protection enough. The death of a Sister, even one in training, would garner significant attention from the wardens, and with a bit of work, they'd find witnesses who remembered Avelin in the company of a group of clan warriors.

They'd bought themselves time, but not freedom.

Once they were safely beyond the outskirts of Brenwick, their pace slowed. Malric led, but never once did he turn to glance back. His shoulders were high and tight, and both Veynar and Cori knew better than to speak to him.

"Did you see the person who saved us?" Veynar asked.

He'd spoken softly, not intending the words to carry all the way to Malric, but he was heard, for Malric froze, almost in mid-step, his entire body taut as a drawn bowstring. Malric spun and stomped back toward Veynar. "What in Caelen's name are you talking about?"

Veynar was too surprised not to answer honestly. "There was somebody on a nearby rooftop who attacked the assassin. I've never seen anything like it. Like bolts of lightning from the sky that drove the assassin back."

Malric stared at Veynar, a furious fire burning in his gaze, but his mouth hung slightly open. He shook his head, as though refusing to dignify Veynar's question with a response. He spun, shoved his hands deep into the folds of his robes, and stomped away.

Veynar reached out, but Cori grabbed his wrist and kept it down. After Malric had put some space between them, she said, "I don't know what's going on with you, but that's not what happened. There was no one else. No 'lightning from the sky' or anything. Malric drove the assassin away with that last charge."

VEYNAR SWEPT the stone walkway leading to the halgard again, gently brushing aside the ants and spiders that insisted the walkway was occupied territory. With death fresh in his thoughts, haunting his memories every time he closed his eyes, he took pleasure in the mercy he offered the insects. Maeryn hadn't assigned him the task, but he'd leaped to it anyways.

Every step he took to understand Lirael's death deepened the mystery that surrounded it. He had a dozen questions without answers, but the only fact he was certain of was that he wasn't mad.

He'd considered the possibility. How could he not? If his memories had only disagreed with friends, families, and witnesses once, he would have called it a fit of delirium, a vision or a premonition without clean explanation. Caelen taught them the world was full of mysteries, and what was one more?

Again and again, though?

There was another explanation. He only had to find it. Avelin had thought she was at fault, but the blame hardly rested on her shoulders. Her corpse in the middle of the street proved her relative innocence.

The search had already cost him more than he wanted to pay. Malric, who believed with all his heart that he'd driven off the assassin the night before, nursed a deep wound in his spirit from Veynar's claim. Cori, who'd never doubted him, not even when he began his apprenticeship under Maeryn, now looked at him with questions in her eyes. If those questions ever became doubts, he feared it would break him.

He hadn't spoken to his family about the matter since visiting the Hall of the Dead. Father no doubt considered the matter settled, and both he and Mother were consumed by their own grief. They bore it silently, as was proper, for Lirael had given up the clan and they'd already mourned her loss.

It would be best to stop asking questions. To resume the normal course of his duties as an apprentice Keeper. He was Caelen's, and all of Caelen's followers who knew how to walk knew what it meant to grieve. The list of friends he'd lost was already almost as long as the list of friends still alive, and he had decades of the Watch ahead of him before he earned his rest. He knew well that time would scar over the memories of Lirael's loss, that though the wound would never close and heal completely, life would go on.

Only he couldn't let it go. The mysteries and the questions gnawed at him like a dog refusing to let go of a bone. Her death had poked holes in everything he'd considered real, and even if he turned aside, those holes would remain, worrying at him until he went truly mad.

So he was here, outside the halgard, not because he was a dutiful apprentice, but because he'd been seized by a madness of another sort, a gamble he hoped would serve him well but very well might land him in more trouble than he was ready for. He apologized to the bugs he roughly swept aside, for his attention was on greater matters.

A strong arm swept aside the furs and stepped into the morning sun. Gavrin squinted as the light struck him in the face, and Veynar used the moment to openly study the enigmatic man. Outside of Maeryn, he was the only Keeper the rest of the clan warriors refused to grumble about. Streaks of gray in his hair flashed against the sun.

Veynar quickly looked away. He'd felt the blows those arms were capable of delivering and had no desire to experience them again anytime soon. He kept sweeping as the Keeper approached.

"You sweep the stones, though Maeryn hasn't requested it. Your broom and feet are here, but your mind is somewhere else," Gavrin said.

Veynar gripped his broom tighter. There was no point arguing with Gavrin's observation, true as it was. He bowed in apology. "Keeper, I'll confess I've been waiting for you."

"For me? Why?"

Gavrin's look was open, revealing nothing but curiosity.

Veynar spoke carefully, cautious about giving too much away and betraying the trust of his friends while still being honest. "Sir, last night I was out with Cori and Malric, and I saw something they did not. I had hoped you might offer me some guidance."

Gavrin nodded, encouraging Veynar to continue.

"We were out and I saw what looked like lightning, though it was straight instead of jagged. It came from no cloud, but flashed as brightly as anything I've ever seen. The light followed what looked like an arrow, but soon after the light faded, the arrow did as well, leaving no evidence of its passing behind."

"A strange tale. Malric didn't have you too deep in your cups, did he?"

"No, sir. I'd had nothing to drink. Neither Malric nor Cori saw it, though."

"If your friends were there and didn't see it, what makes you so certain that you did?"

Veynar offered a rueful smile. "That's the question I've been asking myself since last night. I believe it without evidence."

"A choice full of peril and opportunity. It seems like there's little for me to add."

"I'd hoped you might have an explanation."

"It sounds like a story out of legend. Are you asking me if I'm familiar with any stories of old that match? I'm certain you already know that Caelen's bow was said to strike like lightning and echo like thunder."

Gavrin offered nothing freely, though Veynar didn't expect him to. "I'm asking if you have any explanation for what I might have seen last night."

Gavrin stroked his scarred chin and studied Veynar the same way Veynar had studied him just moments ago. "I think it would be best if you spoke to the High Keeper."

Veynar pushed harder, praying to Caelen he didn't push so hard Gavrin introduced him to the backside of his hand. "You can't help me, then?"

Again Gavrin sidestepped the question, providing the illusion of an answer while giving Veynar nothing to grasp onto. "In such matters, it would be best to speak to the High Keeper. It's her wisdom we should follow."

Gavrin bowed, ending the conversation, and Veynar sealed his lips before he dug himself a hole from which there was no escape. But as Gavrin turned his back to Veynar, an impulse pulled the question he most wanted to ask from his spirit. "Sir?"

Gavrin turned, his posture hinting at the onset of violence. "Yes?"

"My father speaks of you sometimes in the great battles to the east. He told me that your bow never missed."

"Your father is kind, but he exaggerates my skills."

"He also told me that you used to dip your fletchings in the blood of your enemies. That our enemies would break at the mere sight of one of your arrows embedded in the heart of a warrior. Is that true?"

"That they broke because they saw my arrow? I couldn't say. But that I liked to dip my fletchings? Yes. Though often as not it was from game that I had killed."

Veynar bowed in thanks for the answer, then said, "It's just that the arrows I saw last night. Before they vanished, I could have sworn the fletchings were red."

Veynar searched Gavrin's face for any reaction, but there was none. Heart pounding in his chest, he bowed quickly, then hurried toward the halgard as Gavrin had suggested before.

CHAPTER 7
CARVED OF WOOD AND SPIRIT

What, then, is the value of a life? There are those who say it is measured in laughter and smiles, in the love of family and the fellowship of friends. There is a wisdom in such ideas we'd be fools to ignore, but such measures always struck me as too selfish. If we are to make the world safer and wealthier for our children, we must focus on the Making and on the Doing. And so I propose to you this: What is the value of a life? It is measured in what you build and create, what you make with your hands and heart that will live on after you have passed to the other side of the veil.

— FROM *THE WISDOM OF BRENNOR*

Veynar and Cori walked hand in hand outside Caelen's Rest, following narrow trails packed hard over the years the clan had returned to Brenwick. It wasn't one of the trails used by the Watch. Those were farther from the center of Caelen's Rest, spaced far enough away the clan would have ample warning if danger approached.

Not that the clan had to worry here. This far west they were safe from the dangers that ever threatened the east, the monsters and madness the clans confronted daily. Other clans, brothers and sisters all, kept the Watches that mattered most while Caelen's clan took their well-earned rest for the Harvest Festival. Once it was over they would return to the east, and Veynar, Cori, Malric, and all the rest would once again fight to defend all that remained of civilization.

In truth, there was no real need for a Watch here, but their ancestors had learned it was better to maintain the practices of vigilance, even when they weren't required.

Such concerns and thoughts meant little to Veynar. He'd sought out Cori after she'd returned from her Watch and intercepted her before she'd reached Caelen's Rest. "The High Keeper didn't tell you anything?" Cori sounded as surprised as Veynar had felt when Maeryn had summarily dismissed his questioning.

"Not a thing! She ordered me into one of the Keeper's meditative states where she questioned me about all that I remembered. It was a disaster."

"How?"

"Every memory I have slips out of my grasp whenever I try to bring it forward."

Cori frowned. "Isn't that the nature of memory? Always shifting, always changing? I seem to recall the High Keeper once telling us that we shape our memories as much as they shape us."

"That's true for most, but a significant part of my Keeper's training has been learning how to master awareness and memory. I'm no Keeper yet, but I should be able to recall everything effortlessly. Whenever I dropped into one of the recall trances, though, it was like my memories were at war with themselves. I'd see Lirael dead in front of me, and then the next moment I'd remember stumbling exhausted into our family's house that night after a long day at the halgard. I feel so sure of what I saw, but it's like grasping smoke."

Their path carried them up the side of a hill, twisting back and forth to create an easier climb. Cori's shorter, quicker strides easily kept pace with Veynar's longer steps.

"What did the High Keeper say when you told her?" Cori asked.

"That the answers I seek are within me."

"Maybe not a lie, but evasive," Cori observed.

"The same as Gavrin. I'm becoming certain they know more than they're saying. Simply talking about it makes me want to punch one of them."

He apologized as she fixed him with a disappointed glare.

"I'd say you've been spending too much time with Malric, but I know that's not true. He complains about your absence to everybody that will listen."

"So just you?"

That got Cori to smile, but only for a moment. "You should go to the Harvest Festival with him tonight. It would give the two of you a chance to work out your differences, and I'd feel better knowing he had someone at least attempting to restrain his baser impulses."

"You're not going to attempt to switch with anyone?" Veynar asked.

"It's my Watch."

It was a simple fact, but she said it as if it were a deeper truth. Veynar almost believed her. He let his hand brush against some of the taller grass that had grown next to the trail. "Have you decided what you're going to do after the Harvest Festival?"

"No."

Years' worth of anguish lurked beneath the surface of the answer, and Veynar wished he could lift some of the suffering from her shoulders, but the burden was hers alone. "Whatever you decide, I'll support you."

Cori's thanks were curt. Not from rudeness, but from the desire to talk about anything else.

She was a warrior of the clan and a blooded veteran of the Watch. She'd faced countless numbers of the enemy and sent them fleeing. In battle, she was dangerous and reserved, possessing a gift for striking the enemy where it would hurt them worst.

Only Veynar knew—although he was sure Malric suspected and said nothing—that Cori hated her duty.

Many did at some point. Only madmen like Malric basked in it. That was why the clan was as it was. Why children who turned in their swords and bows were disowned by their families. Why Keepers, though necessary, were glared at openly. The clan couldn't afford to lose anyone, but they didn't dare hold on to those who wanted to leave the battlefields.

They reached the top of the hill and took in the view. Pines grew side by side with maples in the valleys where water ran after the rainstorms and birds wheeled in the sky, dancing on invisible currents of air. A fresh breeze played with Cori's hair, tossing it this way and that until she pulled it back and restrained it with a small leather cord.

She caught him looking. "Yes?"

"You're beautiful."

She smiled and gripped his hand tighter as they looked over the valleys and hills.

He didn't want to break the silence, but he'd brought her up here for more than the view. He'd come to depend on her insight when his own failed. "I don't know what's left to do. Every trail I've followed has ended, and I don't think there are any trails left to pursue."

She let go of his hand and reached into one of the pockets of her robes. "I don't have the answers you're looking for. I'm as confused as you, if not more. But I made you something."

Cori opened her hand to reveal a small wooden figure carved from maple. It was of a young woman on her knees, a book resting on her lap. Lirael's face was exactly the way he remembered it, alive in a way that seemed impossible for mere wood. Cori's eye for detail was unmatched, capturing the lines of Lirael's face and hair with subtle cuts that were barely noticeable.

"Cori...this is incredible." He closed his hand around it, brought it to his chest, close to his heart, and he swore he sensed his sister close, some small fragment of her spirit caught in this world thanks to Cori's artistry.

If she ever chose to give up her swords and her bow, there were dozens of woodcrafters across the land who would hire her. Her untutored work was already equal to some of the best sold. How much more could she accomplish if trained by a proper master? She was an artist trapped in a warrior's life, but he didn't dare say that aloud.

Veynar bowed deeply. "I will treasure it."

When he rose, he kissed her. Her lips welcomed his, and he held her close with his open hand. They parted and his hand slipped back into hers. He examined the figurine again.

What would his sister want of him? One corner of his lips turned up at a thought. She'd demand he propose to Cori soon, and he promised her memory that he would, as soon as his Keeper training was resolved and it was permitted.

Beyond that, though? She'd encourage his curiosity. Tell him to follow it wherever it led. She'd pore through books time and time again, searching for some hidden knowledge she'd overlooked.

He embraced Cori again. "It's also given me an idea. Will you come with me? There's something I want to do."

She followed him without question, though from where they had started, their path could only lead to one destination. A quick couple miles of hiking brought them to the short stone wall that marked the edges of the forest park between Caelen's Rest and Brenwick proper.

The sight of the wall inspired a snort of derision, for such a wall could only come from the mind of one of Brennor's followers. The idea that a forest could be contained reeked of city-born arrogance and ignorance.

A true forest was no different from any other creature that wandered the world. It grew or shrunk based on the availability of food and water and the presence of predators. There were forests near the eastern boundaries that had grown hundreds of feet wider in Veynar's short life.

Not here, though. Not where they could be contained and grown with human care. Brenwick's citizens called this a forest merely because it was a collection of trees. It was supposed to be a place that reminded them of the wild they'd come from, but they'd carefully built paths and benches and cleared swaths of trees away to make perfectly circular picnic areas. There was little wild left about this place, but it was as close as most citizens came to their true home.

Veynar judged it even as he appreciated it, for it was still a sight better than the city with its claustrophobic alleys and unnaturally straight streets.

He and Cori hopped over the waist-high wall and strode through the far eastern edges of the park, toward the tree he and Lirael had spent so much time in when he'd been younger. He still held the figurine in his hand, thumb pressed lightly against the book on Lirael's lap. Her voice whispered in his ear, barely more than a child. Even then, though, she'd possessed a wisdom lacking in many who were older.

"Whenever I get confused, I just turn the pages back and go to the beginning, to the last part I understood."

He couldn't turn back time like he could pages, but he could go back to where the mysteries had started.

Red maple leaves crunched beneath his boots. They crunched beneath Cori's boots. He listened to the nearly continual crunching as a group of children chased each other a few hundred paces to the west. A fresh layer of leaves had fallen since he remembered being here last.

If he'd ever been here at all.

The sun was setting to the west, the towers and spires of Brenwick casting long shadows toward the park, the city covering the trees in gradually encroaching darkness. What light remained fought through the red leaves still anchored to the trees, fighting to stay alive as winter grew inevitably closer. The effect was to bathe the forest in a soft red light, warm against the cold gray of Brenwick's stone in the distance.

His and Lirael's tree stood a silent guardian in the quietest parts of the forest. The crunch of leaves faded as they stood still, but Veynar shivered and looked around, somehow certain he was being watched, though this part of the park was empty and quiet.

He dismissed the fear as a ghost of his memories. There was no sign of the violence whose aftermath he was sure he'd witnessed. No blood on the tree or the leaves, no signs of a struggle. Veynar searched the bark of the tree in vain for signs it had been cut by a blade. Search as he might, though, there was nothing around the tree to prove he'd seen something real.

He took a few steps back and put his hands on his hips, studying the tree and its surroundings the way a commander might study the terrain before committing their forces to battle.

Cori completed a slow search around the perimeter of the tree, then joined him.

"Let's assume my memories of that evening are true. That Lirael sent me a note and wanted to meet me here. Let's also assume that Avelin spoke true. What else does that tell us?"

Cori played along. "Avelin implied that Lirael's note came first, because she was already planning on leaving. So she wanted to see you for a different reason."

"Maybe she was just lonely, though I have a hard time believing that."

Cori agreed. "Even if she had been, she would have borne the pain in service of her study. Maybe she had something she wanted to give to you," Cori suggested. "A gift, perhaps."

The suggestion shook Veynar to his bones. Why in Caelen's name hadn't he thought of that? He kissed Cori on the forehead. "You're brilliant."

Her eyes. They hadn't rolled up. She'd been trying to point.

Veynar ran at the tree and planted a foot against the trunk, which redirected his sprint into a vertical leap. Calloused hands caught the rough tree limb, and he smoothly pulled himself up.

His feet and hands knew the way. Instead of climbing to the perch that had been his, he pulled himself over to Lirael's. There was a hole in the tree there where she'd stored little trinkets over the years. She'd always delighted in returning to the tree after a year of Watch to find the same treasures inside. His hand was almost too large to fit, but his fingers crawled around the inside. They stopped on something as hard as steel, with sharp, regular edges. He grasped it between his fingers and pulled it out.

It was a gem, as red as the color of the leaves that surrounded him, and about the size of the tip of his pinkie finger. It was translucent, and when he held it up to the last light of the sun, he could see clear through.

He rolled it across his fingers as he stared at it.

"Did you find something?" Cori called from below.

"I did."

He meant to say more, but his attention was seized, ripped from him like the wind whipped the last leaves from the nearby maples. A presence invaded his mind, and though it spoke no words, no shared language used by the clans, Veynar understood it all the same.

What have we here? A youngling, and sensitive, too.

There was a pause, in which it felt as though the entire world held its breath, awaiting judgment.

This shall be interesting indeed.

CHAPTER 8
EXPLOSIONS IN THE SKY

My brothers and sisters stop and marvel at the wonders that surround them, but I am lost in the future, marveling at the wonders we will someday build together.

— FROM *THE LOST WISDOM OF BRENNOR*

Malric looked around the otherwise empty tent, as though convinced Veynar was speaking to someone else. When he found no one, he pointed to himself and whispered, "Me?"

Veynar reconsidered accepting Cori's advice, but after helping around the halgard all day and nursing a grudge against Maeryn for refusing to share her wisdom, an evening trip to Brenwick with Malric to celebrate the midway point of the Harvest Festival seemed a welcome and familiar form of madness.

The gem from the tree rested back in his family home, hidden beneath the bedding in his room. He'd almost fallen from the tree as the presence filled his mind, but it vanished as quickly as it appeared, making him once again doubt his sanity.

He'd handed the stone to Cori and asked her if she sensed anything, but she'd stared at him blankly, shook her head, and handed it back. On their way back to Caelen's Rest, he'd considered bringing it to Malric, but he could guess well enough what would happen.

Maeryn had said that she'd sensed the gods dancing around him, and they hadn't seen fit to invite his friends.

The discovery of the gem had solidified the story weaving its way through his thoughts, though. Avelin had stolen the gem, likely from the House of Brennor. Somehow, she'd convinced Lirael to deliver it. What had happened after that remained a question. Maybe Lirael hadn't delivered it. Maybe she'd suspected trouble and quickly hidden it. Or maybe she'd known what it was and wanted to deliver it to Veynar when they met. Regardless, she'd been killed because of the gem.

And then the madness began, which he had no explanation for. Everything he'd doubted since finding Lirael's body had been true, from the presence he'd sensed when he first touched the gem to the strike of lightning from the clear sky. Maeryn and Gavrin knew something, too, but for reasons he couldn't guess, they didn't see fit to share.

His mind had wandered over the problem all day, earning him reprimands from the High Keeper for his lack of focus. She'd been harsher with him than usual, he thought, but he couldn't decide if that was true or he felt that way because of her reticence to explain what she knew.

Whatever the reason, he needed to pull his mind away from the problem, and if there was anyone who could do that, it was Malric.

For better or for worse.

"There's no one else here," Veynar said.

"Normally I'd agree, but with all the illusions you've been seeing lately, who am I to say?"

Veynar turned to leave.

"Sorry." Malric reached out and grabbed Veynar's wrist. "I'm sorry. That was inexcusable."

Veynar allowed himself to be pulled back into the room.

"Cruel insults aside, do you think it's wise to return to Brenwick?"

Veynar shrugged. "No one returning from Brenwick has reported any harassment from the wardens, and if they suspected our involvement, I have little doubt they'd visit Caelen's Rest in force."

Malric grunted. "You're forgetting the assassin who killed a Sister-in-training and tried their best to kill us."

Veynar pulled at the folds of his robes, revealing his sheathed blades. "I wasn't planning on visiting unarmed."

Malric studied him for a moment, judging whether or not his friend was full of false bravado. Then he broke into a grin. "You're going hunting."

"No, I really do only intend to celebrate the Harvest Festival with you, but if there's a chance to avenge Avelin's death, I'd be happy to help you take it."

Malric's chest puffed out. "You're a good man, Veynar, and a good friend. Let's erase the stain upon our honor if we can."

The streets of central Brenwick were packed with bodies, a celebratory mass of humanity gathered in honor of a successful harvest. At least, that was what they would say. Mostly they were gathered to drink, make love, and buy seasonal supplies. Veynar allowed himself to be pulled, pushed, and shoved by the crowds, caught like a stick of driftwood in the pounding of the sea against the shore. He knew full well the number of people living in and around Brenwick, but the number meant nothing until he witnessed them all together.

If everyone jostling him tonight had followed Caelen's wisdom, they'd have the numbers to retake the mountain passes and secure their land for generations.

But they didn't and never would, and he surrendered to the mood of the crowd. Malric led him from one stall to another, introducing him to sweets, roasted meats, and varieties of fish he'd never had. Brenwick coins seemed to spill from Malric's pockets, but Veynar had the good manners not to ask where he'd acquired them.

They sampled much but gorged on none. Malric, no stranger to the temptation of strong liquor, avoided all drink besides water, and Veynar followed suit. Time and again, Malric would glance back, a question in his gaze, asking if Veynar's stomach felt sick. Each time Veynar gave a small shake of his head, and their wandering through the streets continued.

They suffered no trouble either from the wardens or from mysterious assassins. The community boards were filled with notices, but none about the death of a sister in training. Like so many of Veynar's memories, it was as though Avelin's death had never happened.

Their journey let them listen in on dozens of conversations, and many followed a theme. Not the murder of a Sister-in-training but concerns about taxes.

Veynar had learned about taxes in his studies, but they were as much a myth to him as Caelen's historic battles. His entire life was an offering, and so there was no need for taxes, nor any money to pay them with. The same wasn't true for the citizens of Brenwick, and from what Veynar overheard, the matter was becoming heated. The King of Brenwick and its lands was named Orlan, and he was advised closely by both the Head

Sister of the House of Brennor and the head of one of the largest merchant houses in the city, House Elowen, named after the original matriarch of the family.

From what Veynar could gather, the two advisors disagreed with one another over the matter of taxation. The House of Brennor was asking the king to raise taxes to fund the development of new inventions and more building. House Elowen had requested lower taxes, arguing that the people shouldn't bear the burden of supporting the House of Brennor's wilder pursuits.

They passed by one argument between two drunk older men that Veynar stopped to listen to. The first gentleman shook his head. "You wouldn't be so quick to judge if you knew all that the House of Brennor has done. It's their medicines that cured my girl when none of the healers knew what to do."

His friend held up his hands. "I don't argue that they're wonderful, and their inventions have helped us a lot over the years, but I'm already paying too much, and I can't afford more just so they can tinker with more contraptions."

"Those contraptions almost always end up helping us."

"Sure, but they'll come around eventually one way or the other. Better to have a few extra notes in my pocket, if you ask me. Elowen has the right of it, if you ask me. Let us keep more money, and we'll spend it all over the city, which is better for everyone. The House of Brennor is becoming a parasite."

The two men started repeating their previous points, only louder this time, as though that would make their arguments more compelling. Veynar gestured for Malric to continue, and Malric led him down a quiet alley, then another, distancing themselves from the crowd. They stepped over a drunk passed out against a wall, and Malric stopped in a narrow alley where two buildings were nearly close enough to touch. Veynar could only barely walk down it without brushing his shoulders against each wall.

"Come on," Malric said.

He placed a hand and a foot on each wall, then flew up the gap like a spider walking between two of its webs.

Veynar watched him, then followed. The close walls made the climb easy, and a few moments later he was on the roof of the shorter building. Malric was waiting for him. Veynar's feet had barely touched the roof when his friend was off again, running lightly across the stone tiles. Veynar followed, a grin slowly spreading across his face. Malric leaped across a man-sized gap without breaking stride, and Veynar did the same.

Another roof passed underneath their feet. A taller building rose in front of them, a story taller than the one they ran upon. Malric leaped the gap between the buildings, planting his foot and transforming his sprint into a vertical jump. His hands grasped the stone edge of the roof and he pulled himself up in one smooth motion.

Veynar made the same leap, refusing to think about the empty space beneath him. His fingers barely cleared the edge of the stone, but it was enough to pull himself up and over. Malric had stopped and waited on the edge, ready to grab Veynar's wrist if something went wrong.

Veynar enjoyed the vista Malric's journey had led them to. The crowds ebbed and flowed far beneath them and the stars twinkled high above. The roof's gentle slope was enough to shed the frequent rains that fell upon the city, but not so steep he feared losing his footing.

They climbed to the peak of the roof and watched the crowd. Veynar breathed deeply, the muscles across his chest relaxing as he drew further away from the mass of people seething through the streets. His shoulders fell.

Malric made a knife with his hand and cut the air. "Care for a sparring match?"

"Is that why you dragged me all the way up here?"

"No, but I figure that if we're up here now, we might as well enjoy ourselves."

Against his better judgment, Veynar considered. Gavrin kept the apprentice Keepers fit, but there was a world of difference between mere activity and training to fight. He'd been too slow in the fight against the assassin. "Let's."

Malric balanced on the peak of the roof and extended his arm. "Classic rules? First solid blow wins?"

"Agreed." Veynar extended his own arm and stretched through his fingertips. They'd done this for countless hours as children, the outside edge of their hand a less lethal alternative than the edges of the swords they had hoped to someday carry. He stepped onto the peak of the roof and found his balance.

Malric attacked first, striking at Veynar's neck. Veynar leaned back and let Malric's hand pass in front of him. Malric stopped his hand and thrust it forward. Veynar swiped it away with the edge of his hand, and it was all too easy to imagine one blade meeting the other.

They fell into the duel, their heavy breathing crystallizing into clouds in the cool night air. By the time Malric landed the winning blow, a smile had extended all the way across Veynar's face. He'd lasted a lot longer than he feared he would.

His expression was matched by Malric's. His friend went to the end of the roof and sat at the edge, his legs dangling over the emptiness below. Veynar joined him.

"Not as bad as I thought," Malric said.

"Thanks."

"You have gotten worse, though. There was a time when you were considerably better than me."

Veynar didn't deny it. "I spend more time meditating these days than I do training, so it's no real surprise."

"Is it worth it?"

Malric had never asked directly, though he'd implied the question a hundred different ways in the months since Veynar had chosen the path of the Keepers. His friend would never understand, not truly. Malric had been born to fight, had known it in the very marrow of his bones even when he'd been young. But he tried to understand.

Veynar wished the answer was easier than it was. He'd never dreamed or desired to join the Keepers. Like most in the clan, he'd respected them but found them more burden than benefit. After the day of his first battle, though, they'd been the easiest way forward, the lowest hanging fruit that a former warrior like him could pick. They were a halfway point, better than the voluntary exile his sister had chosen but worse than the path of a respected warrior.

"I don't know," Veynar confessed. "I'm glad to still be part of the clan and contributing in some small way, but I don't know."

"Do you think you'll ever leave the Keepers and return to us?" Malric didn't quite keep the thread of hope from his voice.

"I don't know that either, but it won't be soon. I want to believe I'd be worth standing beside on Watch, but I'm not. Not yet."

Malric's response was cut short by the sound of a muffled *thump* that drew every eye below to the skies above Brenwick castle. An explosion of bright green sparks expanded in a rough sphere, drawing appreciative cheers and hoots from the audience packed into the narrow streets. More fireworks followed the first, and from their privileged vantage point, Veynar could watch the castle's servants running from place to place, lighting fuses to various arrows and cannons in a carefully orchestrated dance.

The sky exploded in a kaleidoscope of colors and transported Veynar back to a time when the world had held more promise than despair. The fireworks had been less colorful then, and smaller. Brenwick's alchemists had been hard at work since the last Harvest Festival he'd attended.

"Lirael loved the fireworks," Veynar remembered.

"I know. She was always pestering me to get her into the castle so she could see how they were made. I miss her, too."

Veynar glanced over at his friend and wondered at his unknown depths. Once, he would have sworn Malric had sought her hand in marriage, but he'd never courted Lirael, and then she'd exiled herself from the clan and he'd turned his hopes for a successful marriage in different directions.

His stomach churned and he was on his feet in less than a heartbeat, searching their surroundings. He couldn't see any assassins, but after their last encounter, he wasn't sure he would.

Malric scrambled to his feet, hands next to his swords. "What is it?"

Veynar closed his eyes. The sense of unease in his stomach grew. "The assassin from the night before. They're close and coming closer."

Malric's blades whispered their hopes for vengeance as they cleared their sheaths. Veynar opened his eyes and drew his own blades, retreating a couple of paces so he wasn't exposed at the edge of the roof. It had granted them an unparalleled view of the fireworks, but it was a terrible place to fight.

More fireworks exploded above the castle, a rainbow of shades of red falling like bloody rain from the sky. In their light he caught a glimpse of shadow and mist, spiraling and twisting like leaves caught in the wind near the corner of a building.

Veynar extended his arm, pointing the tip of his knife at the approaching assassin. "There."

The deadly mist drifted and spun across a rooftop across the street, a jump no less than twenty paces across. It never slowed, but leaped across the crowded street and toward the friends eager for another chance to kill it.

CHAPTER 9
BLOOD UPON THE STONES

One imperative lives in the center of the heart of every human, a command only the most willful and the most despondent are able to deny, a command written so deeply upon our souls we never question its dictates. If you're wise, you'll use it to your advantage.
That command?
Survive.

— FROM *THE SAYINGS OF CAELEN*

Mist darker than the night swirled toward Veynar. It landed on the edge of the roof with the rustle of raven feathers and launched itself straight at him. A blade extended and thrust at Veynar's chest, the cloaking shadow somehow incapable of disguising the movement of the bared steel.

Veynar used his short sword to turn aside the thrust, and the deadly blade went wide. The mist billowed and stretched, hitting his stomach. Far from a cloud or falling feathers, the mist struck with the hardness of a human joint, most likely a knee. Air exploded from Veynar's lungs as one of the castle's fireworks exploded above, like the whole city was celebrating the blow. He stumbled back, heaving desperately to pull air into his battered body.

Malric struck before the assassin's blade could deliver a killing cut. He came in from the side, his short swords whirling in a blur. The mist retreated toward the corner of the roof, but any hope of sending the assassin over the edge vanished as their blade flashed once, then twice, flicking aside Malric's short swords with contemptuous ease. A heartbeat later and Malric was retreating, needing his two swords to defend against the flickering cuts of the assassin's blade.

Breath finally returned to Veynar's lungs. He leaped into the fray, his short swords seeking the body that had to be hiding within the mist. Though he failed to land a single cut, he tore the assassin's attention in two, and Malric halted his retreat.

They fought together, short swords singing in unison. Once they'd dreamed of fighting their enemies to the east like this, bragged to anyone foolish enough to listen of the conquests they'd win once they were allowed in the Watch. Skilled as the assassin was, one blade against four simply wasn't enough. Only the mist kept the assassin alive, clouding their vision and keeping them as good as blind.

The mist held its ground for a moment, then fled against the coordinated assault, writhing toward the edge of the roof.

Malric grunted and sprinted after, leaving Veynar standing flat-footed for a precious moment.

The mist billowed and stopped and the assassin's blade again lashed out at Malric's heart. He turned the blade aside with one short sword and stabbed into the heart of the mist with the other, but he stumbled forward as he struck nothing but air. Mist coalesced and whipped across Malric's face, and he spun like a child's top as the punch snapped his head around. The veteran held onto his blades, but his gaze was distant as he staggered away.

The assassin wasted no time seizing the advantage, speeding toward Malric, blade out and aimed straight at his heart.

Veynar narrowed his eyes. The longer he watched the mist and the blade, the greater his sense of where their mysterious assassin hid in the mist. They didn't hide in the center as one would expect, and the blade often cut down from left to right.

The assassin fought with their left hand, one last layer of misdirection to protect themselves against the occasional target strong enough to fight back. There, within the shadow, was a darkness even deeper. He sprinted toward the center of the mist with a yell, hoping to distract the assassin's attention from Malric.

It didn't work. The blade rushed toward Malric's heart, but Veynar shifted on his last step and aimed for what he hoped was the assassin within the mist. The assassin noticed and the blade came around, but Veynar lowered his shoulder and leaped, tackling the assassin before they could defend themselves.

He'd expected a more jarring impact, but it felt instead like he'd tackled a young man. There was a higher-pitched grunt, and then he and the mist were over the alley, falling toward the neighboring building. Veynar braced himself, but not quickly enough.

He and the assassin hit the edge of the building, slamming into the roof with all the grace of a drunk horse. For the second time that night the air was forced out of his lungs, and he feared they'd soon quit trying to keep him alive. The momentum from his tackle tumbled him forward and off the assassin's body. He tried to push himself up but his body refused. His arms gave out and he let himself lay on the stone tile of the roof.

The assassin wasn't moving much faster. His tackle hadn't succeeded in stripping the mist from her, but the mist remained still, a small, thunderous raincloud that had lost its way and waited for directions.

Malric leaped from the rooftop, bringing his short swords down in the heart of the mist. They cracked against the stone tiles of the roof, and the mist retreated as he cut wildly.

Veynar cursed at the assassin's recovery. "She's left-handed," he coughed.

Malric grinned viciously and attacked again, adjusting his attacks to the new information. He drove the assassin back fast, her blade slower than before.

A full breath helped Veynar push himself up. He stumbled toward the fight, wise enough not to interfere so long as he was injured and Malric had the upper hand. He only wanted to be close enough to help if needed. His ribs ached as he breathed in, but it was only a matter of time until his friend landed a fatal blow.

The assassin kept retreating, nearing the edge of the roof and the end of her life. Only when she reached the edge, the mist continued retreating and she fell silently.

Veynar cursed and ran forward, peering over the edge with Malric. The mist below obscured their view, but it hadn't fled from the alley. Their heads turned left and right, seeking a way down that didn't threaten to break their legs.

Veynar was still searching when Malric grunted. He shot Veynar a mischievous grin, then sheathed his swords. He stepped over the edge of the roof and twisted, catching his weight on his arms and pressing his feet against the stone of the building. He looked over his shoulder, then dropped and twisted at the same time, pushing gently off the wall with one of his feet.

Veynar cursed for the third time in as many breaths. Malric's drop and twist allowed him to aim his feet at a small windowsill. It wasn't large enough to stand on, but he flexed his legs and slowed his fall. Another half twist and a little jump brought him back to a windowsill on the building Veynar stood on top of, and again Malric's powerful legs absorbed enough of the impact to slow him down. From the last windowsill he dropped the last of the distance to the ground. It was still a hard landing, but not bone-shattering. Malric drew his swords and approached the mist.

Clan sword and assassin blade met in the night, and Veynar watched from above, but only for a moment. The assassin's blade cut and flicked out at Malric as fast as before, and Malric retreated. The clan warrior possessed the shorter blades, but he was trained to fight in the open spaces out east, attacking with wide cuts and slashes that opened enemies from shoulder to hip. Stone walls blocked him in, while the assassin thrust and stabbed her lighter sword like a scorpion's tail.

Veynar shook his head, but sheathed his swords and prepared to match Malric's descent. His heart pounded even faster than before, and his ribs and arms groaned as they supported his weight. He glanced over his shoulder, rehearsed what he needed to do, then dropped, twisted, and kicked.

The first windowsill came up fast. His feet landed cleanly, but he was already thinking about the next move and didn't absorb as much of the fall as he should have. He twisted and stepped out. He hit the second windowsill hard and the wood cracked under the impact. It slowed him, but not enough.

Veynar hit the stone of the alley like a falling sack of potatoes. He bent his knees with the impact and rolled, which saved his legs from breaking, but the alley walls and his lack of control combined to leave him on his back, legs up in the air against one of the walls.

Everything hurt, like he'd volunteered to be one of the dummies for an extended sword demonstration given by one of the Watch veterans. If not for the grunt of pain from Malric, he would have lain there, content to let the world pass him by for a bit.

Veynar rolled to his feet and pulled his short swords from their sheaths. The world spun like Malric had convinced him to go drinking all night and he blinked to clear his vision. Blood dripped from Malric's arm, but he fought with it anyway, so it couldn't have been too deep.

Veynar tried to close in on their foe, but the alley was too narrow and Malric was in the way. He waited, dancing on the balls of his feet, ready to strike the moment he saw an opening.

Malric grunted again and stumbled back. He fell to a knee.

Veynar leaped over his falling friend, noting the spreading blood across the front of Malric's robes. He cut into the darkest part of the mist and it retreated.

What chance did he have if Malric had fallen to the assassin's blade? Malric was the better warrior by far. He had no answer. He just stood between the assassin and his friend, for that was all he could do.

The assassin's blade, dripping Malric's blood, lashed out. He turned the first cuts aside, but the blade kept probing his defense, patiently waiting for him to fail. Never one to disappoint, he wasn't quick enough to respond to a thrust that sliced open the flesh across his right forearm. The sword dropped from his hand, more from surprise than weakness, but the clattering of steel against the stone redoubled the assassin's efforts.

The last of the fireworks exploded in the sky above, the booms echoing and amplified by the narrow streets and alleys. A thunderous roar, fueled by drinking and feasting, greeted the last of the fireworks, and Veynar couldn't even hear the pounding of his heart.

The assassin's blade knocked his last short sword aside and penetrated the last line of his defenses. Without options, Veynar leaped into the darkness, arms out wide. The assassin's blade sought his heart, but he'd caught her by surprise. Her sword still bit into his side, but he wrapped his arms around the assassin, twisted, and spun her into one of the alley walls. She grunted as the back of her head cracked against the stone. Her body slackened.

He let go with his injured arm and grabbed at her clothing, wrapping it around his hand so there could be no escape. Then he let go with his left arm, intending to thrust his sword into the assassin's stomach and end this fight for good.

This was likely the same assassin that had killed Lirael. He brought his short sword back and positioned it only a hand's breadth from where he was certain her torso was. He tensed, but hesitated.

The mist shifted and tried to pull away, but he held tight. Still, he didn't strike, and the mist solidified as the assassin twisted and launched a kick into his undefended side. Ribs cracked under the blow and Veynar gasped and let go of the assassin's clothing.

Another blow caught him in the stomach and lifted him off his feet. She couldn't have come up much higher than his chest and couldn't be much more than half his size, but she struck harder than any brute he'd ever faced. Cold fingers wrapped around his throat and lifted him off the ground. His feet kicked helplessly, but she pressed herself close so they lacked all force.

He didn't understand, his mind and limbs flailing with equal abandon. Her grip around his throat tightened and she pulled her sword from his side. Fiery agony spread across his ribs as blackness crowded the edge of his vision. The cheers of the crowd faded until all he heard was his heart pounding frantically in his ears, a beat so fast no drummer could follow it. The last of his strength faded from exhausted limbs.

It was easier not to fight. Easier to let it all go. He was supposed to be a warrior. Had trained all his life to achieve a single end, and when he'd encountered his first test, he'd failed. He knew full well he possessed the skill. Any warrior training alongside him and crossing blades with him knew as much.

No, his failure had been a failure of spirit. A defect no amount of training could fix.

Offering to serve as a Keeper had never been anything more than a distraction, a way to keep from making a true decision.

Death was the easier release, and he could see Lirael again on the other side of the veil.

The cold hand released his neck and he collapsed into the alley. Warm liquid sprayed against his face, and his lips tasted the familiar metallic tang of blood.

Malric had crawled, bleeding across the stones, to where the assassin had been casually choking the life from him and thrust his sword up and into the place he thought her to be.

He'd struck true.

The mist around her coalesced, shrinking until it was almost nothing. Blood pooled around her feet, spreading out from beneath the protective cover of the mist.

She shuffled away, the mist protecting her until she reached the street and disappeared into the crowd that didn't seem to notice her at all.

"We should—chase after her," Malric said through gritted teeth.

Breath had returned some of Veynar's strength, but not enough to convince him to chase after the assassin. Malric was in even worse condition. His face was pale, and he'd offered no small amount of his own blood to the alley.

Veynar groaned as he pushed himself into a sitting position, his back against the alley wall. He helped Malric up, too. He would need to bandage the wound before they dared to move. Once he caught his breath.

"I think it might be best," he said in between gasps, "if we end our Harvest Festival celebration a bit early tonight."

CHAPTER 10
ON THAT DAY

For the sins of the past there can be no forgiveness, for there is no cure. No war will win back what has been lost.
All that remains is the Watch.

— FROM *THE SAYINGS OF CAELEN*

The Dunmor Mountains stabbed at the clouds far to the east, jagged granite daggers that were as awe-inspiring as they were impassable. None had braved those peaks for generations, but the legends passed down from those that had tried and survived long enough to turn back spoke of nightmarish monsters, wild weather changes, and brutal terrain that demanded blood in exchange for passage. Though he stood on a hilltop miles and miles away, the thought of challenging those broken cliffs sent a shiver down Veynar's spine.

Heavy gray clouds gathered overhead, marshaling their forces to produce what promised to be a thunderous storm. The air was thick with moisture and heat, all the ingredients necessary to unleash torrential rains and deafening thunder upon the weary Watch. They'd hiked twelve miles and gained and lost a few thousand feet of elevation, and still had four miles and a steep hillside to climb.

Veynar and Malric traded strips of dried meat between them as they sat just below the summit of the hill. They ate in silence and watched the valley below for any signs of the enemy. They'd not crossed paths with any yet, but the previous Watch had spotted fresh tracks and suspected a small war party was in the area.

"You seeing anything?" Malric asked between bites.

"No. Think they're hunkering down in preparation for the storm?"

"Could be." Malric didn't sound convinced.

"You have a better idea?"

"The valley over the next hill has trees for shelter and clean running water fed by a spring higher up."

Veynar's eyes narrowed. "Sounds nice, but what does that matter?"

"I think they're there waiting for us, expecting we'll stop there."

It sounded like something they would do. Their ambushes as of late had a deadly creativity to them, pushing the Watchers to stretch their vigilance to the limit. Life along the borders had never been easy, but this last Watch might be the one that broke the clan. He saw the weariness on the faces of his friends and family, the inwardly focused silence of the veteran warriors pushed so far they could concern themselves with nothing beyond their next Watch.

"Should we let the others know our suspicions?" Veynar asked.

Malric tilted his head north. "I don't think we need to."

Veynar's gaze followed Malric's lead. The two veterans of

their Watch, Alvarn and Ylwen, had broken further north, following the ridge of the hill.

"They're coming around from above, so we should approach from below. If anything's hoping to ambush us, we'll crush them between us." Malric couldn't hide the edge of excitement from his voice at the promise of a fight to come.

Veynar had little problem with a quiet first Watch, but Malric was eager to test his bow, blades, and spirit. He forced the same eagerness into his voice. "Then we should get moving, too."

They devoured the last of the dried meat they'd pulled out, took a few swigs of water, then began the hike down the other side of the hill. They followed a well-worn game trail, a narrow path through the tall grass that avoided any sudden ledges or particularly steep descents. An occasional cool breeze from the east refreshed their spirits, but they moved without a word passed between them. Speech risked giving away their position to the enemy and deafened them to the sounds of their enemy's movements.

At the bottom of the valley, they met up with another barely visible trail that paralleled a dry creek bed. They crossed when it was convenient, and Malric led them around the base of the next hill so they could approach the second valley from its bottom.

Life bloomed within the second valley, fed by the trickling stream that cut down its heart. Tall pines stretched toward the summits of the surrounding hills while protecting the dense undergrowth below. Malric nocked an arrow as they approached and Veynar did the same. One well-worn trail, no stranger to human footsteps, ran up the valley along the creek, but Malric took one look at it and shook his head.

They searched for another path, and Veynar found one higher up the side of one of the hills. He crouched and looked closer, then pointed out a track to Malric. It was of a vaguely human foot, recent from the look of it. Ahead, a broken branch hung over the trail, the tip hanging from one last shred of bark at about the height of Veynar's shoulder. He pointed it out, too, and Malric nodded.

Veynar, having the sharper senses and quicker reflexes of the two, took the lead, stepping carefully onto the path. Their pace slowed until it was little faster than a crawl. Veynar explored every step with his toe before placing his weight down, ensuring there were no dried leaves of breakable twigs beneath his foot. Wary eyes swept the dense woods and his ears strained for any foreign sounds.

A soft hiss from Malric froze Veynar solid. His friend stepped directly behind him, then pointed over Veynar's shoulder, his finger aimed upward. Veynar's breath caught at the sight of the Graevath. He'd seen corpses before, as well as seen them at a distance, but the twenty paces separating them were the closest he'd ever been to one that was alive and eager to kill him.

It possessed the familiar pale gray skin of its brethren, but was smaller than most. It balanced between two limbs as though it had been born in the trees and was as still as stone. Veynar couldn't see its face, but it gazed in the direction of the main trail.

Malric whispered so softly Veynar barely heard him. "Mine."

Before Veynar could object, Malric pulled back the bowstring to his cheek. He took careful but quick aim, then released, the arrow hissing over Veynar's shoulder.

Malric's aim was true, and the arrow pierced the creature's heart, slipping between its ribs with ease. The Graevath fell from the tree, but not before releasing a piercing wail. The body crashed into the undergrowth loudly enough to startle birds on the other side of the valley, but at least the fall cut off the inhuman wail.

Malric grinned to hide the shame of his failure. "I bet they know we're here now."

Veynar swung his bow around as he watched for any sign of movement. "I'm not going to take the other side of that bet."

He kept his voice calm, but his heart pounded in his chest like it was trying to escape a locked room. He silently cursed Malric's impetuousness, but the arrow couldn't be returned to the bow, and so he waited for the inevitable counterattack. The Graevath didn't make him stew in his fear for long. Since the Graevath's ambush had failed, they deferred to their natural gifts, the swiftness of their feet and the strength of their limbs. Two of the creatures tore through the undergrowth, crashing through thick live branches as though they were dried twigs.

Another arrow hissed over Veynar's shoulder, catching the taller of the two in the shoulder. It roared in pain but didn't slow. Veynar drew his bowstring back, guaranteed time for one shot, but against which opponent? He aimed first at the unwounded Graevath, then changed his mind, snapping his aim to the taller enemy. He loosed the arrow before settling, and he watched as it sailed clear of the Graevath.

Malric leaped in front of Veynar, short swords in hand, to meet the charge with a yell of his own. The wounded Graevath swiped at him with claw-like hands. Malric avoided the blow easily and cut at the creature's side where it was most exposed. Steel opened the ashen flesh and blood tinged with what looked like mud poured from the wound.

The Graevath roared and twisted, claws raking the air, but Malric dodged low and brought his blades up under the creature's wild defense. One caught on the wiry arm, but the other reached under the chin and punched up into the skull. The Graevath went limp, and in the moment of its death, it looked more human than monster. Its eyes reached for the sky, as though praying the clouds might accept the offering of its spirit.

The uninjured Graevath avoided Malric altogether, hungry for easier prey. Too late, Veynar realized his danger. He stood in the middle of the woods with a bow and no arrow nocked, as good as inviting monsters to feast upon his flesh. He dropped the bow and went for his swords, but the monster was too close. Veynar twisted and dove, and the Graevath's claws scraped across his back instead of opening up his throat. Lines of fire erupted across his spine as he staggered away.

The Graevath whirled as Veynar worked the first of his short swords free. He kept pulling the other at the wrong angle, preventing it from drawing cleanly. His lone blade slapped away one claw and cut at the other, but the Graevath was no stranger to steel. It knew enough to avoid his blade, and a moment later they reached an impasse.

The pause gave Veynar the time and space to draw his second sword, and he held them crossed before him, the blades acting as a shield.

Undeterred by the steel, the Graevath attacked again, swiping at Veynar with its claws from all angles.

He'd seen attacks like this before, though. They'd been demonstrated by the veterans who'd taught him how to wield the short swords of their clan. Those training to join the Watch had great fun pretending to be the Graevath, attacking at angles armed humans wouldn't otherwise expect. Veynar, too, had delighted in using the training sticks to score points against his fellow warriors.

Familiarity allowed trained instincts to take over, his body overruling his mind. His swords blocked the attacks and cut gouges in the creature's arms. A tiny shiver ran up him every time he felt the parting flesh through the hilt of his swords.

Cutting the corpse of a deer he'd brought down he could do, but as his swords cut through the Graevath, he feared he might become sick.

The Graevath's right arm came up and swiped down, hoping to open Veynar from shoulder to hip. Trained instinct responded, and Veynar's short sword caught the blow, slicing clean through the monster's arm. It howled as the arm went flying, and bile rose in Veynar's throat.

The cut was there for the taking. With the Graevath down an arm, there was nothing stopping his other blade from taking its head.

Another dead Graevath. One small step closer to ending the quiet fear humanity nursed every night they fell to sleep.

He brought his sword up and imagined the cut, imagined the look of surprise on the monster's face.

His sword froze, and the monster seized the opportunity, swiping at him with its remaining claw. A third arrow hissed over Veynar's shoulder, close enough he swore the fletching brushed against the side of his ear, and caught the Graevath in the eye. It dropped like a stone, though its claws still ripped through the front of Veynar's robes.

Veynar snapped around, eyes wide. Malric stood tall, bow still outstretched before him. He had a curious look on his face, as though he couldn't quite understand what he'd seen.

Veynar offered a short bow, thanking Malric for his help, and that seemed enough for Malric at the moment. His friend returned the bow and retrieved his arrows. Veynar cleaned and sheathed his swords and did his best to ignore how hard his hands were shaking.

He didn't doubt that Malric's sharp eyes missed nothing, but his friend at least had the good graces not to say anything. Once their arrows were back in their quivers and their weapons cleaned and sheathed, they continued up the valley, though with the noise they'd made in the fight, Veynar suspected their work was done. Others would have come if they'd been in the woods.

He still prayed to Caelen that they'd cross no more Graevath on this Watch, and when they finally returned to camp, he bowed before Caelen's traveling shrine and thanked him for listening to his prayer.

CHAPTER II
THE TRUTHS OF LEGENDS

Be the blade that separates truth from the lies of the world.

— FROM *THE BOOK OF BRENNOR*

Veynar woke to darkness and the rapidly fading nightmare. He would have given almost anything to forget that day, but his mind refused, holding onto it as tightly as a mother clutched to her newborn. Candlelight flickered in the corner of the room, and he'd been buried under so many blankets he feared he would need help to escape the bed. Sweat dripped down the back of his neck and across his torso, soaking into the sheets below.

Distant memories were slowly replaced by recent ones of him and Malric stumbling home, wounded and weary. They'd dripped blood down quiet streets, avoiding crowds and attention. Neither had possessed the strength to speak, and Veynar only remembered bits and pieces of the journey. Hiding in an alcove as a drunk couple passed obliviously by. Tripping and almost falling over an exposed root not far out of Brenwick. Being intercepted by the camp's Watch before reaching home.

All was darkness after that, vague impressions that hadn't pressed quite deep enough to become memories. Of heat and chanting. Of pain.

He was in the healing tent, which told him most of what he needed to know. He tried to move, but the flare of pain that exploded along his side encouraged him to remain at rest. They'd left him alone, and he feared that Malric's wounds had been too severe to survive. The cut he'd taken had been deep.

The border between sleep and waking grew thin. He drifted between the lands of dream and reality, left to navigate his healing on his own. He might have been in the tent for an afternoon or three days. The candle burned eternally but never burned away.

His eyes opened wide when the tent flap opened and fresh, cool air rushed in. Maeryn entered, and he caught a glimpse of Gavrin's back as the warrior turned to stand guard.

"What word of Malric?" Veynar asked. The weakness in his voice surprised him.

Maeryn waved away his concern. "He'll live, despite you two's best efforts to get yourselves killed. What were you thinking, entering Brenwick again?"

She spoke as though she knew more than Veynar had told her.

"Yes, yes. I know you thought you might find your mysterious assassin. And aren't you glad you did? You aren't half as clever as you think you are, which is unfortunate, because you're going to need a sharp mind in the days to come."

Veynar's mind spun, too tired to latch onto any of the revelations and implications Maeryn dropped on him like body blows in a sparring match. "What?"

The Head Keeper pulled up a small stool made from wooden

legs and layers of leather. She sat close to Veynar's bed and fixed him with a stare that made him think she was trying to dissect his spirit. His stomach twisted, and his eyes darted to the tent flap.

"The assassin isn't anywhere near. That feeling in your stomach is from me," Maeryn confessed.

"How?"

She ignored his question and continued to study him. After an interminable silence, she sighed and leaned back. "This will go faster if you go first. Ask your questions."

Those were about the last words he expected from her, and it took a moment for his thoughts to find any form of order. "You know more than what you're telling me."

"That's not a question, but yes."

She refused to elaborate, forcing him onto the next question. "Was my sister murdered?"

Maeryn looked away. She'd come into the tent looking like she'd made a choice, but now she doubted herself, which was as much a surprise as anything she could have said. The High Keeper possessed many impressive qualities, and confidence was high among them. She exhaled sharply through her nose and met his gaze again. "Yes."

"Why?"

"I don't know."

"You're lying!"

Maeryn's eyes blazed. "Say that again and I'll make sure you never walk out of this tent. I don't know. Yes, I have guesses and suspicions, but I don't know. That's part of why I'm here instead of attending to my duties at the halgard."

Veynar swallowed hard, remembering Gavrin outside. He'd do anything Maeryn asked.

Anything at all.

"What do you know?"

"More than you can imagine. But if you want specific answers, ask specific questions."

"Why am I struggling to remember what happened to my sister? Why do my memories conflict with those of everyone else?"

"That I won't tell you, yet."

Veynar ground his teeth together. "Then what questions will you answer?"

"I've answered all of your questions."

He clenched his fists and wanted to scream. He breathed through his nose, letting his Keeper's training wash over him. Keepers valued truth and precision in all matters, a lesson she harshly reminded him of with her answers. What did he most want to know?

"Did Gavrin save us from the assassin when we met with Avelin?"

The High Keeper's face betrayed nothing. "I will not answer that, yet."

The "yet" was important. Maeryn had come here uncertain how much she would tell him, not just now, but in the future. He focused on that. "What must I do to learn the truth of what happened to my sister?"

Maeryn offered him the barest hint of a smile. "That's a good question."

He hated the flush of pride that rose in his chest at that.

She chose her words carefully. "I can't promise that you'll learn the truth of Lirael's death. There are...several considerations that need balancing, and my own knowledge is far from perfect. That being said, I would like to share with you what I know, if I believe it's appropriate. And the way that is decided begins with you telling me everything. Absolutely everything. I cannot stress it enough. Every detail, every impression you've had since her death, I want to know about it. I understand well your lack of trust, and it's justified, though I've only ever had the best interests of you and the clan at heart. But if you want any chance at all of learning the truth, I need the complete story from you, right now."

Now it became his turn to study her, to weigh her words against his experience and seek what was right.

In the end, though, he was desperate to know, and she was the only path forward he could imagine. So he told her everything that had happened since Lirael's letter had arrived in his hands.

She sat in silence when he finished, her head down, chin resting on her hands. "This goes deeper than I thought, then."

She stood abruptly. "Excuse me. I need to confer with Gavrin for a moment, and then I'll return."

Maeryn swept out of the healing tent without another word, leaving Veynar in the dark both literally and metaphorically. He was too hollowed out inside to care. He saw now he'd needed to tell the whole story. Every day since Lirael's murder had added another weight to his spirit, and he'd been drowning unawares. Sharing everything had lightened the load.

The High Keeper returned just as Veynar considered drifting back to the realm of dreams. Cold late autumn air startled him awake, and Maeryn's worried gaze and slow steps made him brace for the worst. She sat listlessly on the stool and finally raised her eyes to his. "The gem needs to be destroyed."

"My sister died because of that gem."

"And we should honor her memory by completing the task she couldn't."

"She was going to destroy it?"

"I believe that she recognized what Avelin had given her,

and she intended to have you pass it along to me, with the expectation I would do so, yes."

She noticed the disappointment on his face. "This bothers you?"

"There is a power to that gem. I don't understand it, although I suspect you do. Why would we destroy it when we could understand and use it?"

"It is not a weapon we should use. It's too dangerous to us."

"How can you know that?"

Maeryn pressed her lips together in a thin line. "It's difficult to explain without telling you more than I think you should know. I don't know exactly what the gem is, but I know what *type* of gem it is, and I can safely conclude it doesn't belong to either Caelen or Brennor. As such, it's too dangerous for us."

Veynar sat up, ignoring the pain that shot up his side and threatened to drive him forcibly back to the dreamworld. "Why won't you just tell me what you know? Why the evasions?"

Maeryn pushed him down and he didn't have the strength to resist. "As Avelin told you, there are secrets in this world that aren't meant to be shared widely. Truths that would destroy the civilization we've fought and bled to build and protect. Some of these secrets are mere knowledge, but others, the ones involving the gems and your sister, are about techniques. Special techniques that would kill you in the blink of an eye, for I assure you, you aren't prepared for them. These I keep from you because I want you to live. I want you to continue to study the path of the Keepers, so that one day you can carry the secrets, too."

"That's what Gavrin does, isn't it?"

Maeryn didn't answer, but from her expression he could tell she believed she'd already said too much.

He knew better than to push for answers she didn't want to

give him. "Fine. I've already told you where the gem is. Destroy it."

"Alas, my eager student, it's not mine to destroy."

The sinking feeling in his stomach warned him what was coming. "I need to."

She nodded. "Once you touched it, the gem imprinted upon you. Which also explains how you had the strength to drag Malric out of Brenwick as injured as you were."

He frowned.

"You were injured badly enough you barely should have been able to stand. By all accounts, you shouldn't even be awake yet. The gem has already marked you."

"Then why can't I simply hand it off to you?"

"I already have my own, and if you were to give me another, I'd be sorely tempted to use it. I'll not bear such a burden, for none can imprint upon two stones and live to tell the tale."

"Then give it to someone else."

"It won't imprint on them without Keeper training. That's why to Cori it's nothing more than a gem. And before you suggest it, no, I won't train another Keeper to take the gem. For better or for worse, an imprint...has meaning. I told you earlier the gods have wrapped their strings of fate around you, and this is part of that. It falls to you to destroy the gem."

"And how do I do that?"

"There is a forge in the Broken Lands, fueled by liquid fire from the heart of our world. It is there you must go."

"How deep within the Broken Lands?"

"Nearly a hundred leagues."

Veynar coughed. "That's suicide! Or at the very least, a guaranteed descent into madness."

"It will be difficult, but not impossible. We can prepare you for the dangers you'll face."

Despite the warmth of the tent and the layers of blankets

covering him, a chill began near his feet, froze his legs, and shot up his spine like an icy dagger. "High Keeper...I—I can't."

Maeryn's hand fell on his shoulder. "I know well what I ask, and if there were a different path, I would choose it in a moment. But there isn't, and this is what must be done. I won't send you alone, though. Gavrin will go with you, and likely Malric as well, simply because I won't hear the end of it if I don't let him join the party."

Veynar appreciated that he would at least have company when he died, but the madness of the request wasn't alleviated by the mere presence of others. "Even so, High Keeper. You know what happened the last time I fought the Graevath. If you send others, I'll be nothing but a burden they must carry."

"You sell yourself too short, child. It is good to be aware of our weaknesses, but I fear you've taken yours and made them into impassable mountains."

"High Keeper—"

Maeryn's patience finally wore thin. "I will hear no more of your complaints, Veynar. I know what I ask, and I know how impossible the task may seem, but we'll ensure you're capable. We must make haste, but it will be days yet before you're healed enough for travel, and there's much to teach you in that time. Get some rest, for you're going to need it."

She left before he could object again, and he cursed her in his heart. All of this was madness, and he wanted no part of it, but she left him no choice. It was nearly too much to bear. He pulled the blankets up higher, as though they would protect him from his future, and tried not to weep over the turn his life had taken.

CHAPTER 12
TO WAKE A GOD

Desperation breeds innovation.

— FROM *THE BOOK OF BRENNOR*

One underappreciated problem of living among a clan of hunters, warriors, and trackers was that there was no way of escaping a person for long. The High Keeper, at Veynar's request, prevented his friends from visiting while he healed, but it wouldn't be long after the healers ejected him from the tent before he'd be forced to confront them.

It wasn't that he didn't want to see them. He longed for little else. He craved Cori's presence in particular, for she carried a certainty within her he'd always admired. While she might question her future, she never questioned herself, and she was slowly teaching him to do the same.

But he was being sent to the Broken Lands, and any future he'd once envisioned for himself was as dead as his sister. Better to let go and make a clean break. Once released from the healing tent, he spent every moment he could training at the halgard with Maeryn and Gavrin. He only returned to his parent's home long after the sun had fallen, taking longer routes so he wouldn't run into her along the way. It was childish, but he hoped that Cori would someday find it in her heart to forgive him.

The hope lasted until the night he found her sitting outside his parent's house, back against the wall, staring up at the dark sky while waiting for him to return. He braced himself for insults and recrimination, but he should have known better. She stood when she saw him. "May we walk?"

He accepted the offer gratefully, for at the very least, it meant he wouldn't have to look her in the eye. She took his hand, though he hadn't offered it, and held it tight in her own. She spoke first, so that he wouldn't have to find the right words.

"The High Keeper has something for you to do, doesn't she?"

Veynar startled and turned toward her, eyes widening. Cori smiled sadly and kept walking. "Don't look quite so surprised. It wasn't all that hard to guess. The healers told me that you and the High Keeper spoke for some time the day you awoke from your wounds. Knowing her, I'm sure she convinced you to tell her everything. The same thing happened to Malric when he awoke, and it's good that she did. More than half the clan was ready to storm Brenwick searching for the person who almost killed you, but the High Keeper convinced them it would be unwise."

Veynar hadn't known that. He'd kept himself so separate from the clan since the attack it hadn't occurred to him they'd go to war on his behalf, though he shouldn't have been surprised. Vengeance ran deep in their blood, a fact the Graevath never seemed to learn.

Cori continued. "Since you've healed, you've thrown yourself into the private training like never before. I doubt that a brush with death has suddenly made you a more determined apprentice, and it wouldn't explain why you've avoided both me and Malric. The only explanation I could come up with is that the High Keeper revealed some of what she knew to you, and it involves you leaving us."

She didn't ask him to reveal anything, didn't pressure him into evasive answers. They continued their walk in silence, threading their way between the huts of Caelen's Rest.

"It sounds obvious when you explain it, but I'm still impressed," Veynar said. "It's a gift to be able to take all these different scraps and weave them into the truth. It's not just observation, although that's necessary. It's insight, too."

They left the last homes of Caelen's Rest behind and wandered the paths outside the permanent camp.

"Maeryn is sending me into the Broken Lands to destroy the gem Lirael hid in the tree. She's scared of it, though she won't come out and say why. Gavrin's going to accompany me, but even so, it's a task I seem unlikely to return from."

Cori made a little half grunt in the back of her throat that told Veynar she saw straight to the heart of him. Saw through his cowardice in being unable to face her and tell her the truth directly. Saw it all, and with a squeeze of her hand, somehow still forgave him.

Her mercy humbled him more than her anger would have.

"Malric is going to be furious when he finds out. He'll want to go with."

"Maeryn's figured that out on her own. She expects that she'll send him along. I'm not sure if she will because she thinks it's best or because it will get him out of her hair."

"Either way, it will be good for him to join."

Veynar heard the unspoken question in her statement. "You would want to join, too?"

"Why so surprised? You're walking into danger. It only seems right that I'd be by your side."

"I'd hoped you might choose a different path. That you could find a life of your own making."

She fixed him with a sharp glare that could have cut the wing off a fly, as she often did when she suspected he wasn't being fully truthful.

"And I didn't think you'd want to risk everything for me."

They stopped in the field and looked up at the sea of stars. Cori spoke gently. "My life is of my own making, you fool. It always has been. And of course I'd risk everything for you."

"Why?"

She blushed at the directness of the question. "I'm not sure you'd like the answer."

He knew she wanted him to let the matter drop, but she'd only inflamed his curiosity. "I'd like to know."

"It's because you're the only one I know who has the strength to be kind in our world, and that's no small thing."

"It's more a weakness than a strength."

Cori shook her head adamantly. "It's not, though, and you shouldn't think like that."

He wasn't sure he agreed, but it wasn't the time to argue. "You'd really disobey the High Keeper to join us?"

"I would." Her answer was resolute.

He'd rather slice off his own foot than bring her into such danger, but her paths were not for him to choose. He swallowed hard, the decision made. "Then I'll be glad to have you by my side."

HE DIDN'T RETURN to his parent's house until much later that night, but sleep was still a distant hope. She'd planted too many new thoughts in him, and so he lit a pair of candles and pulled the gem from its hiding place under the bed. He'd offered to bring it to the halgard, but Maeryn wanted it nowhere near her. The High Keeper seemed convinced it was safe where it was, and had told him only to leave it alone and under no circumstances touch it again.

He'd obeyed without question until now, but Cori's defiance had sparked his own. There was no guarantee the High Keeper and the Elders would allow Cori to accompany them into the Broken Lands, but she'd sworn she'd make herself as obnoxious as Malric if it would help. Lacking that, she said she'd go without the clan's blessing.

Hopefully it wouldn't come to that.

Veynar had wrapped the gem in a cloth handkerchief so that it wouldn't get lost, and he unwrapped it under the candlelight. The gem reflected and amplified the dim orange flame of the candle, lit as though from the inside. He rolled the gem around in the handkerchief atop his palm. Different facets and angles changed the color of the gem in ways that couldn't be explained by light and reflections alone.

It was a strange idea, a fancy he couldn't quite shake, but he felt as if he held the idea of a gem more than he held an actual piece of cut stone.

The weight of the gem and the sharpness of its edges seemed to put lie to the notion. Ideas didn't sit so easily in one's hand, couldn't draw blood if they were pressed tightly into a palm. Yet he couldn't shake the thought that the gem wasn't real the same way the handkerchief was real, or the way the edges of his blades were real.

Veynar watched the gem like an expectant parent watching a toddler on the verge of taking its first steps, but it refused to impress. It sat in his hand, no more than an inert stone, mocking his expectation.

He reached out a finger, then drew it back. Of all the High Keeper's warnings, that one had carried the most weight, the greatest force of her authority. Only when she'd warned him about touching the stone did it look like she might risk having it in her own possession. He'd touched it before, though, and it hadn't harmed him. If the High Keeper spoke true, and she'd given him no reason to doubt her, his contact with the stone had likely saved his life.

He placed his finger firmly on the stone.

And waited.

He sensed the unsettled power within the gem, almost like the force of a rushing river, only contained within the cut facets of the stone. It didn't reach out to him, though, the way it had when he'd grabbed it from the tree. It remained separate, contained. He picked it up between thumb and forefinger, rolling it between the two fingers. He held it up to his eye. "What are you?"

To his dismay, the stone remained silent.

Veynar shook his head, placed the gem back in the handkerchief, and tossed it back on the bed. Foolishness, all of it. A vicious jest played at his expense.

But no—Lirael was dead, and it all had to mean something.

On Caelen's name, all he wanted was to know, to not be tormented by the ceaseless questions. He strode over to the gem, picked it up and again held it to the light, silently demanding that it give up its secrets.

The current of power within the gem answered, swelling like the drums around the clan campfires during the evening's last dance. It broke from the confines of the gem and washed through him. Such was the strength of the gem that it swept away every concern and question. It left no space for thought, and the past and future shrank until all that remained was the present moment. The lingering ache of his wounds faded.

Instincts buried deep within his body fought to convince his fingers to release the gem. His weary spirit found relief within the power coursing through him, but a hidden blade lurked within the gift, threatening to sever his future from the traditions of his past.

The mysterious stone promised him everything, and all it required was that he surrender, that he lay down his burdens before it and give himself fully to its will. No more would he have to worry about Lirael, or his future, or Cori and Malric. All would be cared for.

His reason stood no chance against the temptation, every objection overwhelmed by the magnitude of the promise offered. Only instinct, honed by months of exposure to the Keeper's lore, warned of the dangers ahead. Trained to respond to those instincts, Veynar held fast to his spirit.

An impressive showing.

They weren't words as Veynar understood them, the presence no mere voice in his head. Words were intermediaries, tools used to pass information from one person's head to the next. Powerful as they were, and Keeper's lore held that they were more powerful than the bows and blades that kept the land safe, they were imperfect tools. One could never know exactly the contents of another's spirit, no matter how well described.

This was a more direct connection, Veynar's spirit intertwined directly with another. He heard the words, but they were far richer than mere language.

"What are you?" Veynar whispered.

A fragment of Caelen.

Veynar started and held the gem at arm's length, as though the extra distance would somehow keep him safe.

Mirth echoed through the shared connection.

I wouldn't have predicted any of our families would maintain for so long such a commitment to honesty. It makes you gullible.

"Even well-intentioned lies cut at the foundation of trust, and we can't afford such weakness in battle." The teachings had been forced into him since he'd been young, the response requiring no thought at all.

And do you think that all successful warriors have required such trust?

The question slapped Veynar across the face, for he'd never considered it before, though a moment's reflection revealed the obvious truth. Mercenary units wandered the borders seeking lost treasures, and they trusted only in their shared love of wealth. Again, he sensed the mirth of whatever entity resided within the gem. "You mock my beliefs."

Yes, but I honor your willingness to be wrong.

It was the first note of respect Veynar heard from the foreign spirit. "Who are you?" he repeated.

That answer, alas, does not come for free.

"What do you want?"

The same as any other creature upon the land. I want to live, and to experience, and to spread. For that, I require one who would strive on my behalf. In exchange, what is mine would become yours.

"Are you an enemy?"

Laughter echoed in Veynar's bones. *Would you trust me if I said "no?"*

Veynar detested this other spirit, that played tricks with words as though they were pieces to be rearranged to win a game.

The world is not so easily divided into friend and foe. Caelen and I have had our differences in the past, but I wish his family no harm today.

Veynar strained to detect any sign of deceit, though unsure he would even recognize it. His sense of the spirit, though, was that it made no effort to deceive him. Still, Maeryn must have known something about it and distrusted it, so he didn't leap to trust. "Do you know what happened to my sister?"

No, but there is little that can hide from my eye once I fully awaken. If that is what you most wish to know, we will uncover it together.

"I don't trust you."

Nor should you. I am beyond your understanding, and trust must be earned with time.

"Then help me understand."

The foreign spirit abandoned language all together, pulling Veynar's awareness into a memory that wasn't his own. He inhabited a body much older, and as he was trapped behind eyes he'd never seen through before, he watched as he slivered the greater share of his knowledge and ability into a new form, a transmutation designed to spread his power across the land. A way to expand his reach the way others did. The process took days, but when it was done, he was left with a construct in the shape of a gem.

The memory faded, gently returning Veynar to the privacy of his room, and he had the sense of floating across a vast expanse of time. It wasn't an answer, not exactly, but it revealed a new world's worth of mysteries.

A growing certainty took root, never spoken out lout, but implied. "To accept you is to reject Caelen, isn't it?"

Not by my hand, but by his, most likely. He's long been distrustful of outsiders.

The choice was a stark one, then. A promise of answers, of a power he couldn't quite comprehend, against the clan that had been his family since the day he was born.

Veynar studied the gem a few moments longer, then reached for the handkerchief.

I don't begrudge you taking the time to consider more carefully, but time is not among your allies. Deliberate well, but choose quickly.

Veynar dipped his head toward the gem, then wrapped it in the handkerchief and hid it securely under his bed. Then he reconsidered and took the handkerchief from under the bed and put it in a pocket of his robes. Better if the gem didn't leave his possession.

With that, he laid down and closed his eyes, and to his surprise, he fell asleep faster than he had in days.

CHAPTER 13
A PATH WITH NO RETURN

In the space between awareness and action there is choice, and in that moment, the fate of the clan is decided time and time again.

— FROM *THE SAYINGS OF CAELEN*

Veynar strode toward the halgard as though he intended to conquer it. He'd tied his short swords to his hip and reassured himself the gem still sat secure in his pocket, then marched toward his inevitable confrontation with Maeryn. What point was there in wasting time, when a more direct approach to answers beckoned?

Late autumn air nipped at his cheeks, and when the wind gusted, it snapped his robes and stabbed icy needles through the layered fabrics. Geese honked as they fled south under a perfectly blue and sunny sky. On any other day he would have stopped and basked in the delightful combination of hot and cold, but he barely noticed.

He did notice Gavrin outside the halgard, on the lee side of the building where he could warm himself in the sun like a lizard without having to worry about the wind. A subtle shift of the older Keeper's weight served as warning enough that Veynar shouldn't enter uninvited.

Veynar stopped ten paces away, wary of Gavrin as an enemy, a thought that had never crossed his mind before.

Perhaps the High Keeper had a point. He'd only spoken with the stone for a bit and it had already poisoned his thoughts against those he'd never had reason to doubt before.

But was it poison, or an unveiling of truths he'd been too stubborn to see before?

Maeryn would know. At the very least, what she said or didn't say would serve as answer enough. "I need to see the High Keeper," he announced.

Gavrin didn't move. "She'll be out to see you soon. She's not to be interrupted, even for you." He spoke as though Maeryn had warned Gavrin personally about Veynar.

The path of wisdom was one of silence, but Veynar was too full of silence, and the control he'd prided himself on for so many years was a thing of distant memory, belonging to a young man whose sister was still alive. "Do you ever doubt, Keeper?"

Gavrin's eyes narrowed. "In one sense, every day. In another, never."

"How can that be possible?"

"Questions trouble me the same as they do anyone else. I often wonder if our path is right, or if there's another, better one that exists somewhere else. And more to your point, I sometimes wonder if the High Keeper's choices are best. So yes, I experience doubt every day. But I also have trust, both in the High Keeper and in Caelen. I've known them both long enough to know they genuinely seek the best for us, and that, I've not doubted in a very long time."

The Keeper's answer calmed some of the storm raging in

Veynar's spirit. They should have spoken earlier. "Sometimes it's hard to trust the High Keeper when I know she's keeping secrets."

Gavrin cracked a smile at that. "In this, my young friend, you're in good company. I never faced anything in my Keeper's training like the loss you've suffered, but I, too, hated the way knowledge was handed to me one little bit at a time, like a sweet dessert my parents would only give me a bite of when I wanted the whole thing."

"Is the gem so dangerous?" The question was best directed to Maeryn, but Gavrin was aware of the stone, and his answers were easier to trust.

Gavrin's face hardened, like he was about to dismiss Veynar without answering, but after a brief internal debate, softened. "That's best answered by the High Keeper, but I'll say this: It isn't that we know that the gem is dangerous, but that we fear that it might be. What your sister discovered isn't exactly rare, but each one represents a power we don't know. All of us, including the High Keeper, understand too little, but we know enough that destroying the gem is the safest option for both you and the clan."

"So safe we have to walk through the Broken Lands for weeks?"

Gavrin looked more at ease addressing that problem. "I won't tell you that marching through the Broken Lands is without risk, but with me and Malric accompanying you, I don't think there will be much to worry about."

"Cori wants to join too."

"The High Keeper wondered if she might. She'll be given permission. Four is a good number, and you're all strong, so we'll make good time."

Veynar bowed. "I appreciate it."

"You're welcome. Now, we've talked long enough. The

High Keeper will be a while, so why don't you sit and meditate like I was showing you yesterday? You'll want the practice."

Veynar bowed again and took up a seated position with his back to the halgard and waited, slipping into the meditative trance with ease.

Meditation twisted and played with Veynar's sense of time, but the sun was halfway toward its zenith when Gavrin stirred and called Veynar from his trance. "She's coming out to meet you."

Maeryn exited the halgard and looked straight at Veynar. Her command was as sharp as his hunting knife. "Follow me, child."

He bristled. Despite his age and experience, he was still unblooded, and so the address fit, but it was rude, and intentionally so. The trust Gavrin had restored blew away like dried leaves on the wind. He followed, but his hand brushed against the gem in his pocket.

Gavrin didn't follow as they left the halgard behind. Maeryn ignored the stone path leading back to Caelen's Rest and traveled further east, following the rising sun. She set a demanding pace, but Veynar matched it with ease. "There are powers stirring in Brenwick that I've only heard stories of. Powers dormant long enough we'd begun to think we'd never suffer them again."

"Because of the gem?"

"Possibly. It's more likely the gem isn't the cause, but it's tied up in the mess all the same. If you forced me to guess, I'd say the House of Brennor is stirring up the trouble, though their reason is beyond me. Or, given what you've told me, a third party, as of yet unknown."

"What does that mean for me?"

"You'll need to leave soon, in the next day or two, and I need to decide who I can spare. I fear I'll have greater need of warriors in the months to come than I thought."

Veynar stopped. "You would send me into the Broken Lands without Gavrin?"

"If I believed his skills were more desperately needed here, yes."

"Yesterday you made it sound as though destroying the gem was the most important challenge facing the clan."

Maeryn fixed him with a look that asked what his point was, as though it meant nothing she'd changed her mind so completely. "Yesterday I hadn't sensed the gods moving the way I did this morning. There's nothing wrong with changing a poor decision, child."

"If you have such desperate need of warriors, I should stay."

"You are no warrior, and it's still important the gem be destroyed."

"What if it isn't opposed to Caelen's will?"

The High Keeper's eyes narrowed, and Veynar cursed his impulsive tongue. Maeryn swore under her breath. "You fool. You made contact with it."

"It said that we have nothing to fear from it."

"It doesn't matter what it said! If you contacted it, you know it has a will of its own, and it will say or do anything to find a host."

"But I sensed its feelings! It told the truth."

The High Keeper slapped him across the cheek, her nostrils flared. "You idiot! How deep did you dare connect with it?" She shook her head. "No. Don't answer that."

Maeryn put her hands on her hips and weighed his spirit with her gaze. "I believed I could trust you, that the gem was safest with you. I see I was wrong. You're as thickheaded and impulsive as Lirael was."

The High Keeper reversed direction, marching a few steps

back toward the halgard before realizing Veynar wasn't following. "Come, child. I'll send Gavrin to your home to retrieve the gem. We'll make sure it's put someplace safe."

Veynar thrust his hands in the pockets of his robes, a petulant child caught in the body of a young man. His fingers unwrapped the gem from the handkerchief. "I want to know what you know."

"Someday, maybe. But you're not ready, and I'd only be putting you in greater danger. The traditions of the Keepers exist for a reason, and you're only harming your cause by resisting now."

"So you won't tell me?"

"Veynar! We've had this discussion. Follow, now, or I'll have no choice but have Gavrin force you."

"I want to know!"

The gem burned warm between his fingers, again responding to his desire for knowledge, reminding him of when he'd been younger and his hunger for learning had known no bounds, how he'd listened to the blooded warriors talk among themselves, absorbing every scrap of knowledge, every fragment of wisdom he could acquire. It promised the answers the High Keeper denied him. It didn't hold the weight of the past against him. Held no judgment for his cowardice, nor did it look down on Lirael for leaving the clan to continue her own learning.

You've chosen your path, then.

He had, though he had no idea how to take the first step.

The gem was only too happy to comply, delighted to share in what it knew. It showed Veynar how, and the young, unblooded warrior of Caelen opened his spirit to the gem.

The High Keeper somehow knew, even as it happened, what Veynar had chosen. Her eyes went wide as she realized her mistake, understood what her precious secrets had cost. "Veynar! Don't!"

But it was already too late. The choice was made and the invitation offered.

Like the night before, his senses grew sharper and his muscles stronger, but this time, the transformation carried the weight of permanence. There were paths in which one couldn't turn around, couldn't retreat the way they'd come, and offering his body and spirit in service to this unknown god was such a path.

Layered above the sharpened strength and perception, though, was a greater gift, a knowing that came from some combination of intuition, perception, and knowledge, both his own and that of the god he'd accepted.

The knowing warned him of danger he wouldn't have sensed otherwise. Of Caelen's gifted power growing within Maeryn, the same way power grew within him. To stay was to fight, to pit his untested abilities against Maeryn's vast experience. Some part of him burned with the desire to fight, not out of malice, but out of curiosity, to answer the question of who the stronger warrior was.

The greater part of him wanted no part of the battle. He was becoming something more, but he was still Veynar, who respected the High Keeper even as he disobeyed her orders. Even now, he'd rather cut off his own leg than harm her.

He ran, his legs propelling him across the fields outside Caelen's Rest with all the speed of a deer in flight. He bounded through the grass, pursued by Maeryn's calls for him to return, but she didn't follow herself.

Veynar circled wide around Caelen's Rest, careful to avoid any of the Watch, and made his way toward Brenwick, where the answers surrounding the death of his sister waited.

CHAPTER 14
OF CHOICES AND CONSEQUENCES

It seems at times as though the fate of the world is determined by a choice as small as where to camp for the night.

— FROM *THE SAYINGS OF CAELEN*

Veynar didn't slow until he neared the outskirts of Brenwick. A glance reassured him that neither Gavrin nor Maeryn had followed him. Despite the distance and speed he'd run, his heart beat no faster than if he'd just risen from bed and stretched. He looked down at his hands to ensure they didn't belong to somebody else. They were his, the calluses and scars familiar. The sight anchored him and reminded him that he was still Veynar, only changed.

The transformation continued unabated, oblivious to his exertions. Sounds grew louder and quieter, as though the various sources were running back and forth. His eyes ached from the brightness of the sun, blinding even when he closed his eyes. He found a quiet, shaded alley between two houses and slid down against one of the walls, clutching at his head. "What's happening?"

My host must be prepared.

The worst of the pain passed and he dared to lift his head. His vision was sharper, his hearing clearer, and his heartbeat slow and steady. He didn't think he'd ever felt so strong, so clear-headed.

Where was that clarity of thought when he'd tossed away everything he'd ever known in a fit of anger? "Did you make me do this?"

You'll want to blame me, but no, the decision was yours and yours alone. As it had to be.

"I don't believe you."

Ask your Keeper, if you dare. She knows I speak true.

Veynar knew it, too, though it would be some time before he admitted it.

He took a deep breath, scents from across the area filling his nose. He stared up at the sky, then grunted. What was done was done, and dreams of other paths were pointless. He stood. "I'm guessing there's no going back, is there?"

We are joined unto death. Your death, specifically.

The corner of Veynar's mouth turned up in a smile. He stood, brushed the dust off his robes, and stood. He had his short swords and abilities he didn't understand. Somewhere in Brenwick, his sister's killer waited. He spoke softly. "So, if I'm your host, what does that entail?"

Your body remains yours. You're stronger and faster than before, though be careful. You feel like you're capable of anything, but among my brethren, I was weak. Your clan upbringing closes some of that gap, but most of my brothers and sisters will be more physically capable.

Veynar emerged from the alley and into a street. He turned toward the center of Brenwick and walked, setting a meandering course that ensured he'd notice if anyone tried to follow him. "So you're saying I should have gone with one of them?"

My strongest gifts are not of the body, but of the mind. I think you'll find me a worthy ally.

"You speak as if we're equals, but if my guesses about you are correct, we're anything but."

A matter of perspective. I could overwhelm your mind for a brief time and possess your body, but your Keeper's training is likely sufficient to wrest the control back and contain me. Likewise, you have ready access to many of my powers, but the depths of them can only be unlocked with my cooperation. The remnants I created were a form of partnership with worthy allies, not a means of control. In life, I was capable of much more than you are now, but the truth is that I need you as much or more than you need me.

"When do I hear the story behind that gem?"

When you're safe.

Veynar looked up and around. Other than a few passersby shooting him worried looks as he talked to himself, there was little to see. Except no, there, in the distance, the soft sound of small footsteps running away from him. Not afraid, but determined. Veynar hurried down an adjoining street and poked his head around the corner of a shop. A child in dirty rags ran down the street.

He wouldn't have thought anything of it before. He wouldn't have even heard the steps before.

The boy only ran once he spotted you. Almost as if he'd been waiting.

Veynar took off in pursuit, running lightly, his footsteps nearly silent against the packed dirt of the street. He kept well back of the boy, but hardly needed to worry. The boy never looked back, and the townspeople looked the other way when they spotted his clan robes. They preferred to treat him as though he were invisible, a ghost of their imaginations.

The boy's run didn't last for long. As he approached the center of the city he was forced to slow so as not to trouble others. Veynar also slowed, keeping enough distance that he was certain the boy wouldn't spot him. It didn't take the child much time to weave his way through the city, and even less time for Veynar to guess where the boy led him.

As expected, the boy passed through the main gates of the House of Brennor, unbothered by the guards standing watch. Veynar stopped short, sliding into an alcove where he could keep an eye on the gate without drawing attention to himself. Were he not in his clan robes he might have attempted to pass through the gate. The House was open to all, provided they had sufficient reason to visit, but the moment he approached those gates dressed in clan robes and armed, he'd lose whatever small advantage his discreet pursuit of the boy might yield.

His gaze wandered over the House, noticing much of what he had before, but also some of what he'd failed to see. The difference was subtle, but unmistakable once noticed. The city buzzed around him, a cacophony of sound and activity that unfolded before his sharpened senses. Conversations crept through open windows and spilled into the street while pans sizzled and smoked over flame, promising to warm stomachs and homes both. It was all the stuff of life, mundane and yet there was something meaningful about it all.

Similar sounds, scents, and sights surrounded the House of Brennor, but nestled within, somewhere deep within the walls, was a seed of silence. He leaned out into the street, as though a better angle might reveal the truth of the matter, but a cautioning tug from his spirit pulled him back into the alcove.

You sense a sanctuary.

"What's that?"

A place of peace, guarded by ways older than mine. No harm would come to us, were we there, and we can do no harm to those who enter.

"Is that where the boy is going?"

Perhaps.

Torn between attempting entry and remaining in hiding, Veynar chose the alcove. He leaned back and settled in like a hunter lying in wait. The main gates saw a steady flow of visitors and guests, and both Sisters and Sisters-in-training regularly left and returned. Veynar turned his sharpened senses on all who passed through the gate, but none seemed to be any more or less than they appeared.

The late afternoon sun was dropping quickly toward the rooftops of the surrounding buildings when Malric and Cori walked down the street toward the House. Veynar pressed himself deeper into the shadows, cursing the High Keeper, for their presence had to be her doing.

Their eyes roamed across their surroundings as though they were on Watch, and no amount of trying to make himself small would hide him from their hunt. Malric sighted him first and nudged Cori in Veynar's direction. In answer, he stepped from the alcove and bowed in greeting.

Malric watched him as he would a stranger, his hands never far from the short swords hanging openly on his hips. Cori, too, had made no effort to hide her weapons, straining the unspoken truce between the clan leaders and Brenwick's mayor. Thankfully, though, there was nothing but concern in her look.

"Maeryn?" Veynar asked.

Malric nodded. "She told us you might be here."

Veynar set aside the question of how she could have guessed that. His friends wouldn't know the answer if he asked. "What else did she say?"

"Frustratingly little," Malric answered. "She said that the

two of you had a fight, and that you'd made some 'exceedingly poor choices', which were her exact words, and that we should do everything we can to convince you to return."

There was more Malric wasn't saying, but Cori jumped in so Veynar wasn't forced to ask. "She also said that you might not be yourself anymore, and that you might be dangerous. She sent Gavrin with us, too, but he's waiting a ways behind so as not to spook you, I think."

"So, what's it going to be?" Malric asked. "Will you return with us?"

That answer, at least, was easy. "No."

Malric's hands crawled closer to his blades. "Why not?"

"I need to know who killed my sister, and I finally have the ability to do so."

"What happened?" Cori asked.

"You know that gem we found? It's the way forward." He hesitated. What did he say to his friends that didn't make him sound like a madman? That the gem had become a part of him and connected him to an ancient god who spoke directly into his mind? Malric would cut off his head in an instant, and Veynar wasn't sure he'd even blame his friend.

They waited for him to explain.

"It confers...abilities, I guess. I see more than I ever have before."

Veynar's thoughts raced, but not out of his control. They were ordered and purposeful. He reached his sharpened senses toward Malric. "For example, I know you forgot your two favorite throwing knives this morning, and that when the High Keeper's messenger found you, you were with Faylen."

Malric's eyes went wide and Cori covered her mouth as she laughed.

"H-how?" Malric sputtered.

It was simple enough. When Malric moved, there were none of the bulges under his robe where his throwing knives were usually hidden, and Veynar's nose caught the faintest hint of incense. His friend wouldn't light any unbidden, but Faylen, a woman he'd been interested in for months, devoutly prayed to Caelen every morning.

Veynar wouldn't have made the connections yesterday, or even smelled the incense, but he thought nothing of it today. The conclusions came as naturally as breathing. Still, the amazement on Malric's face was too wonderful to be dismissed so easily, and so Veynar refused to provide the simple explanation.

His mirth faded as a new figure exited the main gate.

A young woman strode out of the Hall, but she wasn't a Sister-in-training. If anything, she appeared to be a hawk in human form, gliding along the cobblestones as if she were soaring upon currents of air searching for helpless prey. She stared straight across the street at him, then walked off in the opposite direction, unhurried but with a determined step.

Veynar pursued, but was stopped by Malric's firm hand on his arm. His friend was torn between his sworn duty to the clan and his personal desires, an echo of Veynar's earlier uncertainty. Malric asked, "Where are you going? We're not done talking."

"To follow that young woman," Veynar said, pointing her out.

"Why?"

"I don't have time to explain, or to tell you everything that's happened, but I believe she'll lead me to the answers about Lirael's death."

"How?"

Veynar grunted. "I suspect she's leading me into some sort of trap."

Malric and Cori shared a glance. "We have our orders to bring you back to Caelen's Rest."

Veynar removed Malric's hand from his upper arm. "You're welcome to try, but I can't waste any more time."

Cori stepped between Malric and Veynar. "We'll help you, then."

Her support saved Malric from his indecision, and with that certainty came a return of his usual nature. A wide grin broke across his face. "A trap, you say? It would be a shame for you to spring it alone."

CHAPTER 15
HUNTER AND HUNTED

There is no greater joy, no greater thrill, than that of being on the hunt, a trusted companion by my side.

— FROM *THE SAYINGS OF CAELEN*

Veynar took the lead, Cori and Malric spreading out behind him. They deferred to him now, the way they once had when they'd been younger and he'd rightly thought himself the best of them. They followed the young woman openly, and she would glance back at times to make sure they hadn't lost her, flashing them a smile every time.

"She seems confident for someone being followed by three warriors," Cori observed.

"If she's the assassin that killed Avelin, her confidence isn't without reason. But you two are strong and won't be surprised, and I'm more capable than before. Whatever surprise she hopes to spring on us will quickly be turned on her."

The woman turned and turned again, pulling them away

from the central parts of Brenwick and toward the docks. The smell of the sea grew stronger as they continued west.

"There's not too much farther before she's going to corner herself," Malric said. His eyes never ceased, examining the rooftops, the alleys, and the windows that they passed. It was good to have him close. It was good to have them both close.

Veynar glanced behind him. "Didn't you say Gavrin was nearby?"

"He was, and I'd suspect he's still close," Cori said.

Veynar wasn't so sure. He saw no sign of the Keeper.

The tall buildings of central Brenwick shrank and expanded, like a warrior growing old and feasting more than hunting. Silk and jewel merchants were replaced by blacksmiths and shops that sold tunics of rougher wool. Teahouses became taverns, and wardens wandered the streets in numbers that deterred even the most daring of cutpurses. Those wardens gave sour looks to the three clanners, but settled at that. The port district might have lacked the sophistication and wealth of the central city, but work crews kept the streets clean and the merchants painted their storefronts every year.

They kept walking until they reached the waterfront, where the woman finally turned south, toward the larger warehouses where ships stashed grain and goods until they could be sold. They passed a dock filled with laborers unloading the sacks of grain desperately needed by Brenwick through the winter months. Veynar slipped through a gap in the line, ignoring the curses thrown after him.

The woman went to one of the large warehouses and stepped inside, shutting the door behind her. It was perhaps two hundred feet long and twenty tall, with a sloped roof to shed the rain that frequently charged in from across the sea. There were no windows, and only the one door the woman had used located on the side of the building and a massive set of doors pointing toward the sea where goods could be loaded and unloaded.

"You weren't lying when you said it was a trap," Cori said.

Veynar had only been in a warehouse a few times before, but he could imagine well enough what the inside would look like. Goods scattered across the floor, possibly stacked high, leaving only narrow walkways running throughout the building. Rooms were usually located up high, accessed by a stair and a walkway running across the upper level of the building. If he was in the woman's position, he'd have dozens of archers lining those walkways, ready to launch arrows into whatever fool tried to go through the door.

Veynar took in the warehouse and its surroundings in a moment. Entering through the side door was foolish, but the main doors opened outward on massive hinges and would cast the inside of the warehouse in light. "We open the main doors."

Malric and Cori recognized the wisdom of the decision. They tugged on the massive handles, and the doors squealed open, the hinges complaining as though nothing had been asked of them in many months. Light poured in, revealing a warehouse filled with lumber, stone, and ingots of various metals. The supplies were stacked taller than Malric's head, and outside of one wide walkway that ran from the main door to the back of the warehouse, the passages between the stacks were narrow. The mysterious woman could hide half an army within and they wouldn't have known.

Cori swore under her breath. "This is a mess. We need more people."

Veynar looked again for Gavrin, but the Keeper remained stubbornly out of sight.

She wasn't wrong. Knowing it was an ambush did little to help them, and no one was forcing him in. He could turn around and find another way.

Only he didn't know how much time he had. The assassin had been waiting for him, and if he returned to Caelen's Rest, who knew what the future held? His disobedience wasn't something easily forgiven. Others had lost their lives for less.

"I'm going in. Whether you help me or not is up to you."

He drew his swords.

Those won't help you, child.

Veynar ignored the gem's warning. If he couldn't trust in the blades his father had given him, there was nothing left in the world to trust.

Malric and Cori followed, as he knew they would. He paused at the threshold and allowed his senses to drift through the open warehouse. The wind carried scents of cut pine and oak as it swirled between the stacks, and something else, almost floral but not quite. No archers waited in the shadows or on the walkways running around the edge of the warehouse.

There was danger here, but where? He walked down the very center of the main walkway, slowly, so as to look down every narrow passage that connected to the walkway. Less than a third of the way in, he found her, sword in hand, near the far wall, cloaked in shadows. She appeared fuzzy in his vision, but remained unmistakable. When he stopped and stared, her eyes narrowed.

Malric caught up to him a moment later. He followed Veynar's look. "Do you see something?"

Veynar gestured toward the passage. "She's there."

Malric leaned forward. "I don't see anyone."

Veynar risked a quick glance at his friend, but there was no deceit within him. Not even Malric would jest at a time like this. The woman strode forward, sword still before her, and Malric looked at Veynar like he was a fool. His stomach twisted as the woman grew near.

This was no place for Malric. This was beyond him. "You need to leave, now," Veynar said.

"I'm not leaving without you," Malric said.

The woman leaped forward, racing down the narrow passage as fast as an arrow. Her sword cut at Malric's head, but Veynar's friend didn't even attempt to dodge. Veynar stepped between the woman and Malric and parried the cut, though the force of even the glancing blow made his arms tremble. There was no mistaking the sound of swords meeting, though, and Malric jumped back, eyes wide as he swore. "What was that?"

The woman gave Veynar no time to answer. She twisted and cut again, and when he blocked her sword, it sliced through his as though it were a child's toy. The top two-thirds of his blade went spinning away from him, clanging against a pile of ingots.

This wasn't anything like the attacks he'd fought against before. The speed was no more than the assassin they'd fought in the street, but the strength was beyond compare. She cut and cut again and to save his last remaining short sword, Veynar was forced to retreat. Her sword seemed to burn through the air, trailing light as it searched for his flesh.

Malric pressed his back against a stack of ingots, and Cori retreated back to the threshold. Their eyes were locked on Veynar, but neither so much as glanced at his opponent.

They couldn't see her.

And he couldn't stay ahead of her. Whatever was in the gem had spoken true. Skilled and strong as he was, Veynar was slower and weaker than the woman, even though she was slight enough he should have been able to break her over his knee.

Behind you.

Veynar risked a glance back and saw a younger woman emerge from the shadows and approach Cori. He turned on his heel and leaped toward her.

The second woman hadn't expected that. She retreated before him, unwilling to cross blades. Her movements weren't nearly so fast as her companion's, and she grimaced as she moved.

She was the one that had attacked him and Malric on the rooftops, the one he'd injured. He lunged at her, sword tip aimed for her heart, but she slid to the side before his blade could pierce her breast. His speed carried him past her, the newfound strength in his limbs so much more than he expected. She swiped at him with her sword, a hastily aimed cut that sought to take advantage of his imbalance.

Cori deflected the cut away from Veynar and allowed him the time to regain his balance. They advanced together on the younger woman, who retreated a pace, then leaped seven feet in the air and landed softly on a stack of cut pine. She skipped backward and Cori cursed. "I lost the shadow."

Veynar watched the younger warrior as she regained her composure. She'd only retreated a handful of stacks away, ready to pounce again when the more experienced warrior forced them off-balance.

He had no opportunity to pursue her. The first assailant, the one he'd followed from the Hall, had chased him for a moment, then turned her attention to Malric, whose eyes darted around the room, searching for the threats he knew were close but couldn't see.

Unable to reach Malric in time, Veynar drew back his broken sword and whipped it at the assassin. More by luck than by skill, his aim and spin were true, and the shattered blade raced to embed itself in the assassin's back.

At the last moment his stomach twisted viciously. Veynar blinked, and it was as though the woman had shifted from one place to another. Impossible, and yet one moment his blade flew true and the next she was no longer there. She spun, impossibly quick, and Veynar's feet slipped as he tried to stop from impaling himself on her outstretched sword. He avoided the blade but went down hard, the back of his head slamming against the unforgiving warehouse floor. The roof swirled overhead before straightening out.

Veynar swiped at the assassin's blade as it stabbed down at his chest, knocking it far enough away that it only cut through the side of his torso. A dagger of ice shot up through his side. Blood spread across his robes. The assassin pulled the blade from Veynar's side, dripping his blood, and prepared to strike again.

Malric finally joined the fight, slashing wildly and shouting. The sheer ferocity of the attack drove the assassin back, but after a pair of cuts that did nothing to threaten the assassin, it was clear Malric's senses couldn't penetrate whatever shroud the assassin used to hide from him. He could only track the dripping of the blood from her blade.

Veynar jumped to his feet, the pain in his side a distant sensation, as though it had already happened long ago. He blessed Malric for his courage and willingness to throw himself into danger on his behalf, but if the fight lasted more than another heartbeat, it would be over.

Veynar leaped to fight by Malric's side, supplementing Malric's wildness and ferocity with cold and precise attempts at piercing the assassin's defenses. Together they forced her back, and when the second assassin approached to even the odds, she found herself facing Cori, who'd found her once again.

The assassins who'd set the trap found themselves pushed toward the back corner of the warehouse, rapidly running out of space to give.

Too easy.

Veynar scoffed at the idea, but the gem had given him no reason to doubt, and so he cast his gaze around the back of the warehouse. A curse escaped his lips. They weren't alone. Most remained well-hidden, but the tip of an arrow and the slight creak of a bow bending gave them away. At least half a dozen archers lurked in the back.

"Retreat!" Veynar shouted, but it was too late. They'd reached the part of the warehouse the archers had been waiting for them to enter. The archers emerged from dark shadows, hidden by the stacks of oak and stone, bows already drawn.

The first arrow didn't come from the hidden archers. It came from behind, trailed by a bolt of light Veynar had seen once before. The arrow caught one archer in the chest, punching through the boiled leather armor like bread and knocking him flat onto his back, empty eyes staring at the ceiling. A second arrow followed less than a heartbeat later, catching another archer in the neck. Veynar glanced back and wasn't surprised to find Gavrin standing at the main doors, an enormous bow in hand. Already a third arrow was on its way through the shadows, and a fourth nocked to the string.

The surviving archers turned their attention toward Gavrin, returning fire a moment after their first companion fell. The Keeper slid to the side as arrows whistled through the space he'd been. He loosed another bolt, knocking flat another archer, but was forced to retreat as two more arrows sought his life.

Cori grunted as the second assassin's sword flashed past her defense and opened a cut down her arm. The wound bled the vigor from her advance, and her opponent pressed her hard.

Veynar couldn't aid her. His opponent had stopped retreating, now effortlessly holding back his thrusts and Malric's wild swings. The weakness that had lured them so effectively deeper into the warehouse was nowhere to be found. Her eyes even had time to wander toward the main door to track Gavrin's fight.

Veynar redoubled his efforts. His body and spirit had more

to give, but every time he summoned the additional strength and speed granted to him by the gem, he lost the balance and precision he'd trained nearly his entire life to achieve.

Another of Gavrin's arrows cut into the last of the archers, who fell with a groan. Veynar's opponent's face hardened at the loss.

Veynar's insides knotted, and when he blinked, the assassin was gone. He twisted and found her next to Gavrin, her sword moving too fast for him to track. Gavrin no longer held his enormous bow, but he must have dropped it behind one of the nearby stacks of stone, because Veynar couldn't see it. He held instead the traditional two short swords of the clan, and they met the flurry of cuts with ease.

Veynar's eyes widened. Gavrin's usefulness upon the battlefield had never been in question, but this—if he wasn't watching it with his own eyes—he'd never believe. The assassin had Gavrin on the back foot, her sword never far from drawing blood.

Reason demanded he help Gavrin, but his heart beat for Cori, and so he launched himself toward their fight. Malric was slower to respond, and Veynar raced across the warehouse alone.

He was halfway to Cori when his stomach twisted again. Veynar braced, expecting an attack of some sort, but his path to Cori remained unopposed. He only stopped when he heard a bubbly gasp from behind him. He skidded to a stop and turned.

Malric stood on his toes, as though he was trying to peek over one of the nearby stacks. But then his leg twitched and he wasn't on his toes, but being held up by the sword thrust through his ribcage. The smaller assassin was hidden by Malric's shadow, but she lifted his body as though he were an infant. Malric coughed and blood spilled from his mouth and splattered against the ground.

The sword flashed and was out, and Malric landed on shaky legs. He wobbled and reached out. "Veynar..."

The assassin's sword flashed again, and Malric's head flew from his shoulders, twisting in the air, and he looked confused. It landed close to Veynar's feet and rolled to a stop, Malric still frowning as though he didn't understand this new perspective. His eyes blinked, then went glassy.

Veynar stood, rooted to the spot.

Gavrin shouted and there was another twisting in Veynar's stomach. Several. Bolts of white-hot light filled the warehouse and the building groaned, though the sound came from many miles away.

Veynar stared, and his stomach kept twisting, like snakes were dueling within his core, and even the gem was shouting, but it was all noise. All meaningless. A sword might have flashed by him, but he stood as still as one of Brennor's statues against the attack.

He was tackled from behind as the building collapsed around him.

CHAPTER 16
KILL YOUR FRIENDS

Why refuse to lie?

It's simple. A liar cannot be trusted, and in battle against the enemy, you must be able to trust the person fighting beside you, as they must be able to trust you.

After all, their lives are in your hands, as yours is in theirs.

— FROM *THE SAYINGS OF CAELEN*

The dream of a full breath was a distant memory. When Veynar tried to inhale, dust filled his nose and his lungs refused to expand. An enormous amount of weight lay atop him, crushing his ribs. He was trapped, arms and legs splayed out, pinned by what felt like a small herd of cattle. There was no leverage to be had, no muscle that could push him free.

His heart pounded as he suffocated, unable to move, unable even to cry. Never had he been so helpless, so immobile. In the darkness his imagination ran free, untethered from reality, and Malric's head blinked, his frown of confusion turning into a scowl of accusation.

Fear flooded his body and caused his limbs to twitch, but not even the strength of panic could free him. He was crushed and dying, slowly squeezed into the earth like one of the ants on the stone walkway to the halgard underneath Malric's unforgiving boot.

A deep voice groaned in his ear and there was movement, a shifting of pressure that increased the weight on his ribs. They creaked like old tentpoles bending under the force of a summer's gale, threatening to crack. More movement, then another long groan as muscles that weren't his trembled. Enormous timbers shifted and finally, finally, he could inhale and force breath through lungs desperate for the taste of air.

With breath came tears too long restrained. His body had remembered, even as his spirit had pushed aside the weight of loss. He was still alive, fate mocking him with every indrawn breath.

A grunt above and the weight eased more. Light appeared, so close he could crawl to it. The strength of the gem still flowed through his limbs, and he pulled at his right leg, still trapped beneath the rubble. It slid free and he crawled, belly scraping against the floor, until he was out.

He flopped onto his back and stared at the sky, dimly remembering there'd been a roof overhead not that long ago.

"Help," croaked a voice.

Veynar stared at the sky a moment more, then worked his way to his feet. Everything hurt and his side burned, but nothing was broken.

He had no weapons, though, nothing to help his savior trapped underneath the debris.

Imagine a short sword in your hand. Focus on every detail you can remember.

Which was easy enough. How many days of his life had been lost as he obsessed over the care of the short swords his father had gifted him? He knew their curve, weight, and design better than he knew his own face. He swore he could feel them in his hands even now, and as he imagined it true, power spread from his core and down his arms into his hands. His short swords were in his hand, whole and as polished as the day he'd first received them.

It would be a shame to beat them against the wood and stone.

Cut.

Veynar did, glad to have someone to tell him what to do, someone to guide him so he didn't have to endure the agony of thinking. The swords cut through roof tiles and pine like paper, though stone mostly resisted his efforts. He cut and cut again, more a woodsman cutting through a tree than a warrior fighting for the life of an ally, but he sliced through most of it and gave Gavrin the help he needed to push himself to his feet.

The Keeper's robes were torn into shreds, revealing an incredible amount of muscle underneath. The muscle shrank as Veynar watched, returning to the lean and wiry frame more suited for long days of walking. Gavrin sported cuts across his body, blood dripping freely, but he took a deep breath that expanded his chest wide as he looked around.

The others. He hadn't thought of the others. Of Malric, there was no need to search. His fate had been sealed. Veynar called for Cori, but there was no answer. He started to climb on top of the shifting rubble for a better look, but Gavrin stopped him. "She's not here."

Veynar didn't understand. She'd been fighting up until the moment the building collapsed.

"Last I saw, they were grabbing her as they fled."

"They escaped?"

Gavrin inclined his head. "The point of bringing the building down wasn't to kill them. It was to save you."

Veynar wrapped Gavrin by his tattered robes and lifted him high. "Why?"

Gavrin's hands moved and did—something—and Veynar's arms went numb. He dropped the Keeper as his arms fell to his side. Gavrin landed on his feet and straightened what remained of his robes. "If you stopped for a moment and thought, you'd understand why."

He did. He had the remnant, which Maeryn rated higher than the lives of other warriors. "You should have saved her."

"If it had been within my ability to save both of you, I would have. Now come, we need to return to Caelen's Rest before more assassins arrive."

Gavrin started over a pile of the rubble, then stopped when Veynar didn't follow. His lips formed a hard line of disdain. "It's not a request."

Veynar remained rooted to the spot. Malric was dead and Cori taken.

Malric was dead and Cori taken.

A cold emptiness spread from his core as his thoughts slowed.

Killed not by the monsters who lurked to the east, but by other humans. Taken without honor. Ever since he'd been a child, he'd held tight to Caelen's teachings, using them to make sense of the world and find his way through it.

Trust and honor. Decency and respect. Kindness to those creatures not involved in the struggle to the east. Violence was an unavoidable part of life, necessary for survival itself, but it was to be contained, a sword never drawn unless there was need.

At the very least, Caelen's sayings were insufficient. More likely, they were lies.

The assassins killed Malric because they could, because he lacked the skills necessary to fight against them. They took Cori because she couldn't fight them either, because they could. Gavrin threatened him, believing his strength sufficient to inspire obedience. They were all the same. He looked up and met Gavrin's eye. "No."

"I saved your life," Gavrin said.

"And I thank you, but I won't leave Cori to them. I won't return to Caelen's Rest while Lirael's murder remains unsolved."

Swords appeared in Gavrin's hands, almost a pair to the ones in Veynar's. "You can't win a fight against me."

True enough, but Veynar didn't need steel to defeat the Keeper. He opened his hands and the swords vanished, blinking away as though he'd cut through the debris with his imagination alone. "I'm not going to fight you, but I won't return with you either."

Gavrin's nostrils flared, then his swords disappeared, too. He crossed his arms over his chest. "Can we at least talk about this somewhere else? This warehouse will be crawling with dockworkers soon."

Veynar could already hear the crowds gathering around the main door. "They'll see us as soon as we leave the rubble."

"They won't if you stay close to me."

Veynar frowned, but followed closely after Gavrin. Rubble shifted under their feet as they climbed over the piles, but true to the Keeper's word, they drew no notice from any of the dockworkers already searching the ruins for survivors. Veynar looked for any sign of Cori, but she was gone.

Better than being dead, but not by much.

They walked around the gathering crowds, never drawing so much as a glance, then slunk into the alleys few warehouses away. Gavrin stopped before they'd gone too far. He looked weary, like he'd been on Watch for two straight days. "I'm sorry about Malric and Cori."

Veynar dipped his head in acknowledgment. "I'll find her and bring her back."

Gavrin looked up at the sky and sighed. "You don't have a clue the forces you're dealing with, Veynar. I understand, truly, I do, but you're being a fool."

"Perhaps, but I can't go back to Caelen's Rest. Maeryn will chain me up and Cori will die."

"She's clan. You won't be the only one searching for her."

"Perhaps not, but what hope does the rest of the clan have against those warriors? Malric was one of our bravest and best, and he was reduced to swinging a sword around like a child learning how to fight in the dark."

Gavrin had no answer to that, so he resorted to his original argument. "Even so, you have no better chance. You've stepped foot into a world of which you know nothing."

Veynar crossed his arms. "A problem you could solve immediately, if you chose to."

"If the High Keeper didn't think you ready, it's not my place to contradict her."

"It's not about being ready. I'm in it, now, and have no choice. By keeping me ignorant, you do nothing but doom me."

"It seems to me that you're doomed either way," Gavrin concluded.

"At least give me a chance."

Gavrin leaned the back of his head against the wall and closed his eyes. Veynar didn't push his case any harder, knowing full well the decision was the Keeper's alone to make.

Eventually, Gavrin sighed and began to speak. "Some of this you've probably already figured out. There are those that came before us who learned to master the world in ways we've not been able to duplicate. Who learned how to master the very stuff of life."

He flexed his hands and the enormous bow appeared. He

opened the hand and flexed again and the bow became a sword in less time than it took to blink. "Even now we don't know the full extent of their discoveries. Long life. Health. The ability to heal, and to be stronger and wiser."

"You're talking about gods."

Gavrin made a sound in the back of his throat. "We call them gods now, but they were men and women, just like us. The only difference was in the mastery they developed. The tales that have come down to us from that time often conflict with one another."

Veynar had learned as much from his study of the legends. "It was a time of greatness, but also a time of strife."

Gavrin nodded. "Power doesn't change a person, though there are some who would claim as much. It reveals a person's deepest desires, and they are only sometimes as noble as they seem. There was goodness and evil, same as there is today, only backed by powers and knowledge that we fortunately lack. It came close to destroying the world."

The Broken Lands, the original home of humanity and the place they could likely never return to.

Gavrin continued, "Near the end of the wars, the gods, as we now call them, discovered a way to transform their essence. It is, as best we can tell, a transmutation, a sliver of soul, mind, and flesh folded and shaped into what appears to be a gem. The idea was to spread their power through the use of willing hosts, to ensure that the knowledge and skills they'd worked so hard to acquire didn't die out because their bodies were killed and destroyed. They gave up their human lives to become these." He held up his hand, a glittering gem in his palm. A moment later and it vanished back into his body.

"The High Keeper and I are the last two of Caelen's servants, and the large part of training to become a Keeper is to perceive and manipulate the strength of the gems."

"That's why I was able to sense the assassins more clearly, and how I knew you'd defended us earlier, even though the other two saw nothing."

Gavrin nodded. "For many generations there's been something of a silent truce between the various gods. I can't speak to their collective wisdom, but they're no fools, and they know full well they once brought humanity close to the brink of destruction. Unfortunately, in the last few years, it seems they've started to move once again. Both the High Keeper and I believe there's a fight brewing. And we're pretty sure one is starting here."

The Keeper held up a hand to stop Veynar's questions before they started. "I can imagine what questions you have, for I have them myself, but the truth is, the High Keeper and I are woefully ignorant. Caelen's geas has always been toward the border and the wilderness, and we've spent far too little time thinking about what happens in the cities and towns where most of the humans and god-remnants live. One of the tasks I was set upon our return to Caelen's Rest was to find out what I could, but this matter with your sister has consumed most of my attention."

Veynar's head spun with the new revelations. "What do you know about what happened to Lirael?"

"Not much more than you." Gavrin looked down, thought for a moment, then said, "Lirael's decision to join the House of Brennor was influenced by her learning what I'm telling you now. She was a tremendously skilled Keeper, and Maeryn was starting to teach her about the god-remnants, but it was becoming increasingly clear your sister's temperament wouldn't make her an ideal match for Maeryn's remnant. Caelen is a hunter, but your sister's obsession was with knowledge alone. There is overlap, but not alignment. We've long considered Brennor a friend, and she felt that if she studied here, she would learn the answers to the questions we had, and she promised to share them."

"She was scouting for you." It cast so much of the past year in a new light and eased the sting of her perceived betrayal.

"No one ever asked her to. I believe she was thinking about leaving regardless, but she'd been torn, and I think promising to send us back information made the choice a bit easier."

When Veynar didn't have any more immediate questions, Gavrin continued. "Anyhow, we weren't really expecting to hear from her anytime soon. Initiation into Brennor's mysteries is a slow process and should have been even harder for an outsider like your sister. We were alert for messages, and we asked a handful of people to keep an eye on you and your family. We heard when you received the message, and I took off after you, though not in time to make a difference."

"So, you were there."

A dark look passed across Gavrin's face. "The park was quite crowded that evening. I was there, but Lirael's departure had also been noted by the House of Brennor, and one of their aelethi had been sent after her, too."

"Aelethi?" Veynar had never heard the word before.

"A word from the old languages. Singular aeleth. Translates roughly to what the Sisters of Brennor would call a saint, but it's the word we use to describe those that have joined their spirits with a remnant."

Veynar gestured for Gavrin to continue.

"You arrived first, but the House's aeleth and I weren't far behind."

"So you don't know who the assassins are."

"No, and I'm sorry. Brennor's aeleth reached you first. She was the one who dropped you into sleep. She and I argued after. She'd considered killing you to ensure the secrets of the remnants were kept, but I'd hear none of it. Ultimately, she attempted to wipe your memory of the event and we brought you to your parents' home. She adjusted their memories, and you know the rest."

Veynar's head spun. Someone had been manipulating his experience in the Hall of the Dead, too. The Head Sister, perhaps?

"The Sisters can so easily alter our minds?"

"Most aeleth have some knowledge of the art. It's what I used to slip away from the warehouse unnoticed, and what the assassins used when they attacked. Some of the Sisters have developed the skill to a greater degree than I'd thought possible. Perception is fragile and easily broken. Most people are already lost in a story of their own making. It was your Keeper's training that allowed you to see past it."

And now the remnant allowed him to see with even more clarity. Why he'd seen their enemies in the warehouse without problem while brave Malric had no choice but to swing wildly at shadows. Veynar closed his eyes and gently shook his head. The void in his chest threatened to swallow him whole if he allowed himself memories of Malric.

"What happens now?" Veynar asked.

"If you have no intent of leaving with me, I'll return to Caelen's Rest without you and speak to the High Keeper. We'll launch our own search for Coriselle." The way Gavrin said it made it sound as though he didn't have high hopes for success.

"And me?"

Gavrin shrugged. "You'll have to find your own way."

"You can't point me in the right direction?"

The Keeper raised his finger and pointed east, toward Caelen's Rest. "I already did, and you refused. Be well, Veynar, and be careful. These are deep waters you've stepped into, and no one has taught you how to swim."

Veynar almost objected, but Gavrin waved it away. "If

there's anyone who can figure it out on their own, it's you. Just, please be careful. You may not be Caelen's anymore, but you're still family."

And with that one final warning he left Veynar to his loneliness and grief.

CHAPTER 17
ALLIES IN THE DARK

I admire it. I respect it. There are many days when I wish the world worked as the hunters believe, but I am no fool, and any man or woman who puts their faith in trust is a fool.

Rely on selfish interest and incentive, instead.

Only then can you move the world.

— FROM *THE WISDOM OF BRENNOR*

He had to keep moving. One step in front of the other. Shuffle or sprint, the pace didn't matter. Only the movement. The action.

He'd stood still when Gavrin left him alone in the alley, lost in a new world without a map or a guide, filled with limitless possibility and lethal threats. All directions had seemed equally valid, and it was easier not to choose. Easier to stand rooted and let the world wash over him. Perhaps the trees had always had the right of it.

Only the memories had caught up with him, a persistent hunter who'd never lost sight of its prey. Malric died again and again, helpless against the assassin with the remnant. And he had watched.

He started walking, hoping to escape the grip of the past. Walking required thought and attention, keeping his mind too busy to wander the corridors of its memory.

Gavrin had finally told him the full truth, confirmed by the impressions his remnant provided. Its presence lurked in the back of his mind, quietly consuming the sights and sounds of Brenwick. The companionship wasn't unpleasant, and easy to ignore if needed, but always there at his request. It still unfolded, revealing more of itself while securing itself more deeply to his mind and spirit.

He had to keep moving, and he walked from one end of Brenwick to another, then turned around and retraced his steps. His sister's killers were here. Cori was here. No reason for him to leave.

He could have walked until day turned to night and back into day, but Cori didn't have the time. Halfway back through Brenwick he whispered, "What do I do?"

Instead of a direct answer, a memory surfaced, pulled from the tempest and placed before him like he was an elder at a feast. The assassin had left from the House of Brennor. The remnant had called it a sanctuary.

There was no conscious decision. He had to keep moving, and so his feet carried him in the direction of the House. With a direction and purpose, his thoughts fell into order and a greater awareness of his surroundings returned. The afternoon was busy as many of the markets rushed toward their close of the day, and the streets were filled with the energy of hundreds of people, each with their own purpose. The Harvest Festival drew to its conclusion and the shopping was appropriately frenzied.

He drew attention as he passed, and he looked down at himself. Easy enough to see why. Clan robes drew attention regardless, but his were bloody and torn. His hands and hair were caked in dust and grime from the battle and the collapse of the warehouse.

Gods, he was tired. His body ached from the blows he'd taken in the fight and in the aftermath. How long had it been since he'd slept?

He slapped his face until his cheeks stung. He couldn't rest, not with Cori in danger. Clothes. He needed clothes and a bath.

Veynar didn't have any of the notes Brenwick used as currency and no way of acquiring some in short order. He passed an alley where clothes hung up high between two second story windows. Some appeared to be about his size, and he climbed the wall and took them down. The tunic was a bit large and the pants a little small, but they were close enough they wouldn't draw attention. He folded his robes and hid them behind a pair of barrels.

His throat tightened as he stepped back from the barrels, realizing there was a real possibility he might not see the robes again.

Veynar turned on his heel. No matter. He wasn't one of Caelen's anymore. He didn't deserve to wear the robes. Maybe he never had.

A stop by the river that cut down the southern side of the city served as a substitute for a bath. He rinsed the worst of the grime away, the cold water stinging needles across his skin as it flowed calmly toward the sea. Clean and clothed, he left the riverside a new man, reborn into a new life.

He returned to the same alcove he'd used before, a lifetime ago, when Malric had been alive. Evening approached, and the main gate to the House of Brennor was busy with citizens both coming and going. The guards were attentive but not disruptive, letting most visitors enter without question.

The feeling of the sanctuary was stronger than before.

Veynar felt its presence in his bones. It made him feel like he was in a quiet forest clearing, the sun warm against his skin as a cool breeze blew through the trees.

"Sanctuary isn't just a building, is it? Or a rule everyone agreed to follow."

Again there was no answer that translated into language. Just a feeling of a power, one greater and older than the power locked within the remnant. Not enough of an answer to satisfy his curiosity, but enough to confirm what he needed to know. He could trust the promise of sanctuary, and so he emerged from the alcove and made his way toward the gate. A group of merchants walked parallel to him, the Hall clearly their destination. Veynar slipped in behind them, not so close he'd earn any strange looks, but close enough that an outsider might have considered him one of the group.

They passed through the gate without challenge and Veynar breathed out a sigh. He broke apart from the merchants, who had come to give their offerings for the week and followed his sense of the sanctuary. Unfortunately, it didn't take him through the exquisite gardens he'd visited earlier. Instead, he turned off to the side and followed the silence.

It led him to a three-story stone building near the corner of Brennor's grounds. Lights blazed within, filled with a warmth that promised comfort and rest. He looked for guards, but there were none to be found. He shrugged and reached for the door.

As soon as he touched the door handle he lost control of his hand. His fingers wrapped tight around the curved metal, and a new power entered his body. There was a touch of the familiar about it, a distant relation to the power of the remnant within him. The remnant, though, was the weaker power, a faint echo of the force that lurked within the handle. The power wandered through his body, deep and steady, like an enormous wide river of unfathomable depth.

The power passed through him and returned to the door. A lock slid open and he pulled. A blast of warm air smacked him in the face, smelling of fresh bread, tea leaves, and the malty aroma of beer being brewed. The sanctuary reminded him of one of the inns he'd sometimes visited as the clan wandered away from the Broken Lands for brief respite between their Watches. He'd never spent the night in one, but the clans would frequent the common rooms when the opportunity presented itself.

Veynar had never set eyes on one like this, though. The tables came in all shapes and sizes, from small round tables that barely fit two drinks to long tables that could hold a feast for a large family. High backed booths circled around the edges of the common room and appeared to be the most popular choice of seating. Thick upholstered cushions encouraged long hours of conversation, and the smell of food and drink would have pulled in hunters from miles and miles away.

He entered and closed the door behind him, acting as though he'd been here many times before. Another glance around the common room made it clear he wouldn't be fooling anyone. His common clothes had allowed him past the guards at the main gate without question, but even the servers gliding between the tables wore clothes that made his look like a beggar's garments. He saw none of the garish colors he sometimes saw on the streets of the city, but the quality and cut of the fabrics was far beyond his simple clan robes. The knowledge of such things wasn't one he'd developed personally, but he found he could cast an expert eye upon the stitchings and designs draped over the sanctuary's other patrons, and he was impressed.

Veynar ignored the temptation to hide in one of the booths. Against the far wall was a raised bar, the wood polished from countless years of heavy use and considerate care. A man stood behind the bar, pouring drinks as requested, speaking with patrons quietly when he wasn't otherwise needed. He'd noticed Veynar's arrival and taken him in with eyes that missed little. He had the look of a man who knew a great many things and would share that knowledge if asked kindly enough.

Veynar pulled up a stool and sat, sighing in relief at the chance to rest his legs. He didn't feel exhausted, but his body behaved as though it was. The bartender came over. "What can I get for you?"

"I'm afraid I have no coin, so your advice is all I seek."

The bartender studied him closer, then grunted. "You're one of Caelen's."

"Was." The answer came out too quickly, his tongue unguarded. Only one word, and yet the changing expression on the bartender's face told Veynar he'd said far too much.

The bartender reached under the bar and pulled out a small cup suitable for rice wine, then followed it with a small, corked bottle. He gently pushed both toward Veynar. "Advice I can give, but the look in your eyes tells me it would be a crime not to share this, too."

Veynar fixed the bartender with a hard look, which the older man waved away. "No tricks from me, though I wouldn't extend your trust too far. Now, how can I help?"

Like most in the clan, Veynar rarely drank. Liquor and wine were hard to come by in the distant reaches of the land and dulled senses that needed to be kept sharp. Celebrations were limited to the small respites when they passed through towns and villages, and even then were limited affairs. It was too easy, after seeing what they saw on Watch, to fall to the tempting promises of bottomless bottles.

Veynar uncorked the bottle and poured the clear wine into the cup. He sipped. The wine cooled his parched tongue. It was a sweeter wine with a bite at the end, and it warmed the parts of his chest that had been cold since Malric died. Muscles loosened, and his shoulders dropped. He poured himself another cup, promising it would be his last, and drank it quickly. He bowed in thanks, almost knocking his forehead against the bar. "I'm looking for any information about who killed my sister. I think they've been here recently."

The barkeeper attended to another patron, giving Veynar an opportunity to sip at a third cup absentmindedly. He returned a moment later. "There's advice I can give and advice I can't, my new friend, and I'm afraid you've asked for the latter. I won't tell anything about other patrons to you, just as I won't tell other patrons anything about you."

Veynar looked around the room and compared the state of the others to his own condition.

He couldn't miss the strength within the common room. He assumed everyone possessed a remnant, guessed the door wouldn't open for anyone but. Far more than he'd guessed, and for the first time in his life, he wondered if his clan was weaker than he'd always thought.

The strength in the room ran parallel with the wealth. If the clothes weren't evidence enough, the room itself was. He'd never been in a nicer inn. If this was his world now, he'd need the coin to move through it, same as he needed good boots on the edges of the Broken Lands.

He shook his head, but his thoughts wouldn't clear. He'd only been in Brenwick for a little more than a day and already he was thinking like someone born in the city. What he needed was to find Cori, and in so doing, find the murderers. "Is there anyone I could ask for information?"

"Of course, but I think you'll find that such information rarely comes cheap."

Veynar nodded. "I understand." He pointed to one of the

booths. "I'm going to drink there, alone, but if you could spread the word around, I'd appreciate it."

The bartender gave a slight bow. "Certainly, sir. Enjoy your rest."

ONE DRINK FOLLOWED ANOTHER, each easier than the last. It didn't seem like long before the last of the drink was swishing around in the bottom of his cup. The world had grown dull again, darkness crowding the edges of his vision and every sound muffled, as though he'd wrapped a blanket around his head. He couldn't drink fast enough to keep the memories away. Every time he squeezed his eyes shut, Malric was there, dying in front of him all over again.

Drink spilled from his cup and he swore. It hadn't been his doing. He looked up and a new face swam in his vision, framed in golden hair and revealing a smile that would cause ladies across the land to beg for his hand in marriage. "Rough times?"

Veynar tried to straighten, then decided it was easier to slump back in the high-backed chair. "I've had better days."

He spoke slowly and precisely, but his words still slurred.

"Haven't we all? I've heard word that you're looking for information. Fortunately for you, I have exactly what you need."

"How do you know that?"

"Because I'm the sort of person who has found a great deal of success in knowing things and learning secrets. Say, for example, that you were involved in a fight down at the docks earlier today that destroyed a very expensive warehouse, a loss the owners are eager to recoup, in blood, if necessary."

The implied threat cut through the fog clouding Veynar's mind. He sat up straighter.

The man smiled again, reminding Veynar of a snake preparing to eat. "I see I have your attention. Good. I also happen to know that one of Caelen's clan was taken hostage during the fight, and I happen to know where they're hiding her."

If the table hadn't been between them, Veynar would have picked the man up by his expensive shirt and demanded answers. Circumstances forced him to settle for the latter half. "Tell me."

"Certainly! For a price, though, and I hear you carry no coin."

"What do you want from me?" Veynar asked. Even in the state of his drunkenness, he could recognize the man's intent.

The man took a folded piece of paper from a pocket, opened it, and slid it across to Veynar. "There's a warden who's been giving me a particularly hard time as of late. It would be best if he didn't report for duty tomorrow morning. Or any morning thereafter."

Veynar recognized the face. It was the warden who had accompanied the Sister when she'd visited Caelen's Rest. He took the paper, which also had an address scrawled across the bottom. "You'll be here when I return?"

The man spread his arms out wide and patted the long seat. "Likely still in this very booth. It's one of my favorites, you know."

"I do now." Veynar stood, drank the last of his drink quickly, and stumbled toward the door, on his way to murder a warden.

CHAPTER 18
A PERFECT NIGHT FOR MURDER

Sometimes we must destroy before we can create.

— FROM *THE BOOK OF BRENNOR*

Night had fallen by the time Veynar left the sanctuary. The House of Brennor's grounds were quiet. The Sisters would be cloistered within their rooms by now, and most visitors would have left before the falling of the sun. He wasn't bothered by the guards as he left out the main gate and turned down the street, lit by the lamps placed at regular intervals.

An icy air blew in from the sea, cutting through his thin clothes and stabbing into the flesh that was as good as unprotected. The drink cleared itself from his system quickly, leaving him in a melancholy mood.

He didn't think of the task given to him by the stranger, nor of Malric's death. He didn't dare stop to contemplate either, certain that if he did he'd never find the strength to move again. Movement was his only refuge.

So different, the streets of Brenwick. They were thoughts he'd had before, only sharper now. Lamplighters allowed people to walk day or night. The shadows, as always, held their dangers, but thanks to the lighting, the shadows were few and far between. He thrust his hands into the pockets of his trousers, desperate for any warmth.

Twice he had to ask for directions, but both times the strangers were kind and courteous. Wardens roamed the streets, but they never bothered Veynar except to wish him a good evening. Without his robe, he was nobody to them.

He still preferred the silence and emptiness of the plains, of an endless sky not bounded by tall buildings, but it was unfair of him not to recognize Brennor and his servants for what they'd accomplished here. Brenwick was largely a good city, filled with people that cared. It was different in almost every way from the life he knew, but that fact remained.

The moon was just rising over the tops of the buildings when Veynar reached the address given to him by the stranger. It was a taller building near the center of the city, not all that far from the House of Brennor. According to the scrawled notes, the warden lived on the third of four floors. Veynar figured he could climb to the window, but he wasn't sure which window, and the night's drinking had already dampened his enthusiasm for unnecessary effort. The front door was open and the stairs were easier.

Veynar ascended the stairs, footsteps quieter than a mistress sneaking from her lover's room. Unadorned walls stripped whatever meager warmth the building might have otherwise had. The tent he lived in near the border contained more decoration, and for good reason. Their lives were already lean, stripped of the fat the citizens of Brenwick took for granted. Too lean, though, and life lost meaning. A weary warrior battling madness and the sharp claws of the Graevath needed more than bare walls and a meager meal to return to.

Footsteps echoed on the stairs above, descending toward him, but it was best not to be seen on the way to commit murder. "Can we hide, the way Gavrin or the assassins did?"

Mention of the assassins brought him too close to Malric's memory, but the voice of his remnant returned, grounding him firmly in the present.

The skill must be trained, but if you surrender your body, we could briefly vanish from sight.

The steps were about to turn the corner. "Do it."

He slid to the right side of the landing so he wouldn't be in the way. The remnant's power swelled like a wave about to break against the shore and covered him like a blanket, shaped by a will not his own. To his sight, nothing had changed, but when a young man appeared on the landing above Veynar, he charged down the flight as though Veynar wasn't there. The youth took the stairs three at a time, and his eyes never so much as glanced toward Veynar.

The remnant's power folded upon itself and returned to its original resting state. Finely-tuned senses tracked the manner of it.

He called upon the same power, manipulating it into the same shapes he'd just felt. When he erred, the remnant nudged him in the right direction.

You learn quickly.

He'd have to, if he hoped to survive this new world.

He allowed the veil to drop when he reached the third floor. The hallway was empty, all the good little citizens of Brenwick tucked tight into their beds. He stopped outside the warden's door and wondered how best to proceed, but the weight of everything built up behind him, like an enormous boulder rolling down the hall, and he couldn't afford to time to stand around and plan. Like any polite assassin, he knocked on the door.

The moment the door clicked open, Veynar flung his entire weight against it. The door slammed into the warden, who stumbled back into a small but tastefully appointed living room. Veynar followed the warden and took in countless details at a glance. The room had the look of a space not often occupied, the furniture spotlessly clean and precisely placed. A small shrine sat near the north wall of the room, the cushion in front of it the only well-worn object in the room. Two candles had been freshly lit, casting a warm and melancholy glow over a charcoal drawing of a smiling couple.

The warden recovered and went for his swords hanging on the nearby wall. He moved slowly, closer to a casual stroll through a park on a sunny afternoon rather than a desperate grab for a weapon. Veynar's fist found the warden's stomach with ease, folding the lawman over his arm. He pushed the warden back toward the far wall.

The warden staggered but recovered, raising his fists and taking a fighting stance. He led with a practiced combination, a jab with his left followed by a swing with his right. He moved too slowly, and Veynar could read his movements as easy as one of Maeryn's countless books.

Veynar slapped the jab away and stepped inside the warden's swing. He drove his knee forward and caught the warden square in the stomach. Again the warden staggered, his legs quivering as he fought to support his unsteady weight. Veynar credited the warrior, though. He kept his feet and sought an opening.

Veynar stepped forward again and the warden's eyes went wide. Veynar's right arm snaked out and he caught the warden by the throat, driving him backward. The warden clutched at Veynar's wrist and tried to rip it away, but he might as well have tried to bend iron. Veynar slammed the back of the warden's head into the wall and the man's eyes lost focus for a moment, rolling in different directions. The warden's hands slipped from Veynar's wrist, and Veynar lifted him, one-handed, from the ground.

His victim's eyes regained their focus as his face turned red. The warden kicked and tried to claw at Veynar's face, but Veynar was unbothered. What power the kicks possessed quickly faded as the warden failed to draw air into his lungs.

The man's pulse pounded beneath Veynar's fingers, a desperate heart fighting for a few more moments of life. The warden's face changed color again and his kicks grew feebler.

Veynar blinked, as though realizing for the first time where he was and what he was doing. His stomach churned as he looked up at the warden's face, spit leaking from the side of his mouth.

Veynar let go and stumbled back. The warden collapsed to the floor, lungs gasping for a breath they'd given up hope of ever receiving.

Veynar's hands trembled and a shiver wracked his body. He took another step back and shook his head. His knees trembled and he couldn't breathe, cords wrapping tight around his chest. His skin crawled, filled with the power of the remnant, but what was his and what wasn't? Was his mind even his own?

The warden's breathing evened as he slowly stood. He looked at Veynar closely for the first time. His eyes narrowed, then widened a moment later. "You!"

He started again toward his swords, but Veynar raised a hand. "Don't."

The warden obeyed, but every muscle in his body was strung tight as a bow, ready to snap at a moment. Veynar had no fear for his safety. The warden couldn't threaten him, even with his swords.

He required the warden's death to pursue his sister's killer.

But who was he fooling? He hadn't even been able to kill the Graevath when he'd been on Watch. What chance did he have of killing a warden?

The real fool is the one who sees only one path when so many exist.

The remnant's remonstration kicked Veynar's thoughts into motion.

"Can we talk?" he asked.

A silly question considering the circumstances, and the confusion written on the warden's face was no less than Veynar deserved.

"Please?" Veynar backed two steps away to prove his sincerity.

The warden leaped for his sword. He pulled it from the wall and drew it in one smooth motion, holding it level with Veynar's heart. He debated for a moment, then thrust at Veynar's chest.

Only Veynar had seen the tension in his muscles, had known of the warden's decision possibly earlier than the warden had. He slid to the side as the warden began his thrust, the slammed the side of his hand down against the warden's outstretched wrist. The sword cut through nothing but air, then dropped as the warden's hand opened.

The warden stared, openmouthed. "You weren't this strong before."

Veynar ignored the question. "Please?" he repeated.

The warden shook out his injured wrist and stared at the sword lying useless on the floor. "I suppose we should, then. Can I get you some tea?"

Veynar shifted awkwardly on the cushion, but no position remained comfortable for more than a moment. The warden's footsteps moved confidently around the kitchen, the man a master of his domain, no matter he'd almost been killed at home just before. He came out carrying a tray, the tea already steeping and two cups waiting. He kneeled across a small table from Veynar, bowed, and placed the tray on the table. Steady hands poured two cups of tea, and the gentle fragrance released some of the knots in Veynar's stomach.

Poison.

Veynar's hand froze in midair, and the warden shook his head at the hesitation. He picked up his own cup, took a sip, then returned it to the table. Veynar bowed a silent apology, then took a sip as well. It was flavorful tea and well-prepared.

"I—I don't know your name," he confessed.

"And yet you came here with the intent to kill me. Why?" The warden asked as though merely curious, as though it wasn't his life that had almost been ended.

"I'm searching for my sister's killer."

"I'm afraid if your search led you here, you've gone very far astray."

"I know you didn't kill her, but there's a man who knows more than he should, and he promised to set me on their trail if I killed you." Veynar took another sip of the tea, which steadied exhausted nerves.

"So why didn't you kill me?" the warden asked.

"It wouldn't have been right."

The warden scoffed. "Funny thing to realize when you're choking the life out of someone."

The answer had been close enough to the truth, though, and Veynar's shame wouldn't allow him to provide an explanation that was any closer. One of Caelen's warriors would never have hesitated.

The warden ran the tip of a finger around the rim of his cup. "My name is Roneth. If you don't mind me saying, you're in over your head, and I might be able to help."

"You know who killed Lirael?" It seemed everyone in this city besides him knew.

Roneth shook his head. "I don't, but I have been working with the Head Sister at the Hall. She's been searching, too."

"What has she learned?"

"If it's anything specific, she hasn't told me. They hold tight to their secrets there. What I do know is that there's a new force in town opposing Brennor. Could be the same people that killed your sister. That's who the Head Sister has me chasing after."

Veynar's head spun. That matched with what Avelin had said. Whoever they were, they'd killed Lirael over the remnant currently sharing space with Veynar's spirit.

The warden said, "I've been trying to root them out the last few days, but they're buried deep. Could be why they seized an opportunity to have me killed."

Veynar turned the full force of his attention onto the warden. The cold air from the walk, followed by the fight, had finished clearing the drink from his blood. Exhaustion shaved the edge off his awareness, but he retained enough to put Roneth's demeanor under the closest scrutiny. The man's heart thumped steadily in his chest, and his eyes fearlessly met Veynar's.

If the man lied, he was one of the greatest in the world.

"Let's say I believe you," Veynar said.

"If you did, then you'd know the one who sent you to kill me is probably part of whatever group killed your sister."

Veynar set his empty teacup down and rose, bowing before turning to leave.

The man in the bar had lied and used him. Had probably been laughing the entire time to himself, too.

Veynar's knuckles popped as he squeezed his fist tight. He hadn't been able to kill the warden, but he had little doubt he could kill the man who had sent him here.

Anyone involved in Lirael's death would die, but not before telling everything they knew.

CHAPTER 19
THE PRICE OF KNOWLEDGE

There can be no peace without threat of violence. No order without threat of consequence.

If we wish to build the future, we must be willing to destroy today.

— FROM *THE BOOK OF BRENNOR*

The moon sat high in the sky by the time Veynar returned to the sanctuary, bathing the streets and buildings in its cold light. Come winter the snow would sparkle under its silvery gleam, but tonight it muted the world's colors.

Veynar stumbled through the door holding an empty bottle he'd liberated from the warden's stash before leaving. A slow look around the common room told him that little had changed in his absence. Several guests had left, no doubt sleeping the sleep of those at peace. The kind of sleep he'd forgotten since the day he discovered his sister dead at the base of a tree.

The man who'd asked him to kill the warden sat in the booth waiting, as good as his word. When he saw Veynar stumble through the door and almost trip over the leg of a chair, the corner of his mouth turned up in a smile he was quick to hide. Veynar swayed between the chairs and tables, earning scowls from many of the patrons.

Inebriation alone they had little quarrel with. It was the despair and desperation that echoed through the room with every step, the lack of pride in one of their own. He possessed a remnant and the world was his to shape as he pleased, and this was how he presented himself? Their judgment was silent but final, and if he were to cross paths with any of them outside this sanctuary, they might kill him as a matter of pride.

He slumped into the booth. "It's done."

The man's eyes flashed with delight, congratulating himself on the ease with which he'd manipulated Veynar. "A drink to celebrate?"

"Brought my own." Veynar tipped the bottle to his lips, then frowned. He held the open bottle upside down and stared at it as though it were a riddle he couldn't unravel.

"Dear new friend, it appears you're dry. Allow me to get us another."

Veynar shook his head, then grimaced. "No. Cori."

"Of course, of course. There's no time to waste. Come with me. I know where they took her after the fight in the warehouse."

"How?"

"I make it my business to know what happens throughout Brenwick. You're fortunate I was here tonight."

Veynar nodded, then half-stood, half-stumbled out of the booth. He made it to the front door after hitting only one chair, a feat that failed to impress his new friend as much as it should have. The cold night air slapped him across the face as he exited, and he stuffed his hands deep in his pockets so they wouldn't freeze. He missed his robes. The blonde man emerged behind him and pulled the collar of his coat up. "Follow me."

The man was considerate enough to walk slowly so that Veynar didn't fall too far behind. They walked west toward the docks, though not quite the direction they would have traveled if their destination had been the destroyed warehouse. Most of the people they passed were wardens, patrolling through the night so that Brennor's beloved citizens could sleep through the night in peace.

Veynar's guide kept glancing back, as though ensuring Veynar's inebriation hadn't faded.

The smell of the sea had grown strong by the time his guide stopped outside a small nondescript building. "In here."

The building's windows were darker than the night sky, but Veynar followed without question. The man produced a key from his pocket and a moment later was inside, beckoning Veynar to follow. He spoke softly. "Quiet, now."

Veynar nodded and followed, only the tip of his boot caught on the uneven entry and he stumbled, knocking into a small table by the door. A book fell to the floor, thumping louder than Veynar's heart.

His guide hissed, but didn't seem too distraught. Whatever role this place served during the day, it was empty and silent now. Veynar's eyes adjusted to the dark quickly, and he followed his guide down the entryway.

Richly appointed rooms sat on either side of the hall. Bookshelves rose from the floor to the ceiling and were crammed full of more books than Veynar had ever seen in one place. Leather chairs faced one another across from a fireplace, still warm from that day's use. "Looks comfortable," he said, and went into one of the rooms.

His guide grabbed his arm and whispered. "Not here. They took her to the cellar."

Veynar blinked, then nodded slowly. "Right. That's why we're here. Lead the way."

Down the hallway, then a right, and down another short hall and there was a trapdoor. Veynar's guide held a finger to his lips, then bent over and gently tugged on the ring embedded in the door. It opened on silent hinges.

There wasn't a sound from below, but Veynar was hardly in a place to criticize his guide for a bit of theatricality. He followed the man down the wooden ladder.

The cellar floor was dirt. Racks of wine bottles, dusty with age, lined the right wall. His guide lit a lamp, his motions practiced and experienced. There was a larger room beyond, which Veynar guessed was their final destination.

The guide lit two more lamps, bathing the cellar in flickering firelight. Once, long ago, the room might have been used for the storing of food, but it had been emptied out and put to other uses since. Iron rings were bolted into the ground and the wall, and manacles of various sizes and lengths of chain were scattered around the room. Against the far wall was a collection of tools whose purposes Veynar didn't care to guess. Blades of all shapes and sizes, from tiny sharp scalpels to the long swords favored by the wardens. Some were serrated, and in the light of the lamps, it was too easy to see the chunks of flesh caught by the blades. There were hammers and tongs and other tools Veynar didn't even recognize.

There was blood on the floor. Too much blood, though it was hard to tell what was fresh stain and what had decorated the room long before. If Cori had been here, Veynar didn't care to imagine what had happened.

His guide's smile was vicious, confirming Roneth's guess earlier that night. Of course he'd been involved. He couldn't have known so much about Cori otherwise. Veynar should have seen it earlier, but his mind had been too clouded, his emotions too easily manipulated.

A cold shell crashed shut around Veynar's heart, suffocating the anger that threatened to burn his spirit to a cinder.

A sword appeared in his guide's previously empty hand. "You drunk fool. I promise, at least, to make it quick."

He approached lazily as Veynar blinked away his confusion. When he was two steps away, he raised the sword for a powerful overhand cut.

Veynar stepped forward and drove his fist into the guide's stomach, then followed it with a roundhouse left that snapped the guide's head around and sent him to the floor. The sword dropped from the man's hand and vanished before it could strike the ground. The guide tried to scramble away, but Veynar was still on his feet and too fast, and he snapped a kick straight into the man's face.

As the man slid into unconsciousness, Veynar dropped into a smooth squat beside him, eyes sharp and glittering in the lamplight. "Make it quick?" Veynar grabbed the man's chin and forced him to look. "I won't," he promised.

HIS GUIDE WOKE IN IRONS. A pair of manacles with a long chain between them had been secured to the ceiling such that he could just barely stand flat-footed on the dirt floor of the cellar. Blood dripped from his broken nose and one of his eyes was swollen shut. Veynar leaned against a wall across from him, arms crossed.

The shell that had slammed shut over his heart hadn't opened since. Whenever it wavered, he imagined Cori here, and once again, his blood turned to ice and his heart slowed until healers would have worried for his health.

His guide swore. "You lied!"

Veynar uncrossed his arms, pushed off the wall, and walked slowly toward the center of the room. His guide tried to shift away, but the manacles prevented any escape. Veynar brought his foot back and kicked, the boot blurring as it smashed between the man's legs. The guide's eyes rolled up in his head and he sagged against his chains, no doubt wishing for the oblivion of unconsciousness.

When the man regained his focus, he formed a knife in his hand and worked at his chains, but the blade wasn't strong enough to cut through the steel formed in the heat of Brenwick's forges. Veynar watched the man struggle for a while, then made a fist and advanced again.

"What do you want to know?"

Veynar twisted his hips and put all his weight into a punch to the man's kidneys. Again he sagged, manacles cutting deep into his wrists. The knife dropped from his hand and disappeared. The guide growled. "You don't have the slightest clue. You have no idea. You kill me and what happened to your girlfriend is only the beginning of your worries. Whatever pain and suffering you think you know is nothing."

In answer, Veynar formed a blade and stared at it. He'd practiced while the man had been unconscious, and it was almost natural now. The short sword felt every bit like the ones his father had ordered crafted for him. Perfect balance and sharp enough to shave the wing off a fly.

The man's eyes went wide and his bout of courage failed him. "What do you want to know?" he screamed.

Veynar stabbed. He didn't cut deep, just thrust it a ways into the guide's side and twisted it around a bit. The guide screamed, his pain echoing in the small room.

Veynar's heart fluttered and his stomach felt sick, but as soon as he imagined Cori's fate and the agonies she'd endured in this room, the sensations faded. This man had information and he needed it to save his friend, if she could still be saved. What else mattered?

"Why won't you ask me a question?" the man said.

Veynar drew the edge of the blade softly across the man's armpit. He screamed as blood flowed freely.

"I don't know where they took her! I knew they brought her here because it was close to the warehouse and I heard some of the other guys talking about it. After that, I don't know. Word was that the bosses wanted more time with her, but I don't know where."

Veynar let the blade disappear. When it formed in his hand again, the blade was clean of blood. That was convenient.

He asked his first question. "Why would your bosses want her?"

The guide made no effort to hide anything. Words spilled from him almost faster than Veynar could track. "She's a clanner, and she knew you, so they must have figured she had at least some Keeper's training."

"Why would they care about that?"

The guide hesitated and Veynar lifted his sword, inspiring an admirable level of cooperation. "Gods, you don't know anything, do you? They want Caelen dead, too."

Veynar almost reminded the guide that Caelen had died hundreds of years ago, then realized the truth. He spoke about the remnants. His bosses believed Cori would know enough to help them.

The power in his remnant stirred. *Or they believe they can use her as bait to draw you in, as they are now.*

"Too? Who else do you want dead?"

The man didn't answer, but the power in Veynar's spirit did. *Brennor.*

"Why do you want Brennor dead?"

The guide growled with unexpected ferocity, and Veynar retreated half a step, despite the fact his companion was in chains. "Because he stole our land!"

"What?"

"The land that Brenwick sits on? Do you think it was his? Our people were here first, living peacefully, and then he came with his lies and false promises."

He belongs to Daevor. The voice was as certain as it had been about anything since making home in Veynar's spirit. Unfortunately, the name meant nothing to Veynar. He'd studied all the gods as part of his Keeper's training, but he'd not heard of that one.

"If you had to guess where they took her, where would they have done so?"

Blonde hair snapped back and forth as the guide shook his head. "I really don't know. This was our gathering place when we met, but the bosses kept their own accommodations, and not even I'm fool enough to attempt to figure out where those are."

"Tell me about your bosses."

"Eryndel and Ardyn, master and student. Strong enough I don't think I'll ever hold my own against their blades, and deep into the mysteries. They were raised to hate Brennor and all the rest, and their movement is already too late to stop. There are too many of us."

Veynar took his blade and stabbed it into the guide's heart and he died a moment later. He let the blade vanish.

"One less now," he said.

CHAPTER 20
NEW FRIENDS, OLD PROBLEMS

Pity the hunter who finds himself alone.

— FROM *THE SAYINGS OF CAELEN*

Veynar didn't make it out of the room before his stomach rebelled. The blonde man hung limp from the chains, the thread of his life cut without so much as a second thought. Had he children, or a lover he returned to? Friends that would miss him? Veynar's conscience posed one unanswerable question after another, tightening the screws in his gut that made him want to vomit. He stumbled to a wall and slumped against it, heart pounding violently.

He reached for the cold certainty he'd known just moments before, but it slipped from his grasp. Sweat dripped from his brow, though the cellar was almost as cold as the air outside. He closed his eyes and swore.

Malric was dead. Cori's blood mixed with the blood of the guide in this very room. The man would have killed him if given the chance.

All true, and yet it didn't loosen the screws in his stomach or return him to that detached state when everything had seemed so clear.

Something small plopped into a puddle of blood. Veynar pushed himself off the wall and turned around on shaky legs. He couldn't raise his eyes to the dead body, but they roamed across the bloody floor. There. A lump of some sort. He walked over and squatted, reaching out with thumb and forefinger to pick it up. The shape was familiar, though the color was different.

A gem, much like the one he'd accepted into his own body.

In answer to his unspoken question, the remnant in his spirit said, *Kill the host, and the remnant is yours.*

"What good does it do me? Can I absorb it too?"

You can but I wouldn't recommend it. The strength of two gems is too much for a body to take, and my brothers and sisters rarely get along. Even a meager connection, like the one you once formed with me, may be enough to kill you.

The voice's warning was the same as Maeryn's, yet it didn't sound so certain. If anything, it sounded like it wanted Veynar to form a connection but was talking itself out of the idea. "What do I do with it, then?"

Hide it. Learn from it. Bargain with it. Destroy it.

Veynar sensed there was much more the remnant wanted to say, but it hesitated and held back. He could attempt to force it to reveal what it hid, but it seemed unwise to force its hand. Better not to anger the god-fragment lurking within his spirit. He put the gem in his pocket and left, climbing the ladder at the end of the hall and closing the trapdoor behind him.

The overstuffed chairs called to him, promising rest, but Cori was still missing. Perhaps he'd been too quick to kill the guide, but he didn't think the dead man had taken too many secrets to the other side of the veil. He'd only known enough to lure Veynar into the trap.

With any luck, the house would reveal more. It wasn't just a random building, but a place for conspirators to gather. Perhaps they'd left tracks behind he could follow.

He began his search in the first of the sitting rooms, though he held little hope. There were no burnt-out logs in the fireplace and the room hadn't been dusted in several days. Still, he took note of everything he could. He ran his finger along the spines of the books. He was no scholar, but as near as he could tell, there was no theme to the collection. Histories were intermixed with memoirs and travelogues. Some of the books seemed quite ancient, naming places that were currently deep in the Broken Lands. Nothing guided him to where they might be hiding Cori.

Veynar crossed the hall to the other room, a hint of warmth still lingering in the dying embers of the fireplace. He started again with the books, though there was nothing more to be found. Fortunately the room held more than old books, many of which hadn't been cracked open for years. Papers lay scattered upon the side tables. Bent and crinkled and stained from where mugs had rested and sweated upon them, they drew his attention. He flipped through them, reading quickly. One sheet of paper was a brief tract condemning Brenwick's overcrowding. Another was a map printed out by the city detailing the sites of blessing for the conclusion of the Harvest Festival. Yet another was a newsletter detailing the taxes the House of Brennor wanted to levy, and to what uses they might be put. The one that caught his attention, though, was a long list of names, all women. He ran his eyes down the list and froze near the bottom. Lirael was there.

The list had no description, but Veynar had a suspicion. He ran his eyes over the list again and nodded. Avelin's name was also present. It was most likely a list of Sisters and Sisters-in-training. Combined with the guide's confession and the warden's concerns, a story was finally starting to emerge.

His remnant had seemed familiar with the blonde man's complaints. "Do you know who they are?"

Followers of Daevor.

"I've never heard the name."

No reason you would. I thought they were dead, and I suspect many others thought the same.

"He spoke true, then, about what happened?"

True enough. He came from a clan not that much different than yours. Only Brennor wanted to build here, and he wasn't one to take no for an answer.

"So Brennor killed them off?"

More or less. Apparently less, as the survivors want revenge.

Again, there was more the remnant wasn't telling him, but the details of a feud hundreds of years ago didn't much matter to Veynar today. "Does knowing any of that help us find Cori?"

The remnant was silent, which was about the answer Veynar had expected. He folded up the paper with the list of the Sisters' names and slid it into the pocket with the gem. The room held nothing more of interest, so he made a slow walk through the rest of the building. Most rooms hadn't been used recently, but there was a metallic smell in the kitchen that almost reminded him of walking past a forge. The wood-fired stove was warmer than the surrounding air, but there were no pots or pans around with evidence of what had been made.

By the time he finished walking through the house his heart had calmed, and so long as he didn't think about the body below, he was well enough.

He'd been rash. The guide might not have known where Cori was, but he would have known how to contact others. Veynar could have used him somehow. Instead he'd killed his best way to find Cori.

He tapped his fingers against his leg. The trail he'd found had gone cold. What was left to him?

He sat in one of the overstuffed leather chairs and stared at the ceiling. Despite his exhaustion and the haunting memories of what he'd done, he found his thoughts falling into order with ease. Ideas sprang up one after the other and he examined each, weighing its benefits and risks before discarding it. He'd never felt quite so clear, so focused in the midst of chaos. It was an echo of what he'd felt below, only turned to solving a problem instead of killing a man.

"Is that you?" he asked.

It is.

"You were a scholar?"

Amusement. *Of sorts.*

Again Veynar saw little reason to push. It wasn't as useful as speed or strength, but he appreciated the remnant's influence. The answer wasn't one he liked, but it was clearly the best way forward, even if there was a decent chance it killed him. He sighed, wishing he could take the chair with him. His body wanted to melt into it the way the gems melted into their hosts. It was such a nice chair.

Regardless, it was time to see if he could make some new friends.

Veynar made no effort to sneak past the guards at the main gate. Attempting to reach the Head Sister by stealth posed a collection of risks he saw no need to run. Two of the guards appeared alert, but the other two looked ready to fall asleep standing. Given the late hour, it was unlikely anyone had passed through the gate in some time. He bowed and said, "I must speak to the Head Sister, please. It's urgent."

One of the almost-sleeping guards snorted. "Nothing is so urgent you need to see her tonight. Scram."

"I'm afraid I must insist. I'm one of Caelen's warriors, and there's trouble afoot."

One of the more alert guards looked him up and down. "Where are your robes?"

Veynar glared at the guard, which did nothing to intimidate him. "We don't always wear our robes, and I didn't want to draw attention to myself tonight. I assure you, it is urgent. It has to do with the deaths of apprentices Lirael and Avelin."

That got through to the other alert guard, who'd stood behind the other three, watching the exchange with interest. The others glanced back at him, and Veynar directed his next words that way. "Warden Roneth would support my claim. I met with him earlier tonight."

It was enough. The head of the guards nodded. "Follow me, then."

Veynar bowed in thanks and obeyed, the other guards casting questioning glances their way as they stepped into the gardens. They made their journey in silence, allowing Veynar to turn his full attention to his surroundings. Though the night was cold, the garden was warmer. Maybe it was just the effect of the high walls blocking the wind from the sea, but it felt like something more. As he passed through the other side of the garden he felt the chill on his arm before they reached the warmth and protection of the Sister's House. Veynar's guide spoke with the two guards on duty at that door and then they were through. They walked down dimly lit hallways, the sound of their footsteps swallowed by thick carpets.

Veynar's mind was turned toward the meeting with the Head Sister, but the remnant silently urged him to keep his eyes roving, to let his fingers glide across the polished wood and the heavy curtains. He saw no harm in it and agreed and was surprised by the satisfaction emanating from the presence in his core.

He formed the question in his mind. "Why?"

Because despite all my history with Brennor, he knew how to build. All of this was beyond us, and now it's so common you barely even bother admiring it. Such wealth and beauty didn't exist in my time.

They stopped outside a heavy door with another two guards standing on duty. Again Veynar's guide explained the situation, and after a hurried debate, one of the door guards entered. Each of the guards shifted uncomfortably, as though nervous about the consequences of waking the Head Sister. It was a fair amount of time before the guard returned, but when he did, it was with relief. He nodded to Veynar's guide, who led him through the open door.

The room on the other side was bigger than Veynar's tent, with nearly as much space as the house Veynar's parents used when they camped at Caelen's Rest. It was richly appointed with thick chairs, cushioned benches, and a fireplace that had just recently been stoked back to life. Bookshelves lined one wall, and a small but elegantly crafted writing desk sat in a corner. Veynar could well imagine a scribe there, scratching out notes as the Head Sister held her important meetings.

His study of the room would have ended there, but the remnant's opinion of the building had twisted his perspective and he looked closer. The wooden paneling on the far wall was exquisite, polished to a gleam that reflected the firelight and made the room feel brighter than it was. His boots sank into the carpet, and the landscape paintings across the wall almost made him feel like he was outdoors. Even he, who had little desire for sturdy walls and protective ceilings, felt at his ease here.

Several doors connected to this room, but Veynar's guide

gestured for him to remain in place, and so he did. He didn't wait long for the Head Sister to appear.

Veynar hadn't thought much of her when they'd first met in the Hall of the Dead, but here she exuded a different, stronger aura. She still looked tired, but she walked with a quick step, and the firelight reflected in her eyes could have well been the fire of her spirit. Her eyes narrowed when she saw him. "I wondered if it was you."

Veynar bowed deeply and apologized for the lateness of his visit. "Much has happened since you and I spoke last, and I bring worrying news. I believe Daevor's clan is alive and well and mean the House of Brennor, and maybe Brenwick, great harm."

The Head Sister pursed her lips, then grunted. "Well, I can't throw you out after that."

She looked up at the guard. "Perhaps you'd be so kind as to grab us some tea? I suspect we might be here for a while."

Veynar began with a question. "Why did you try to hide the truth of Lirael's death from me?"

The Head Sister didn't answer at first, then said, "That is not a question I feel comfortable answering quite yet."

He sensed in her reluctance the same fear that had kept Maeryn from answering his questions. That clinging to secrecy even when it no longer served them.

"I already know about the remnants, and I've seen firsthand some of the powers they grant. I also know Avelin stole a remnant from you and gave it to Lirael, so I know why she died. There's no need to hide anything."

The Head Sister's shoulders relaxed, as though she'd decided to surrender the burden of the secrets she carried.

"Very well, then. The decision to hide the truth from you was nothing more than what I've trained my Sisters to do. The presence of the remnants is a closely guarded secret no matter where you are. We intercepted the letter Avelin sent, and I sent one of my Sisters after Lirael. When my Sister discovered she was too late and Lirael was murdered and you were there, she took steps to ensure the secret remained. Speaking bluntly, if Gavrin hadn't also been present in that park, she would have killed you and the secret would have been safe."

"And then you did the same in the Hall of the Dead."

The Head Sister nodded. "The course had already been set, and you were under Maeryn's protection. My hands were as good as tied, and so I continued the illusion."

Veynar leaned back in his chair. One at a time, the mysteries fell away. All that remained was to find the Daevor assassins and bring them to justice.

The Head Sister gave him a moment, then said, "You said you had information about the Daevor."

Veynar nodded, and he told an abbreviated version of the story—that the Daevor had found him and lured him into the building, but that he'd turned the tables on the would-be assassin and killed him instead. He made no mention of his remnant or the one that had been within the Daevor. It wasn't that he didn't trust her, exactly, but that he was painfully aware people killed for the remnants, and the less said about them in general, the better.

She listened with her full attention, the same way High Keeper Maeryn did, and the mere presence of that attention eased some of the tightness in Veynar's chest. It made him feel like he wasn't alone, that he had allies in this fight he didn't understand. He finished by saying, "I won't rest until I find Lirael's killer. And Cori."

The Head Sister sat and considered what Veynar had shared

for some time. She turned her next question in a different direction. "And what would you have us do with this information?"

"I don't care what you do with it. All I hope is that you'll share some of what you know in return and point me in the right direction. Cori might still be alive. The way I figure it, both you and I want justice for Lirael. We can work together."

The High Sister tapped her long fingers against the armrest, and her next question caught him completely flat-footed. "Have you heard of Daevor? Few people have."

Veynar confessed that he hadn't.

"They were supposed to be wiped out. Brennor wanted this land. Offered them anything to let him build. He promised them wealth, shelter, and beauty. I can't say why they refused him. Brennor's own records are less than charitable. But they did, and he took the land by force. His followers were already far more numerous, and the smaller clan had no chance. He killed those who resisted and all those who claimed to be Daevor's disciples. It was assumed that the few who survived would join other clans. Apparently we were wrong. Enough of them held together to keep their clan alive."

She fixed him with a stare. "I won't deny they've been wronged. How does that make you feel? Does it make you want to ally with them? I know you have no particular love for Brennor."

"How I feel about their past hardly matters. Daevor's people killed my sister and my best friend, then kidnapped Cori. I won't stop until they're dead."

"I wish I could believe that," the High Sister said. "Did you know Brennor and Caelen were good friends? As different as sea and sand, but they loved each despite those differences. Maybe even because of them. The alliance was always meant to be two parts of a whole. Cities and civilization for those who craved order, and the wilds of the worlds for those unsatisfied or incapable of surrendering enough freedom to live in peace with so many neighbors. The shattering of the world broke the spirit of the alliance, though. Your people became defenders and protectors, a role they were naturally suited to. We built and grew, thanks to the peace you provided. And in time, we became two different peoples. I sometimes wonder if we could have made different choices and gone down a better path."

"Lirael was different. She believed in Brennor and what he's built."

The Head Sister nodded, and the grief on her face was the first genuine emotion she'd shown since Veynar had walked through the door. "She was different, and she did believe. She was an incredibly gifted student, but I think she was still Caelen's at heart, even after she swore her oaths to the order. Unfortunately, I think you are much the same as her."

The hairs on Veynar's arms raised on end and his stomach twisted. He spoke in his head to the remnant. "What's happening?"

She's gathering power.

He couldn't believe that she would fight him. They wanted the same things. When her blow came, it wasn't from a sword but from the force of her will. Memories that weren't his own, that weren't even real, flashed in his mind's eye. They weren't true. He knew, could define the boundary between what was real and what wasn't. Two paths unfurled before him, one the path he'd walked the past few days, and the other of her imagining, a terrible weaving designed to pull him into Brennor's embrace.

In the vision she wove, Maeryn exiled him because of his relentless curiosity, his push for the truth. He'd wandered Brenwick until a Sister found him and brought him here. Details blurred like old memories, leaving only the comfort he'd felt upon speaking with the Head Sister. She'd listened to all that he learned. Offered the House of Brennor as a home for him, molded him into a protector that would save the House even though he hadn't been able to save his sister. She promised him hard work but ample reward.

He slumped back in the chair, head pounding as his spirit sorted truth from tale. He lived two lives, both terrible, but one promising him welcome and the truth promising nothing at all.

What surprised him most was how much he wished he could just accept the lie and surrender the responsibility for his life. If he gave it to the Head Sister and Brennor, the weight of his actions would never bother him again.

It would have been so much easier if she would have allowed him to hate, but even as she tried to weave her lies into his heart, he sensed her motive, a deep-seated desire to do what was best for him. She knew so much more than she was letting on, and the well of her compassion was deep, causing her no end of anguish as she fought to establish order in a broken world. She believed that if he didn't give his whole spirit to Brennor, he would eventually come to grief. These lies were designed to save him from that, even as they shaved the sharp edge of his freedom away.

Alone, he might have surrendered. Might have let go of his memories and accepted the lie.

Except he was no longer one, and the remnant within held to truth more tightly than a man lost in the Broken Lands clung to his last canteen. The lie, no matter how appealing, couldn't satisfy.

The vision faded, leaving him with two complete sets of memories, only hers faded quickly, untethered to the truths he knew in his bones. He couldn't let her know that, though. He bowed deeply as though grateful. "Your offer is too generous, High Sister."

Her posture eased, only a bit, but she was convinced her illusions had worked, just as they had before.

He continued, "I didn't come expecting such a welcome, and though my heart yearns for it, I have grown distrustful of my spirit. I know it is rude, but may I have some time? My haste has doomed me often enough these last weeks, and this is not a decision to take lightly."

The Head Sister showed no sign of disappointment. "Of course. Please, go with my blessing, but be safe. There are dangers out there you still know nothing about. And always remember, you have a home here. Someplace safe. Here, at least, you'll always be welcome."

CHAPTER 21
FISHING FOR AN ASSASSIN

Chase the doe across the plain if you wish. Better, though, to convince the doe to come to you.

— FROM *THE SAYINGS OF CAELEN*

The doors to the House of Brennor closed behind Veynar and he shivered as the first light of dawn threatened to rise above the buildings to the east. He wasn't sure if it was the cold or the lingering impressions the Head Sister had left, but he wrapped his arms around himself in an effort to keep the warmth within his body.

The last survivors of Daevor's clan wanted revenge against Brennor. He'd made the Head Sister aware, which was a good thing, but she hadn't seen fit to share any of what she knew, which closed off the route he'd planned to take. His interview with her had answered some of his questions, but left him no closer to finding Cori.

She had to be alive. Not because he believed. In the darkest corners of his heart, the truth lurked, waiting for him to acknowledge it. No. Cori had to be alive, because if she was dead what was the point of fighting?

He shuffled over to the gardens, unwrapping his arms as the warmer air caressed exposed skin. The smell of late summer lingered, a guest who didn't want to leave even though the celebration was long over. Where did he go from here? What else was left for him to do? He could wait. Try to track the movements of the Sisters and Daevor's followers. In time, he might work his way toward where Cori was being held.

He didn't have the time. Whatever odds Cori had of being alive shrank with each passing moment. He needed to aim straight for the heart of his enemy.

His hand brushed against his pocket and the gem within. He reached into the pocket and rolled it between his fingers, too careful to bring it out in full view of the Sisters. He didn't know how numerous the gems were. The number of patrons within the sanctuary made him think the number was a lot larger than he would have guessed, but they couldn't be common. They had to be valuable. Daevor's followers would want this one back.

They could have it, for all he cared. Let Brennor and Daevor fight each other to the death. What difference did it make? So long as Cori lived, the rest of the world could burn.

The plan formed in his mind instantly, branching down different trails depending on how Daevor's followers responded. He sensed the influence of his remnant's comingled spirit, his thoughts racing faster and reaching farther. He pushed the gem deep into his pocket, grinned, and started the hunt for a piece of paper. The day was young yet, and if he hurried, he could have everything in place before the city woke.

He found a quiet roof with a vantage point that allowed him to look over the building where he'd killed the blonde-haired aeleth. From where he sat he could clearly see the note nailed to the door at eye level, where it would be sure to draw attention. All that remained was to wait.

Under clear skies and a calm breeze, the sun quickly warmed the air, as though fighting to prove winter was yet a ways away. Hiding behind the peak of the roof on its eastern side, the last of the chill that had settled in his bones overnight burned away. Warm and at rest, he felt the full weight of the exhaustion that had haunted him for the past day.

He couldn't remember when he'd last slept, or when he'd eaten a full meal. He rested his head against the roof and closed his eyes. It would be easy to rest, if just for a while, until someone discovered his note.

If you sleep, you'll never wake in time to see who arrives or where they go.

Right. He was tired enough that he might sleep through the day and the next night. Anything short of a bird landing on him would fail to stir him. Muscles ached as though he'd covered miles and miles of sharp terrain, and he supposed that in a way, he had. He suspected the gem's influence was all that kept him upright and reasonably alert, though even that edge was wearing off.

There are limits to my powers, and strengthening your mind is no different than strengthening your body. In time, the cost comes due.

Whenever his eyes started to close he'd either slap his cheeks or gently bang his head against the roof tiles. The streets filled as dockworkers rushed to their jobs and the docks filled with the hundreds of other workers who supported and managed them. The noise of the streets sounded as though it came from far away and grew more distant as the morning carried on.

With the end of the Harvest Festival tomorrow, the streets would be especially packed as workers rushed through the last full day of work. Tomorrow was a feast day, and every hand in the city would be helping with and partaking in the celebrations.

A man appeared at the front door in the late morning, and Veynar finally sat up. Dressed in dirty trousers and a tunic that looked older than some of the bones resting in the Hall of the Dead, the man stared at the note and scratched his head, as though it were written in a foreign language. Then he went in, leaving the note nailed to the door. He was inside for a bit, then came out, eyes wide. He ran off.

Veynar stayed where he was. Whoever it was, it wasn't someone he needed to worry about.

It didn't take long for the laborer to bring someone new to the house. This man wore finer clothes, though not as nice as the fabrics worn by the citizens who lived closer to the center of the city. He read the note, then tore it from the door. He looked up and down the street, then, seeing nothing suspicious, followed the laborer into the house. The new visitor reappeared only moments later, face red. He stormed down the street, and all who saw him coming possessed the wisdom to get out of the way.

Veynar shaped his remnant's power into a shroud of invisibility, then climbed down the roof and followed. He slid through the crowds, careful not to bump anyone. The man looked back once or twice, but never for long, and his eyes never so much as paused as they passed over Veynar.

They didn't travel far. The man reached another warehouse, smaller than the one Gavrin had destroyed yesterday. Two men lounged in front, apparently bored dockworkers, but the swords tucked in the shadows and their roving eyes gave their true purpose away.

"Is there any way of telling if they're aeleth or not?" he asked his remnant.

Not until they use whatever gifts they've been given, and even then, depending upon the nature of the gift, it can be difficult.

Windows ran along both sides of the warehouse, and so Veynar retreated a street and tried a different approach that brought him to the back. The warehouse had no rear entrances, and so there were no guards to observe his approach from the other side. He crept into the alley and took a look through the first window. He had to press his face close to peer into the darkness within.

The warehouse had been converted into some sort of small bunkhouse. Bunks were stacked high against the far wall, and a crowd had gathered around the messenger. Veynar could see almost all the interior, and there was no sign of Cori. After a brief but heated discussion, a group left the warehouse. They split up and walked in different directions, and Veynar didn't dare guess where they might lead. He couldn't follow them all.

That didn't matter, though. They'd come to him.

VEYNAR FOUND a vantage point on top of a roof that overlooked the Lover's Square. It was perhaps not a coincidence that he chose the very rooftop the statue had fallen from only a few days before, when the assassins had sought Avelin's life. He risked a precious moment examining the place where the statue had once stood, running his fingers along the stone too newly quarried to be so worn by weather it would collapse on its own.

There was little time to examine the area further, for already the hour of the designated meeting drew near. He'd intended to be in position earlier, but it was still almost an entire bell before the time he had scribbled on the note he'd affixed to the would-be assassin's door.

Some small part of him hoped that they would bring Cori to the meeting, and if they did, he would happily trade the gem in exchange for her life. More likely though, Daevor's followers would use the opportunity to eliminate him as a problem once and for all. They probably imagined him a fool for giving them a time and a place where they could easily find him.

At least, he hoped that was what they thought. So long as they underestimated him, he could hunt the hunters. He took up a position near the top of the roof, hiding behind the peak until he could just barely see into the square. The wind blew in cold from the sea, and despite the preparations for the conclusion of the Harvest Festival, there weren't many people out. Those who were hurried from place to place, and Veynar offered a small prayer to whatever god watched over him. Without people lingering in the square, it would be easier to spot anyone taking up position to wait for him.

It wasn't long before he regretted his premature thanks. He was used to the cold and the wind and all the various arrows of pain and misfortune that weather could throw at him, but he was also used to his clan robes. His cloak, his hood, and all the clothes and gear he had accumulated over the years had softened the blows of inclement weather. The tunic and pants he had stolen were woefully inadequate to the task. To keep himself warm, he practiced forming his swords. With each repetition, he improved, until it took little more than a thought to summon them.

"How does it work?" he asked.

That is a question that can only be answered after years of study. It is one better answered at another time, for I believe our first guests have arrived.

Veynar looked down and agreed. A short man with a beard shaped like a dagger sat on a bench, looking around and stretching his feet as though weary from a long day. Only he looked like the sort of man who could walk for a week with little rest, and the quality of his gaze was not that of a civilian looking for a friend or something interesting to observe. It was that of a hunter looking for his prey.

Veynar held tight to his sword and imagined dropping from the roof and killing him, the way the shadowy assassin had killed Avelin. He hadn't kept the closest track of time, but he was reasonably certain the noon bell was still a ways off. The only reason to be that early was to prepare an ambush.

"Can we cast one of those veils over ourselves while using a sword?"

It is only a matter of focus.

A matter of focus not so easily achieved, as Veynar soon discovered. Once the sword had been formed, it required far less of his will to keep in hand, but the amount wasn't zero, and so he had to hold one idea in his head even as he worked with another. His first two attempts failed, and it was only on his third that he sensed the veil surrounding him.

Impressive, but beware. The quality and strength of your veil is not what it would be otherwise. Your divided attention has a cost.

Veynar thanked the remnant for the advice and settled in to watch. The bearded man turned out to be the first of many. Two figures appeared on adjacent rooftops, and though Veynar had to squint to make them out, even in broad daylight, he could sense them.

The ability to see truly is also part of your abilities. You divide your attention into thirds, and so the veils they cast are more effective.

Veynar bit back a curse. It would be easier, perhaps, to let the sword drop, but he wasn't confident of his ability to return it to his hand if danger arose without warning. Thankfully, the assassins' full attention was fixed on the square below, and though the rooftop watchers did occasionally cast a quick glance across the adjoining roofs, it was clear from their bearing they expected him to walk willingly into a trap of his own making.

At noon, the bells began to ring, and as the ringing of the last bell echoed across the square, the younger of the two assassins from the warehouse—the one who had first attacked Malric and Veynar earlier that week—appeared. Ardyn, if he remembered the blonde man correctly.

There was no sign of Cori anywhere. Despite the time of the meeting passing, Veynar didn't move. He looked around the square, checked the rooftops, and even ran his eyes down nearby streets and alleys, searching for any sign of where she might be hidden. In retrospect, choosing the Lover's Square carried certain drawbacks. Although he could keep a pretty close eye on the streets and on the square itself, he couldn't see into the buildings, and it was altogether possible they had Cori in a room near the square. Though he wasn't sure he believed that likely. If they were here to trade in good faith, they would have brought her somewhere visible.

He gripped his sword tightly. The woman was close and had no idea that he was here.

It would be nothing at all to draw back a bow, take careful aim, and end her life. She would likely cross the veil never even knowing she had been in danger. He waited for his stomach to rebel, for his conscience to force his limbs to tremble. He imagined driving the arrow straight into her heart and basked in the pleasure he would feel at her death, but his body failed to react in any way. His heart beat as steady as it ever had, and his breath came slow and even. It wasn't the same icy cold that had gripped his spirit in the basement of that building, but a longer-lasting echo, an indifference to the idea of killing a fellow human.

Ardyn stood in the square and waited. She crossed her arms, tapped her feet, and Veynar thought she seemed awfully impatient for a hunter. She looked around at the half-dozen men and women who had filled the square, seeking any indication that he'd been spotted, but each answered with a subtle shake of their heads.

The assassin dug into one of her pockets and pulled out a crumpled piece of paper. He assumed it was the note he had gifted them earlier that day. She read it quickly, then crumpled it again and threw it to the ground. She made a sharp gesture with her hand, and everyone in the square began to leave. The assassin was the last, and she took one final look around the square before departing.

Veynar finally let his sword vanish. Many of the people in the square were traveling in different directions, but he had eyes only for Ardyn. If anyone was going to lead him to Cori, it would be her.

He shifted all of his focus into his veil and followed after. He ran across the rooftops for a bit, then had no choice but to descend and follow her through the streets. Though they weren't as crowded as they could have been given the festival's impending conclusion, there was enough traffic that he didn't worry overmuch about being seen. He kept several buildings of distance between them and was careful not to knock into any passersby, keeping close to the walls and alcoves in case he needed a place to hide.

She was more careful than anyone he'd followed so far. Twice she doubled back on herself, and once she walked all the way around a building only to continue going the same direction as she had been originally. At times, her shape grew fuzzy in his vision, which he took to mean that she had cast a veil over herself. During such times, she would always take one or two corners and then let the veil drop.

Veynar patiently proceeded, feeling for the first time like he was at home in the city. This was hunting, tracking prey—nothing more than what he'd been born and raised to do. The environment might have changed, but the principles remained the same.

Yet despite her precautions, she never seemed to cast her eyes in Veynar's direction, and she gave no sign that she noticed she was being followed.

All told, their journey covered more than a mile of distance, though Veynar figured that if they had taken the shortest possible route, the distance would have been less than half that. The assassin's journey ended at a house near the center of the city that could best be described as a mansion. Tall stone walls sealed it off from the noise and activity of the street, and four attentive guards stood at attention at the front gate. The assassin walked inside with barely a nod at the guards.

Veynar studied the mansion carefully. He didn't know what this place was, but it had to be where they were keeping Cori.

Some degree of that coldness from the basement returned to him as his swords formed in his hands. He could kill two before they knew what was happening, and with the use of his veil could likely kill the other two with little risk to himself. The only problem was that he wasn't so sure he could kill them all before one of them rang the bell beside the front gate.

He gripped his swords and prepared to sprint at the guards. There was only one way to find out.

Out of the corner of his eye, he saw light from above—a strike of lightning on a clear day that blinded his sight. Then it struck, and all went dark.

CHAPTER 22
A REMNANT REVEALED

The past is never what those who write the stories about it would have you believe.

— FROM *THE BOOK OF BRENNOR*

He awoke to a pounding headache and increasingly familiar surroundings. The polished wood of the walls reflected the bright light pouring in through the windows. Outside, he could see the tops of the trees that made up Brennor's garden. He grimaced and put his hand to the side of his head. It was tender, but considering how hard he must have been hit, there should have been a bruise the size of an eggplant. He sensed, more than saw, Gavrin off to his side.

"What did you hit me with?"

"Blunted arrow."

Veynar grunted and pushed himself up on one elbow. "Seems unnecessary."

"I got the sense you weren't thinking very clearly. Figured I'd give you a bit more time to think it over."

Veynar waited for his vision to stop swimming. "That's where Cori is."

Gavrin sighed. "Yeah, I was worried about that."

Veynar startled when another voice joined the conversation. He hadn't realized they weren't alone, the back of the couch he'd been placed on blocking the view behind him.

"Do you have any idea whose place that was?" the Head Sister asked, as though the answer should be obvious, as though anyone possessing even the rudimentary working parts of a mind should know, as if she didn't realize he was clan and didn't care one bit whose mansion it was.

She seized upon his silence as an opportunity to give him a lecture, as though he were a Sister-in-training. "That's the Elowen household, friends of the king and one of the longest-lasting families in Brenwick. They wield a power in this city at least equal to the House of Brennor."

Veynar was in no mood for a talk. "It doesn't matter who they are. If the assassins are lodging in the mansion, there's no doubt they've thrown in their fortune with that of Daevor."

"You're practically a child. What do you know about the intricacies of Brenwick's halls of power?"

Gavrin butted in. "He may not know much about Brenwick, but he is no fool, and he is one of Caelen's most skilled warriors. You would be wise not to be premature in your dismissal."

The Head Sister crossed her arms. Gavrin's word carried weight with her, and for the first time, she seemed to take Veynar's accusation seriously. "Even if I believed you, and I'm not sure that I do, one does not simply move openly against the Elowen household."

Veynar opened his mouth to argue, but the Head Sister held up a finger for silence, then began pacing the far side of the study. An unpleasant silence settled across the room while the Head Sister argued with herself.

Veynar turned to Gavrin. "How did you find me?"

Gavrin leaned forward in his chair. "The High Keeper asked me to find you. She wants me to bring you back to Caelen's Rest."

"But how did you *find* me?"

Gavrin shrugged. "Nothing so impressive as you might think. I had considerable help from the Sisters. They spread throughout the city to look for you, and once you were found, they reported directly to me. Even with their help, it took too much time."

It served as a good reminder to keep a better eye on his surroundings. He'd felt so superior on the rooftops over Lover's Square, confident he wasn't being seen. Now he'd made the same mistake, and if it had been an enemy instead of Gavrin, there was a very real chance he'd be dead in an alley. If he was going to survive, he needed to keep his awareness open at all times.

The Head Sister stopped her pacing and fixed Veynar with a stare. "Beyond the confession of this one man, which only you heard, what evidence do you have that these assassins are interested in us?"

"None. But he wasn't lying."

The Head Sister pursed her lips. "It's too little to bring to Orlan. We've had our differences with House Elowen over the years, but I never would have imagined it would come to this. There's nothing I can do with so little."

"What about me? I don't need to prove anything more."

Gavrin shifted in his seat as though sitting on something uncomfortable. "Caelen's bound by the same laws she is, Veynar. You've already stomped all over them, but no more."

Veynar swallowed hard and spoke softly. "But you know I'm no longer one of Caelen's."

Gavrin winced. Even after all this, the old man didn't want

to lose him. That subtle gesture warmed his spirit, reminded him that he wasn't alone, no matter how he felt. But he had to continue, because if he stopped even for a moment, he wasn't sure he'd ever move again. "So what's stopping me?"

Gavrin tapped his chest.

The Head Sister watched their exchange like a hawk, and when they reached their impasse, chewed on her lower lip. Veynar swore he could hear her mind racing. "Is there anything else? Anything you can tell me that would help me keep my House safe?"

Veynar searched his memory. He was about to say no when he stopped. "In the house where I heard the man's confession, there was a sheet of paper that had been well used. It listed the sites the House of Brennor publishes every year with the locations used for the blessings at the end of the festival. If they were going to strike, that would be the time. They'll know exactly where all of you are."

The Head Sister nodded. "That's not any evidence we can bring before Orlan, but it's something. If that's where they plan to strike, we can counter them. We step up protection at the sites and make it so that no matter what they try, they can't get to us. Sisters already perform the blessing in pairs, so we can have those who are adept with the remnants be ready to fight."

Veynar had reached the end of his patience. "Good. I'm glad that's settled." He pushed himself to his feet and grimaced as his head reminded him of the abuse it had so recently suffered. "Wish you wouldn't have hit me quite so hard," he told Gavrin.

The ghost of a smile played across Gavrin's face. "You've always had a hard head. I needed to be certain you'd cooperate."

The Head Sister's voice froze him in place. "I'm sorry, but I can't let you wander free, not knowing what you intend. Besides, now I know that you're an aeleth."

Veynar opened his mouth to object, but before the Head Sister could explain, Gavrin interjected. "When I came searching for you, the Head Sister and I compared notes. Thanks to the extra knowledge she had, we probably know what happened to you better than you do."

Veynar wanted to make an empty boast, to tell them that if they knew what had happened, they should know they couldn't stop him. But Gavrin was there, and though he looked relaxed, it was in the manner of a cat, ready to pounce at a moment's notice. Whatever skills Veynar had been blessed with thanks to his remnant, he suspected he'd have no more luck against Gavrin than he had before. He couldn't leave unless they let him.

He fixed the Keeper with his hardest stare. "Cori is in that home."

Gavrin nodded. "And we'll find a way to get her, but there's more at stake than just her life, and you know that."

"I know it, but I don't care."

Gavrin's eyes flashed. "Whether you're lying when you speak such words or not, you spit upon the sacrifice of all the brothers and sisters that have fought in the Broken Lands on your behalf."

The words stung, flushing Veynar's cheeks with shame, but he couldn't bring himself to bow an apology. What good were his skills if they weren't used to protect the people who needed them most?

"I have a compromise," the Head Sister said.

Both heads turned toward her.

"I'm performing a blessing tonight, too, and if what you say is true, there is no doubt Daevor will come for me. My Sisters and I are skilled and powerful, but if the Keeper vouches for you, then you have my trust as well. Protect me tonight until I return home safely from the blessing. If they attack, you can keep me alive. Then I'll grant you the full force of the city for your strike against House Elowen."

"And if there is no attack?"

"Then you've been in my sight the entire time, and we can see what the future holds. But you have my word I will do all I can to help you find your friend."

Veynar looked toward the door, imagining rushing for it and sprinting out into the cold night beyond. There was every chance that the delay might cost Cori her life. If Daevor's attack succeeded, what good was she to them?

It wasn't as though he had a choice. The Head Sister was kind enough to provide him an illusion of one, but he imagined that if he refused, he'd simply be imprisoned or restrained and sent back to the clan. They'd make sure he stayed out of trouble until the conclusion of the Harvest Festival.

He swore under his breath but couldn't quite bring himself to agree to her terms.

"Perhaps I can sweeten the deal some more," she said. "I could tell you the history of the remnant you carry. It was Atheron's, a scholar who reached a remarkable level of power. He's unique, even among the stories of the gods."

She settled back into her chair, knowing full well that she had baited a hook to perfection, and all she had to do was wait for him to bite.

The curiosity caught him, but it was the lack of choice that he surrendered to. He collapsed into the chair across from her. There were times when it was worth fighting against the tide and swimming as hard as one could, but there were other times where it was best to simply let the current take one wherever it would. He had little doubt he was trapped in one of the latter.

He gestured with a resigned wave. "Well, please go on."

"Atheron was among the later generation of beings that we now call gods, and he learned to separate his spirit just as the world was breaking. Because he was among the last, he never split into as many parts as some of his predecessors. In the chaos that surrounded the breaking, it was thought, for a time, his skills had been lost for good."

Veynar leaned forward, interested despite the circumstances. The remnant in his spirit kept quiet, neither supporting nor arguing with the Head Sister's tale. "Why?"

"The Breaking was a time of incredible violence, and though Atheron was more than capable of it, he wasn't proficient. Not in the way many of his contemporaries were. Most came from martial traditions, but Atheron was a scholar."

Veynar's hope in his newfound abilities plummeted faster than a loose boulder rolling downhill. He lived in a world filled with remnants, and somehow he'd found one of the few that was a scholar? What good did that do him?

The Head Sister saw his look. "It's not the trouble you might think. You've been raised as one of Caelen's, so you're more than capable of fighting already. Isn't it better to have a remnant that compliments your existing skills?"

Veynar didn't answer, and the Head Sister continued. "We don't know as much about Atheron's life as we do many of the others, but we know he was obsessed with the acquisition of knowledge, potentially to the exclusion of all else. We unearthed some documents that implied Atheron was—morally flexible—shall we say, when it came to the pursuit of learning."

"Is that true?" Veynar asked silently. Bad enough he'd accepted a scholar into his spirit, but that was perhaps no better than he deserved for his hasty choices. But if the remnant was dishonorable on top of that?

I've never cared for the laws of the Kings and Assemblies I've lived under, and my methods sometimes went against both tradition and convention. I'll not deny that. But my own morals have always been consistent, even if they haven't lined up with what was expected of me.

Not quite the reassuring answer Veynar craved, but good enough to prevent him from falling into the brink of despair.

The Head Sister, oblivious to the silent conversation, neared the end of her story. "Anyhow, it was said that Atheron could tell a person's life story at a glance, and knew as much about the world as any man living or dead. He could be a powerful ally if you learn to use him well."

Veynar cocked his head to one side, eyeing the Head Sister as though he were an owl. "How is it that you've come to know so much about Atheron, and that this is his remnant?"

The Head Sister shifted and rearranged her dress. "The House of Brennor has long kept track of as many remnants as we can."

The answer hid more than it revealed, but she pressed her lips tightly together, and Veynar knew there was nothing more he would get from her tonight. She'd bargained well, though. Knowing more about the remnant would help him use it better, and simply knowing more about it helped, too. He leaned back in his overstuffed chair, the events of the past few days and the exhaustion of so much effort finally catching up to him. He closed his eyes and told them to wake him up when it was time to leave.

CHAPTER 23
HARVEST'S FINAL BLESSING

Chase not the doe through the fields, but wait instead where you know she will soon be. Patience surpasses persistence, but the hunter who masters both qualities will never go hungry.

— FROM *THE SAYINGS OF CAELEN*

The Sisters had been kind enough to give him a coat, for which his thanks seemed meager recompense. Gavrin, after much debate, had helped Veynar acquire a bow and a quiver of arrows from the Sisters' armory. Depending upon the nature of the Daevori attack, the bow might be of considerably more use than the swords his remnant shaped. Suitably armed and clothed, he'd followed the Head Sister into the streets.

The sun had fallen below the sea and the stars were out, though clouds rushed inland, blown on a wind that wasn't interested in resting overnight. Veynar stood on the corner of a rooftop behind a statue which provided precious little shelter from the wind. He shivered despite the coat and wrapped his arms tighter around himself, holding on to every scrap of warmth.

No more than forty feet separated him from the streets below, but he might as well have been standing in a different world. Not a single eye would look up tonight, and he had no need of Atheron's veil to protect himself from discovery. The streets were bathed in the warm glow of the fires, and the smell of roasting meat tormented his long-empty stomach.

This was why the clan had come all the way from the edges of the Broken Lands, to celebrate the close of a year with the people their sacrifice protected. He saw them, in pairs and in small groups, intermingled among the citizens of Brenwick. Tonight, at least, the differences between clan and city were erased, due in part to the acceptance preached by the Sisters, but mostly to the copious amount of alcohol running through everyone below. Warriors stood side-by-side with carpenters, merchants, and chefs, singing songs, drinking, and feasting on the meat as it was pulled from the fire.

A few days ago, tonight had been all he'd been waiting for. One night of fire and feasting, a night where differences were put aside and friends were made, if only until the sun rose the next morning. Instead, he stood on this roof alone, cut out of the whole not only by his loss, but by what he had gained, the remnant in his spirit.

He should have been down there. He would have gone with Cori, their hands intertwined, smiles plastered permanently on their faces. Malric would have joined them, disappearing time and again, always returning with another tale, each growing more ridiculous as the night went on.

He allowed himself a few moments of grief, then sealed it away, for it helped nothing. A wooden stage had been built near the center of the square, tall enough that whoever climbed on top of it would have their feet slightly above the heads of the crowd. A small altar had been placed in the center of the stage, a brazier of wrought iron that would have risen to Veynar's chest if he'd been next to it. From his vantage point, he could see the wood within, ready for the fire the Head Sister would carry.

The Head Sister had increased the protection around the stage. Veynar's dim memories of earlier blessings included only one or two guards, but there were eight now, four near the steep stairs and one at each corner. All together they formed a ring around the stage that none of the celebrants were foolish enough to break.

Veynar let his eyes drift across the celebration, across the windows that looked upon the square, and over the surrounding rooftops. An archer seemed the most likely method of assassination. They could hide almost anywhere, and a single arrow dipped in poison would nearly guarantee success. Far better that than attempt to push through the guards and strike with a blade.

The Head Sister's guards clearly thought the same, for more of their attention was focused on the windows and rooftops than on the crowd. Veynar was glad he wasn't the only one looking out for the Head Sister's safety. She needed to survive to make Cori's rescue an easier matter.

Storm clouds built in the west, choking off the last of the light from the stars. The air felt heavy, wetter than normal, and Veynar figured there was snow on the way. A fitting conclusion to a Harvest Festival, even if a bit early. He pulled his coat closer and resumed his fruitless hunt for assassins.

The ringing of the bells heralded the arrival of the Head Sister, surrounded by six guards who joined the eight at the stage. Together, they formed a solid ring of muscle that would have even intimidated Gavrin had he attempted to approach with a knife. For the moment, the Head Sister was ignored by most as she lit the wood in the brazier with the torch she'd carried from the House of Brennor. The dry wood caught quickly, and soon the flames flickered before her face. She pressed her palms together and bowed her head, her mouth moving as she silently prayed.

Veynar watched for a bit, then returned to his hunt for the assassins. Now that the fire had been lit, it wouldn't be long before the final set of bells marking the end of the festivities, followed by a farewell blessing uttered by the Sisters. The assassin had to be close.

But if so, Veynar couldn't sense them. He was the only one foolish enough to be on the rooftops. No matter how hard he squinted, he couldn't make out any archers, even as he sought signs that one was using a veil. The windows around the square seemed the other likely place one could shoot from, but all were sealed tight against the cold of the night.

Had he been wrong? They'd never had much evidence of an attack.

The Head Sister continued the ceremony. She raised her hands and slowly, the crowd in the square quieted to receive her blessing.

A feeling of unease grew in the pit of Veynar's stomach. Not the twisting sensation he sometimes felt when other remnants were used close to him, but the kind of unease he'd felt when he was out on a hunt and something wasn't right. He was missing something, but he couldn't guess what.

He looked down, searching for any sign of trouble, but still there was nothing. He checked the rooftops again, but they were empty as far as his eye could see. The Head Sister had told him to stick to the rooftops, but he wanted to be closer, in the crowd, feeling whatever it was they were feeling. He took one last look around the rooftops, afraid the assassin would appear as soon as he abandoned his post, but he remained alone.

Veynar climbed down a ladder, then moved into the square. Among the crowd of bodies and close to the fire, he grew warm. Despite everything, some bit of the spirit of the festivities got into him, and he appreciated the revelers and the freedom of their celebration.

He searched the crowd for any eye not fixed upon the Head Sister, or any gaze filled with malice or hate, but all he found was the diffuse joy of the holiday and merrymaking. Fathers held children and wives close while young couples held each other even closer. Yet the feeling of something being wrong continued to grow. He made a wide circle around the stage, ending on the side with the stairs, and still there was nothing he could point to.

Disaster happened too quickly for him to understand at the time. Later on he'd remember that there was a deep *thump* that echoed deep in his bones, but it was followed less than a heartbeat later by the rapidly expanding storm of sharpened stone that mowed down the unfortunate third of the crowd that was closest in the square to the explosion. The blast ran through him like a punch he felt everywhere at once, then passed through him to the person behind.

The building on the north side of the square exploded outward, but only near the bottom. Stone cracked and glass shattered, and all the fragments were blasted into the crowd. Those unfortunate enough to be closest became something less than human in the blink of an eye, bone, muscle, and tendon an unrecognizable mixture as they were shredded by the forces arrayed against them. Those a bit farther away weren't much more fortunate. The sharpened debris was as deadly as any storm of arrows and fired indiscriminately. They fell by the dozen. Some were fortunate enough to die quickly, but the others, struck in the legs or torso, only fell where they stood, cursed to witness what came next.

The building, three stories tall, tilted like a tree cut more than halfway through by a woodsman's axe. Stone groaned, crumbled, and cracked. Dozens of windows shattered as the structure of the building gradually failed, showering the square with sharpened glass.

Most were still turning when Veynar realized what was about to happen. His mind, aided by the remnant, gifted him the time to act. He sprinted through the crowd, the power of the remnant filling his spirit and his legs. He pushed through the guards, all too human, turning toward the sight of their destruction. Three steps carried him up the steep stairs, and the Head Sister was in his arms as he leaped, the first screams from the crowd coming from below.

She was light in his arms, seemingly no heavier than an infant, and he landed, legs flexing with the impact. He threw her over a shoulder and ran as the weakened building finally fell toward the square.

There were a few who recovered from the shock of the blast quickly enough to react. Others that had turned toward safety and were starting to run.

Most haunting were the families, the mothers and fathers who realized their doom but couldn't scoop the children up fast enough to save them. Veynar watched one father abandon his family without a look back and another whose last act was to hold his children and wife closely. He ran between them all, their stories meaningless, because Cori's ended if he didn't save the Head Sister.

He made it to an alley as the edifice crashed behind them. The sound was deafening as people and buildings died together, the screams of women and stone blending together in a cacophony that threatened to drive any who heard it to madness.

He kept running, grateful not to be crushed but sensing the

danger behind. A wave of dust and pressure chased him down the alley and struck him as he reached the next intersection, blowing him off his feet. He landed hard, but cradled the Head Sister from the worst of the impact.

A deathly silence followed the madness and Veynar worked his jaw, wondering if he'd lost his hearing for good. He tried to speak but heard nothing. His world was as quiet as when he was on Watch in the Broken Lands, only he lay in an intersection in the middle of one of the busiest cities across the land.

There was more happening. He wasn't sure what, but beneath his palms, the ground was rumbling, as though the entire city was being invaded by stampeding giants.

He closed his eyes and swore. The other blessing sites. The attacks hadn't been just against the Head Sister, but against the entire House of Brennor.

Each surrounded by civilians.

His hearing slowly returned, and as it did, he began to wish that it wouldn't. Screams shattered the night. People called for friends and loved ones, dazed, as though they weren't quite sure where they were.

Nor should they. In the span of a few moments, they'd gone from one world to another, and Veynar didn't think the places they knew would ever be the same again. He lay where he fell, unwilling to move, hoping that if he just stayed where he was, someone else would come and take care of it all.

The Head Sister stirred at his side, sitting up as she came out of her daze. Flakes of snow fell from the sky, mingling with the dust in the air and melting as they landed on her ashy face. She looked back, face filled with grim determination as she pulled him into a sitting position. "Come on. We need to help however we can."

VEYNAR WALKED THROUGH A LIVING NIGHTMARE. The dust, darkness, and snow worked together to strip color from the world and forced him to walk through a broken field of gray. Others wandered among the rubble, either looking for loved ones or simply stunned. Nothing of the square remained.

He saved at least one life, a young man who'd almost made it to safety but had been trapped by the stone. Veynar's strength allowed him to lift the rubble that had trapped the man to free him. Other than that, there was little he could do. Little anyone could do. Death had been decisive in its choosing, and the wounded were already receiving all the care the survivors could muster. Healers and neighbors from unaffected parts of the city came, first one at a time, and then in droves as word of the attack spread.

The Head Sister directed the efforts at first, but it wasn't long before there was no need. There were more people who'd come to help than survivors who needed it. Veynar kept close to her, in case the assassins came around to check on their work. His eyes wandered the rooftops and the crowd, but he saw nothing that caught his attention.

Eventually he found himself standing beside the Head Sister, looking upon the destruction, and he was empty inside. There'd been friends of his in the square, too. Clan warriors who'd fought bravely out in the Broken Lands so places like this could exist. Only to be killed like this, crushed by stone, lives ripped away by the very people they were sworn to protect.

Thankfully, he was no longer Caelen's. His oath to protect, as far as he was concerned, was as dead as the corpses crushed beneath the stone.

The Head Sister turned to him. "Evidence will be too long in coming, if we ever get enough to make a case in front of the King. I imagine they'll have been careful, and I can't afford a hasty mistake. I can't move against them."

Veynar's heart hardened. It didn't matter anymore. He'd tried to play by the Head Sister's rules. No more.

But she wasn't done. "I can't move against them, but there have always been other means. If they turn to assassins, so will I."

She looked up at him, and there was a hint of a plea in her voice. "Veynar, will you kill them all? I'll offer you all the money you ask for. Just kill them, and make sure the action can't be traced back to me."

It wasn't even a question. He nodded once, bowed to her, and left, vanishing from her sight as he threw a veil up.

CHAPTER 24
A LONG COLD NIGHT

Building, I believe, is a rebellion. Perhaps the greatest rebellion of them all. A protest against the nature of the world. Look around. Decay is everywhere. It's the way of all things. There are those that demonstrate their strength through destruction, but they're fools. Leave almost anything alone for long enough and it will die and decay. Destruction is terrifyingly easy. It is those that build that show true strength.

— FROM *THE BOOK OF BRENNOR*

Veynar stood at an intersection as the wind whipped flakes of snow past his face. One street took him toward the small warehouse where he'd found the first collection of assassins, and the second took him straight to the Elowen household. His heart pulled him toward the mansion, but the remnant tugged him toward the warehouse. It was the first time he'd sensed its desires so clearly. "Why?" he asked.

You need to learn, and the warehouse is the easier target. Second, you don't know for sure she isn't there. Best to start small and work your way up.

"What do I need to learn?"

So much, but tonight, you need to learn how to hunt human. There's no more dangerous prey.

Veynar debated a moment longer, then turned down the street that would eventually bring him to the warehouse.

His route took him past other blessing sites, where more buildings had collapsed upon the Sisters. For all their guards and precautions, all Veynar's warning had done was give the falling buildings more bodies to crush. He'd been so close to unraveling it all but had still failed. He'd prepared for the attack and still couldn't stop it.

The blessing sites were buzzing with activity, though it was starting to fade as hope of finding more survivors ebbed. He skirted around the sites, not wanting to be reminded of his failure and unwilling to endure the temptation of wanting to help. Light snowflakes were being blown about by the wind, the first harbingers of the storm to come. If there were any people still alive under the rubble, and he hoped there weren't, it wouldn't be long before a blanket of freezing snow muffled their cries for help.

He pulled the veil closer around him as he neared the warehouse and was surprised to find it blazing with light and bustling with activity. Outside the sites of the blessing, Brenwick was quiet, its good citizens huddled in their homes against the storm and the dangers of the festival. The warehouse was anything but. He suspected there were nearly two dozen men and women around. A handful for standing guard, swords tied at their hips, but most were carrying heavy burlap sacks over their shoulders. Veynar's first guess was flour or grain, for the sacks molded themselves to shoulders as they were carried.

He slid into a shadow and observed the ordered commotion. The bags were being hauled out of the warehouse and placed into carts, and there seemed to be an awful lot of them. The wind picked up and blew the scents of the warehouse toward him. It had a metallic tang, familiar, though he needed a moment to remember where he'd smelled it before. It had been in the kitchen of the building where he'd killed that man.

The workers finished loading the first of the carts, and after a supervisor carefully counted the bags within, the cart was sent on its way, a driver and four guards walking alongside. Veynar bit his lower lip. The Head Sister had asked for him to kill them all, and a smaller group had conveniently separated from the rest. He followed after the cart, and once it turned the corner so it was out of sight of the warehouse he nocked an arrow in the bow he'd borrowed from the Sisters.

Veynar interrogated himself, expecting some sort of rejection or complaint from his spirit or body, but found nothing. He hadn't been this certain back on his first Watch. After seeing the room where Cori had been held and now living through the attack on the Sisters, what question was left? To kill the Sisters they had murdered hundreds, if not thousands, of innocent men and women, including celebrants from the clan.

He pulled the bowstring back, took aim, and released the arrow. Given the distance, he aimed a little higher than normal, but the arrow barely dropped. It struck the driver just below the neck with such force that he pitched forward, knocked clean out of his seat. Veynar nocked and loosed a second arrow before the body hit the ground, punching straight through a guard. He released a third as the guards realized they were under attack and started to twist. It caught a turning guard in the chest at an odd angle and spun him around.

Veynar dropped the bow and sprinted toward the cart, his veil still draped over him. The guards squinted, then went wide-eyed as he appeared beside them, short swords in hand.

He thrust one blade deep into the closest guard's chest and left it there, spinning around the falling body as he cut at the last guard, who fumbled to draw his sword. Veynar's spinning cut caught him in the neck, an ugly strike, but fatal, nevertheless. Both blades vanished, and when they reappeared in Veynar's hand, they looked as polished as the day he'd gotten them from his father. He hopped into the cart and sliced one of the heavy sacks open.

The bag held a dark mixture of powders. As he'd guessed, the metallic odor came from them, and now that he was close, he caught a whiff of brimstone. He reached down, grabbed some, and brought it closer to his face. It was some sort of black grit.

It's worse than that.

"You know it?"

I do, and it shouldn't exist in this world. It was the pursuit of materials like what you hold in your hand that eventually led to the Breaking. Those of us who survived agreed: Never again.

"What should we do with it?"

Atheron was slow to answer. *It needs to be destroyed.*

The remnant shared with Veynar a plan that brought a smile to his face. He climbed to the front of the cart, took the reins, and gently urged the horse forward. They drove forward until they were far enough away, then found a place to tie the horse. Veynar stopped the cart before it came in view and hopped off. He ran his hands along the horse's side. "I'll be back soon."

A short walk returned him to the warehouse. It still bustled and showed no sign of having noticed the tragedy that had befallen the first cart. He looked for any sign of Cori, but couldn't see any from across the street. Regardless, he needed to get closer. He circled around the buildings so he could approach from the back. The rear was quiet, and he held his veil close as he stepped into the alley running alongside the building. The first and second windows he tested were locked, but the third had been cracked open. Veynar slowly pushed it open further, then poked his head inside.

The window opened over an empty bunk, on the opposite side of the building from where he'd peered in before. No lamps had been lit near the bunks, and so the wall he looked in from was in shadow. No one paid the area any attention, their focus entirely on the opposing wall, where the sacks were stacked nearly as high as Veynar was tall.

His original plan had been to sneak into the warehouse, but there was no need. He could see everything, and it was clear Cori wasn't in the building. He pulled his head back and rubbed his chin. The remnant had given him the idea, but figuring out how to make that idea real was up to him.

A nearby streetlamp provided inspiration. He tore a few strips of cloth from his tunic, dipped them in oil from the lamp, and wrapped each around an arrow. He lit one and held the shaft of the arrow as a makeshift torch.

He hurried back around to the north side of the warehouse, where he could look through the massive open doors. Most of the sacks were still against the wall of the warehouse. He pulled out his bow, nocked the second arrow that had been dipped and coated in oil, then lit it from the first.

Veynar took a deep, steadying breath, then stepped into view and raised his bow. As he drew the string back to his cheek, the first of Daevor's adherents saw him, but it took her another precious moment to realize what was happening.

By then it was too late. Veynar released the string, and the arrow flew true, leaving a streak across his vision, much like Gavrin's arrows did. The arrow buried itself in one of the sacks, the point digging deep, carrying the fire within.

One of the workers shouted, and they scrambled, but the

fire reached the powder, and Veynar's vision went white. The force of the blast knocked him clean off his feet, more powerful by far than the explosion that had almost killed the Head Sister. He hit the ground and curled into a ball, protecting his head with his hands. After the dirt and dust stopped falling, he lifted his head. His ears still rang, but he could see well enough.

The place where the warehouse had stood was a smoking pile of rubble. All the windows in the surrounding buildings were shattered and chunks of debris had punched holes through any wall that sought to slow it.

Veynar stood and propped his bow against the wall of the alley. He drew his swords and stepped into the wasteland he'd created. Most of Daevor's servants were dead, but a few who'd been out in the street loading the cart survived, though few would thank him for what life remained. The force of the exploding powder did terrible, indiscriminate damage to the human body. Driving cold steel into their hearts was the greatest mercy he could offer.

At least, that was what he told himself.

He worked his way through the street quickly, for it wouldn't be long before he had visitors. His sword plunged into one body and then another, stilling their cries. The last of the survivors was a woman, gray haired and bitter, as tough as the stones she crawled across. Her left leg had been shattered, and from the trail of blood she left behind, there were other wounds as well.

Veynar stood in front of her, and she stopped. She looked up at him and it was as though she were a child, all the defenses of a lifetime of hard living stripped from her on this, her final night on this side of the veil. "Are there any more warehouses like this?"

She shook her head, unable to form a coherent reply. Her eyes begged for mercy, for succor, maybe for forgiveness.

Something stirred within Veynar, but Cori, Malric, and the bloody scene in the square silenced it before it troubled him. Whoever this woman was, she'd delivered the same and worse, putting her beyond human kindness.

And in following this path, you do the same.

He knew that well enough, and he accepted the cost.

He took the tip of his sword, placed it between her ribs, and plunged it into her heart. She struggled but only for a moment, then went still.

Veynar took one last look around. "Do you think my hunt was successful?"

More than I had ever imagined.

Help would soon be coming, and likely the wardens after. He hurried down the streets, taking one corner after another until he reached the post where he'd tied the horse. It was skittish from the distant explosion, but he soothed it the best he could. Once it had calmed down, he climbed back into the front of the cart and took the reins.

With so much of the powder at his disposal, it seemed a shame not to deliver some of it as a gift to the Elowens, who'd been so kind in sharing it with him.

CHAPTER 25
BLOODED

Upon the completion of a hunter's first successful Watch, when it is said by all who shared the Watch that their duty was performed admirably, a hunter shall earn the title Blooded, and it shall be theirs until the day they pass through the veils of death.

— FROM *THE SAYINGS OF CAELEN*

Cart and mind plodded through the streets of Brenwick. Veynar cast no veil over himself, but he was as good as invisible, regardless. Late night had become early morning, and the snow fell steadily. Some activity remained at the blessing sites, but it was mostly a handful of determined friends and family desperately searching for survivors that were certainly dead.

Veynar rolled through like a ghost, covered in gray dust and white snow. His bow was stowed safely in the cart, and his swords, they could be called at any moment. The city was as quiet as he'd ever seen it, and he wondered how long it would be before it had even a fraction of the vibrancy it had possessed earlier that night.

The strike at the warehouse had gone smoothly, but luck had played an outsized role. If they hadn't left the doors wide open and the powder ready to be ignited, the story might have been very different. He couldn't count on the same fortune at the mansion.

It wouldn't be long before his enemies knew they were being hunted, if they didn't already. Then he'd have to fight his way through more guards and deal with more precautions. He had surprise and a cartful of the powder, but he was still only one man.

You can strike as though you are many, though.

Atheron opened up locked memories, sharing battles and ambushes he'd been a part of. The memories faded, but the lessons learned seeped into Veynar's spirit, and he looked at the tools he'd been given in a new light. He considered the terrain around the mansion and the number of guards he might face. Some would be aeleth, a thought that sent a shiver down his spine.

He drove the cart in a circle as he shaped and reformed his plan, though ultimately, he had little choice. He lacked the time he would have liked to scout the area and learn the habits and routines of the guards. Daevor would be on the move soon, and who knew what that meant for Cori's future.

He pulled to a stop outside an apothecary's shop, in need of supplies. The door was bolted closed, but a window hadn't been firmly latched, and with a bit of jiggling, Veynar opened the window and crawled in. He took what he needed, prepared a few surprises for the Daevor, then returned to the cart carrying his new possessions. If he lived through the night, he promised himself that he would pay the apothecary for the stolen materials.

Then there was nothing left to do except straighten his spine and make his way toward the Elowen mansion. Several roads led to it, but only one served his purposes. He rolled the cart into position, then hopped out of the driver's seat and jammed a piece of split wood in front of the front wheel. He turned to the horse and ran his hand along the creature's side.

She was an old horse that had seen better days. If he could have, he would have escorted her back to the clans, where she would have been cared for until she died, but all he could do was set her free and hope she found a better home. He formed a short sword in his hand and cut through her harness, the remnant's blade slicing clean through the worn leather. A gentle pat on the rump got her moving. "Be well, friend. I hope you come to no harm."

Veynar waited until she was away, then grabbed bow and quiver from the cart. He nocked an arrow he'd prepared for the occasion, rested it on the very back of the cart, then took one last deep breath. He kicked the split wood from underneath the wheel and positioned himself behind the cart.

The snow fell heavily now, obscuring his sight of the mansion's front gate, but he assumed it would stand much the same as it had before, with four guards standing watch despite the weather. The cart didn't want to move now that it was at rest, but he called upon the strength of his remnant and leaned into the cart, grunting with the effort. It began to move, and though the angle of the street wasn't much, a slight decline kept the cart rolling forward. Once Veynar was sure it wouldn't come to a stop, he gave it one final shove, grabbing his bow from the back before it escaped his reach.

The guards noticed the cart a few moments later, their shouts echoing down the empty streets. Though the cart wasn't moving quickly, it weighed as much as a horse, and any man who stood in front of it was a fool. Veynar drew the bowstring to his cheek and waited. Where an arrowhead had once been, there was now a small vial, filled with two powders separated by a small wad of cotton. The knowledge of the making of it came from Atheron, for he'd never been taught such things. He wasn't sure if such knowledge even existed in this age.

He squinted and guessed at where the vague outline of the cart was. It crashed against the main gate as the guards scrambled out of the way. Veynar loosed his arrow. Even with the weight of the vial, his arrow barely dropped the width of a finger. The vial smashed against the spilled powder and shattered, the two powders within finally coming into contact.

Veynar took cover behind one of the adjoining buildings as the world erupted for the third time that night. The flash was brighter than any bolt of lightning, and the sound abused eardrums already aching from the torture they'd suffered throughout the day. He waited for the dust to settle, then poked his head out into the street to gaze upon the destruction he'd wrought.

His throat tightened at the sight. He'd been raised as a hunter, taught only to loose the arrow when he was as good as certain of his kill. He took only what was needed to feed his clan and no more. The same ethos applied to a Watch, who killed only that which threatened the clan, villages, and cities they protected. They destroyed no more than was necessary.

The same could not be said of his efforts tonight. The guards were dead, and the gate blown open, but who knew who else had been hurt? Every window in the area was shattered, and as his hearing returned, he heard the cries coming from behind the broken glass.

Veynar clenched his jaw and turned back into the alley and ran. He circled around the enormous estate, an eye on the wall. When he found a promising section he sprinted to it and began climbing. He expected every guard on duty would converge upon the main gate. He poked his head over the wall, made sure he wouldn't surprise anybody on the other side, then scrambled over and dropped silently.

Somehow, the Elowen's space seemed even larger once inside the walls. The estate was enormous by Brenwick's standards, but wasn't that large in absolute terms, perhaps about two hundred paces to a side. Only it had been designed to feel spacious. The stone wall ran along the entire perimeter, and the gardens ran just inside that, an inner ring about forty paces wide. A canal bordered the other side of the garden, narrow enough he could leap over it easily, though small wooden bridges between the inner yard and the outer garden were plentiful.

The gardens here were as meticulously kept as those in the House of Brennor, though they were more expansive. He slipped into the gardens, and it was as though he'd stepped into another world. The wall muffled almost all the sound from the city, and tall maples and pines blocked the view of any tall buildings. If not for the wall blocking his sight, he almost might have believed himself in a forest, back on Watch.

Almost. Beautiful as the gardens were, the influence of human hands was too clear. The trees ran on in straight lines. Each species of plant kept to itself, isolated from the rest and prevented from mingling. Not nature, but nature if it were ordered by someone like Brennor. Aesthetic, yes, but incomplete.

He darted along the garden paths until he reached the inner edge. He took cover behind a tall maple and studied the yard ahead.

The entire estate's attention was focused on the main gate. Men, women, and children ran down the wide path toward the scene of the destruction, most still dressed in their nightclothes. A cluster of small buildings sat just inside the main gate, though thankfully, it looked like damage to them had been minimal. Veynar recognized a small stable, but wasn't immediately sure what purpose the other two buildings served. As he watched, it became clearer. Most of the people running around were entering and leaving those buildings, and given their dress, it was probably where they lived. Servant's quarters of some kind. A lump formed in his throat. The blast had thrown the doors in a different direction, but he'd been saved by luck alone. If the roads had been angled differently, he would have angled the cart differently and risked the welfare of the servants living there.

He pushed the thought aside and continued his study. At the other end of the wide path was the main house, built in a style that would have fit better in the city a hundred years ago. The building was almost entirely wood; the beams shaped and joined by master carpenters. It stood only two stories tall, shorter than most of the trees that surrounded it. The effect was that it felt like a wealthy home in the middle of the forest, rather than one in the middle of the city.

Strange. He'd come here to kill those that lived inside, but much could be discerned about a person from the place that they called home, and he felt an affinity for the spirit that would design a home like this. He didn't know anyone in House Elowen, but if their personality matched this design he didn't think he would mind them.

He shook his head. Cori was in that house, and he stood here admiring its construction, like a prisoner complimenting the thickness of his manacles. He was getting too tired, his focus wavering.

His distraction had succeeded even better than he could have hoped. Not a single eye watched the main house, and every guard and servant was at the gate. He slipped from the shadows of the tree, hopped across the canal, and climbed onto the veranda that circled the house. The polished wood sang gently under his steps, but no one was around to be alarmed. He slid open the first door he came to, stepped inside, and closed the door behind him. His eyes needed only a moment to adjust to the lack of light within.

The same principles that had guided the builder of the house had guided the design of the interior as well. Unlike the House of Brennor, rich with carpeting and decoration, the walls here were nearly barren, the floors no more than plain polished wood. Three long calligraphic scrolls hung on one side, each a short poem. On the opposite wall hung a painting that drew Veynar's eye. It had been painted on a scroll nearly as tall as he was. A waterfall dominated the length of the scroll, the water captured in ink in such a way Veynar had no problem imagining himself there as it crashed into the pool below. A hunter stood on the rocks near the top of the waterfall, his bow aimed at a deer grazing in the meadow near the pool at the bottom.

He could have stared at it all day, if given the chance, but he didn't have that long. At some point, the people helping at the gate would return, and he'd lose the ability to move freely through the house. He formed his swords in his hands, padded down the halls, and cracked open doors as he passed, searching for Cori.

The rooms were all empty. Some might have served as bedrooms in times of need, but Veynar got the sense there weren't that many people living here. Some rooms had long tables and plentiful cushions. Others had small shrines. The house had the feel of a place that saw more guests than residents.

His breath caught when he opened one door that revealed a large training room. Various wooden weapons lined the walls, and the room held the lingering stink of sweat. Ardyn knelt in the center of the room, and her eyes were locked on him. The last time they'd met, she'd been fighting Cori in the warehouse, the apprentice of the two Daevor assassins.

The remnant in his spirit doused the fury that erupted in his chest. Alone, he would have charged into the room, swords drawn. Instead, he was gripped by that same icy cold, a detachment that tore mind and spirit apart. Ardyn spoke first, her voice deep and calm, reminding him of the powerful flow of a large river across the plains. "I wondered if you had found us."

She gestured for him to kneel across from her, and he noticed her sword was on her left, where she couldn't easily use it. It was a sign of peace, though he wouldn't trust her so easily. He gripped his blades tighter, but she made no reach for hers. He wavered, then let his swords drop to his side.

The training of his youth still held too much sway. He still preferred not to fight, if he could. He knelt across from her. "Where's Cori?"

She tilted her head. "We'll free her if you return the remnant you stole from us."

Veynar reached into his pocket and pulled out the gem. He held it between his fingers and lifted it high so she could see. "Here it is. Bring her out."

The assassin tilted her head further. "I don't think you understand. We want that one," she said as she pointed to his chest.

Veynar dropped his hand holding the gem. "You want the remnant inside me?"

"It belongs to us."

Veynar frowned, and the confusion was echoed by Atheron. *I don't belong to anyone, but certainly not them.*

Not that it mattered. The only way to separate a remnant from its host was to kill the host, and he was in no hurry to die. He stood and flourished his swords. "I'm afraid we won't come to an agreement."

The woman stared at him for a moment, then sighed with resignation. "You cannot win. I have a core remnant, and yours is but a sliver."

Veynar couldn't guess what that meant, but it sounded like an empty boast. "Come then."

The woman grabbed her sword, pulled the blade from its sheath, and cast a veil over herself, and a strong one at that. Veynar saw her, but her form was indistinct and fuzzy. Combined with the darkness of the room, she'd be difficult to track.

He held his swords ready and she came at him, sword nearly invisible in the dark, trying to take his head.

CHAPTER 26
LEARNING FROM DEATH

I've heard it said that mistakes are valuable, for we can learn from them and improve. The only problem is it's hard to learn when your mistake kills you.

— FROM *THE SAYINGS OF CAELEN*

She moved fast, faster than Veynar thought a human could, even with the gifts the remnants offered. In the dark, small space of the training room, her form fuzzy against his sight, there were times when it seemed like she was everywhere at once, her sword attacking from every direction. He met what attacks he could, thankful to have two blades to her one, but she slipped past his defenses time and again, never able to land a fatal blow, but never more than a heartbeat and a mistake away.

There was no sign of her injury, no weakness he could exploit. Beyond that, he was tired, exhausted from days of activity and too little rest. The remnant had kept the worst of the weariness at bay, but even Atheron had limits.

He parried one cut cleanly but was too slow to defend

himself against a spinning back kick that sent him flying into a wall. Panels cracked but held as the back of his head smashed against the wall. Blood trickled from the wound down the back of his neck, itching as it dripped its way down his spine.

She was on him before he could recover, her blade a force of nature, as inevitable as a summer storm looming on the western horizon. Veynar feinted with his left hand, but she wasn't fooled. He cut with his right, but his blade deflected off her sword. This close, his shorter swords should have had the advantage, but he was too slow. Her knee came up.

He twisted his hip slightly, and her knee struck his leg, numbing it instantly. She tapped her foot against the floor and thrust her knee again, and it was all he could do to lower himself and take the blow in the gut instead of lower. His stomach felt as though it had been churned like butter, and for the first time he was grateful he hadn't had anything to eat in ages. Her sword came down, and his blade was too slow. It cut through the bicep in his left arm and his hand opened, dropping the blade.

The control granted him by the remnant snapped and left him raving mad. He cut at her, then cut again and again, heedless of the wounds she opened on his chest. She had no choice but to retreat against the ferocity of his attack, but all his anger did nothing to threaten the assassin. Her sword was always where it needed to be, and though he struck at her with all his strength, he couldn't overpower her.

When his attacks slowed she responded, her sword cutting a gash across his chest that made it feel as though someone had opened him up and stuffed a fire inside his ribs. He stumbled back as the strength left to him fled his body.

It was just as well. Doors were opening near the front of the house, no doubt the guards returning to their positions. Even if he somehow left this room alive, the odds of him reaching Cori were plummeting faster than a corpse falling off a cliff.

Stop trying to fight better and start fighting smarter.

A wave of memory flooded through body and mind, experiences not his own that became his through Atheron's will. Of fights won and lost, of strategies and tactics.

The room gave him precious little to use. His fallen sword on the floor was of little use without his second hand, and she was too competent to trip over it for him.

She raised her sword to cut him down.

He summoned what little strength remained and created a veil as she began her cut. Her eyes narrowed, searching for him as he shifted away from her blade. The edge sliced through hair at the top of his head, the side of the sword sliding smoothly across his skull. He stabbed into the opening, plunging his short sword into her chest. Frantic, he pulled the blade out and stabbed again and again, even as she fell, her eyes blank. He fell on top of her, still stabbing. He didn't stop until his blade punched clean through her back and stuck in the floor.

Veynar gasped for air, sweat dripping down his brow and across Ardyn's face. Somehow, she looked even younger dead.

He wanted nothing more than to roll over and lay beside her, let their blood mix together on the otherwise spotless floor, but if he did, Cori's last slim hopes of survival would fade to nothing. She'd said they'd trade Cori. Possibly a lie, of course, but he chose to accept Cori was still alive. He knelt over the dead body as some small fraction of his strength returned. Atheron burned in his core and he stood.

The other guards were spreading throughout the house. They spoke in quiet whispers not even Veynar's remnant-assisted hearing could pick out. They shuffled quietly, having heard the fight but not knowing exactly where the noise had come from.

Veynar let his swords vanish, then made one reappear. Not that he could use two at the moment anyway. Even the tip of one wobbled, his arm too weak to hold it steady. He was about to stumble toward the door when movement out of the corner of his eye caused him to spin. For one terrible moment, he thought Ardyn had somehow lived through his assault.

But no, she was dead, well on her way to the other side of the veil. It was only the remnant, crawling out of her body to rest on her bloody and shredded chest. Atheron tugged him in that direction.

He needed to get to Cori before he lost the last of his strength. "What good does yet another gem do us?"

She was a powerful host. We can learn from her.

Their connection meant he didn't have to express his confusion out loud. They'd been carrying the blonde's remnant since the night before. Why hadn't they tried to learn from that?

He carried a remnant, but he was nothing. She was a true disciple, advanced. Hold the gem in your hands.

"I thought no human could handle the strength of two remnants."

I'm not seeking to absorb it. All I want is to learn from it.

"We don't have time."

It might very well be the only way we have a chance. If you haven't noticed, your body is close to failing.

Veynar cursed and shuffled back to the corpse. He picked up the gem. "Hurry."

Calm your mind.

Veynar grimaced but closed his eyes and returned his attention to his breath. The guards' footsteps grew closer, but he forced himself to breathe in slowly, filling his lungs as full as they would go. Then he exhaled completely, pushing out the last of his air, even as his chest burned under the agony of movement.

It served the remnant's purposes well enough. Atheron formed a connection with the gem, similar to the one Veynar had first formed with him. For a moment, nothing happened.

Then it felt as though someone had found the key to his mind and opened it wide, filling it with lifetimes' worth of knowledge. Unlike Atheron, who'd shown him the mercy of revealing his knowledge one piece at a time, often when he'd most needed it, this was a dump. His mind pounded against the confines of his skull, too full of knowledge to exist in such a small container.

Veynar's eyes twitched, an involuntary spasm that worked its way through his body until every limb was shaking. It was all he could do to keep his feet. The whole world trembled, rejecting him for what he'd done. With every breath he drew fire into his chest, and with every exhale ice emerged. He fell to his knees and shook, digging the sword into the floor for support.

Lifetimes of agony passed, though when sense returned to his body, it felt like only a moment or two. Guards whispered to one another down the hall. They'd heard him fall to his knees, knew someone was in the room ahead.

He ordered his body to move, but it wasn't yet under his command. The learning, if he could call it that, still coursed through his veins. As knowledge alone, it meant little, but in time he would integrate it with his body and make it meaningful.

Still, he had hallways filled with guards and didn't know where in the house Cori was. He needed to live to make any of it matter.

He would, though. He swore it.

Control slowly returned to his body, and he stood. His legs were shaky and tired, and who knew if he had the strength left to fight the battles ahead, but he'd rested a few moments, and

Atheron's endurance supported his. He cast a veil over himself as the door opened to reveal two guards, swords drawn.

He wondered what they saw. Was it like when the assassin had attacked him and his friends that night, a dark mist without definite shape? Or did they see him as something else entirely?

Either way, they stabbed out at places he was not, and he found it no difficulty at all to keep the veil raised as he cut them down. From their lack of reaction, they never even saw his blade as it took their lives. They fell loudly, though, alerting the rest of the building to his location.

These two wore different uniforms than the guards outside the warehouse he'd blown up. They were dark blue, which he took to mean they were from House Elowen instead of from Daevor. It mattered little. They stood between him and Cori.

The need to save her had become everything. He loved her, yes, but it had become something more in the past few days. A burning need, not just for her sake, but for his. A quest to prove he was strong enough to matter.

Another pair of guards came racing around the corner, also dressed in blue. Like the ones he'd just killed, their eyes revealed they could barely see him as he moved, and he cut them down faster than a farmer cutting hay. They were far from the last, though, and the hallway quickly filled with new arrivals. Veynar had no choice but to keep going until his sword dripped as much blood as his chest.

A FINAL PAIR of blue-robed guards waited for him on the stairs. They died as quickly as their compatriots, their deaths nothing more than a brief inconvenience.

Veynar let the veil drop and sagged against the stairway railing. Seven stairs led to the top, but from the bottom it looked like he was trying to climb an impossible summit. There was a thump from a room upstairs, as though a body had fallen. He summoned the last of his strength and trudged up the stairs. Two young men waited for him, their edges blurred in his vision. Veynar swore. They weren't wearing the blue uniforms he'd come to associate with House Elowen. They drew their swords in unison and attacked.

The fight was animalistic in its ferocity. Neither of the two had the training Ardyn had, but they were fast, strong, and eager to spill his blood. He knew they cut him deep, but he hardly noticed. He slashed and cut, spun and kicked. They slammed him into walls, nearly threw him down the stairs, and opened a gash on his leg that roared in agony every time he took a step. They took what little he had left and devoured it, beasts that leeched not just his blood, but his strength and spirit.

Yet when the battle was over, he stood on shaking legs, and they were dead, blood spattered across the walls like a painter throwing a tantrum. He swore he heard a muffled scream from a room ahead, and he shuffled forward, leg and chest burning with every step, his sword gripped tight in his hand.

Veynar slid open the door and blinked against the brightness of the light within. Before his eyes could clear something smashed into the side of his face. His jaw went suddenly loose as he spun to the floor, weightless and beyond the pull of the world. He barely felt it when he hit the ground.

Daevor's most powerful assassin kicked him in his stomach, and he went sliding backward, slamming into a far wall.

He tried to move but couldn't, his body beyond its endurance.

But he had to move.

Because Cori was here, and against all odds, she was still alive.

CHAPTER 27
A MEETING OF ASSASSINS

Many fear the stranger, and perhaps not without cause. But I say unto you, beware the person you have the most in common with, for that is where your true enemy lies.

— FROM *THE BOOK OF BRENNOR*

Cori was alive, but Veynar hadn't come in time to save her from suffering. Hundreds of fresh wounds had been carved into her flesh. The cuts ran up her arms, across her stomach and breasts, around her legs, and across her face. Most had begun to heal into scars, but a few were fresh, Cori's blood trickling across wounded skin. And that was only what he could see. Who knew what else she'd been forced to endure in her captivity?

Her wrists and ankles were tied tight with a long leather thong, and a gag had been stuffed and tied in her mouth, forcing her jaw open. A long stretch of rope tied her tightly to a heavy wooden chair. Her eyes were wide with fear.

All Veynar's exhaustion vanished at the sight of her. He

pushed himself to his feet, took a step toward her, then froze as a sword appeared at her throat.

Daevor's head assassin, Eryndel, stood beside the chair, at ease, as though the death of her apprentice and the slaughter of Elowen guards meant nothing at all. The tip of her blade was steady, no more than a finger's width from Cori's vulnerable neck. "Another step closer and she dies."

"What have you done?" Veynar growled.

"No more than your High Keeper would have done, were our roles reversed. I need information, and this is how I acquire it. She was initially resistant to telling us what we needed to know."

Veynar twitched, anger burning just barely within his control. The assassin's blade moved a hair closer to Cori's neck.

"Nothing justifies this," he said.

"Don't be a fool, boy. It makes me think less of you. Anything can be justified if the circumstances are dire enough, as they are these days. You've accepted Daevor into your spirit. Can't you feel it? The world thinks that the gods are dead, that they've faded into the past. There are even aeleth who believe as much, that they're among the last of a dying breed. But you know different, don't you? You can feel it in your spirit."

"The gods are moving," Veynar said. He didn't have a clue what the assassin referred to, but he suspected the statement pointed in the general direction of the assassin's thoughts and would be vague enough to keep her talking. The longer she talked, the less she was killing Cori.

"They're sharpening their knives. Preparing for the war to come. Jostling for position, so when the war starts, they're on the winning side."

Veynar had heard enough. "You tortured my friend."

"Only because she wouldn't share what she knew. Caelen needs to die. He's too stuck in the ways of the past, too resistant to the change the world needs to see. It took some convincing, but your friend finally told us everything I needed to know. Once I'm done in Brenwick, I'll visit Caelen's Rest. It'll be easy compared to this."

Veynar settled into a fighting stance, careful not to approach any closer and give the woman the justification to kill Cori. His vision wavered, not from illusion or a veil, but from the sheer exhaustion that had settled upon his bones and into his spirit. One question tickled the back of his mind. He'd barely survived the fight with Ardyn, and the older woman was very clearly the more dangerous of the two. She could kill him in the blink of an eye. So why hadn't she?

"What do you want?"

"The knowledge she doesn't have. I need to know how many remnants Caelen has separated himself into and who has them."

"Why would I help you destroy my clan?"

A ghost of a smile crossed Eryndel's face. "Do you think by now that we don't know you, Veynar? You care more for Cori than for Caelen or your clan, and there's no use pretending otherwise."

He wanted to deny her, to throw her words back in her face, but he wouldn't lie. "Her life for the knowledge?"

What other choice did he have? He couldn't defeat the assassin, and if he could save Cori's life, that was a price he'd willingly pay. As Eryndel said, they knew him well.

The assassin nodded. Cori shook her head, trying to argue through the gag, but his spirit was at peace. So long as she lived.

"Then let her go. I'll tell you everything you want to know."

Cori screamed, the sound coming out as nothing more than a muffled, high-pitched whine. The assassin grinned. "Though you may be one of Caelen's, my trust in you is low. Give me the names, and I'll let her go."

Veynar held up four fingers. "I'll tell you two of the names. Then you let her go, and I'll give you the last two."

The sword drew a thin line of blood across Cori's neck. "Give me all four."

"Maeryn and Gavrin!"

The assassin snarled. "That's not four, and those two were obvious. Who are the others?"

Veynar gave two more names. Hunters with long histories and many successes.

The assassin removed the blade from Cori's neck. "Good boy."

Tired as he was, Veynar saw every moment of the betrayal, saw the shifting of weight that revealed the assassin's intent. Atheron's awareness ensured he missed nothing. His eyes went wide and he reached forward, but he was too far away. The assassin's threats had made sure of that. She reversed the grip on her sword and stabbed behind her.

Cori, warned by Veynar's expression, flung her body away. All she accomplished, though, was to shift the heavy chair the width of a finger. The assassin's blade stabbed into her chest, and she screamed once more into the gag, a muffled cry of agony that broke Veynar's heart even as the sword pierced hers.

A rage unlike anything Veynar had ever known took hold of him, hotter than any fire, burning thought and pain away.

Eryndel was already turning toward him, bringing her sword up, tip bloody.

His stomach twisted hard enough he sensed it through his anger. He knew now what it meant.

Knew how he was going to be killed.

He stopped, reversed his blade, ducked low, and thrust it back and up.

Eryndel vanished from his sight. His thrust struck flesh and buried itself deep even as the assassin's longer blade cut over his head. He twisted his blade as he pulled it out, and there was a grunt behind him. He spun low and cut, his sword slicing through the meat of the assassin's thigh.

Eryndel dropped her sword as she clutched at the gaping wound in her stomach. A faltering step away from him put more weight on her injured leg than it could handle, and she collapsed, confusion written on every line in her face. He stood and towered over her, though he didn't trust himself to stand for much longer.

She looked up at him, raging against her fate. "How?"

He leaned over and stabbed at her heart. Bloody hands caught at his sword, but he just put more of his weight behind the weapon, and it slid between her hands, cutting skin from the palms as it did. The tip reached her chest and with a final thrust, he ended her life. He waited for a moment to ensure she was dead, eyes cold, then pulled the sword out.

Cori's cough behind him reminded him of why he'd come. He swore and turned around. His legs barely carried his weight, but he stumbled over to her and cut her bonds with his sword. She removed her gag, and though she seemed to be in tremendous pain, she wasn't bleeding to a quick death.

"How?" he asked, shivering as he heard the echo of the assassin's unanswered question in his own.

Cori's hand went to her chest. She pulled aside the cut fabric, revealing the wound. It wasn't that deep. Cori tried to speak, failed, then tried again, her voice coming out like a croak. "Moved. Hit a rib."

Veynar wrapped her in his arms and squeezed her tight. Her body stiffened, and he feared that he'd hurt her. "Come on. Let's get you out of here."

She moved hesitantly as feeling gradually returned to her limbs. Veynar supported her to the hallway, then leaned her against a wall. "One moment."

He returned to the room, where a small gem had appeared beside the assassin. He picked it up, pocketed it next to the others, then returned to Cori. She stood still, eyes fixed on the corpses in the hallway. "Did you do all of this?" she whispered.

"I did," he answered, and he couldn't help but feel a note of pride. Now, finally, he was strong enough to be helpful. Strong enough to keep his friends safe.

If only he'd found the strength in time to save Malric.

They made their way down the stairs and into the bloody hallway that came after. He guided her over the bodies he'd left behind. Her steps were slow and cautious, but he got her to the front door. She saw the damaged gate. "That was you, too?"

He nodded. "A long story. I promise I'll tell you someday."

They didn't make it to the gate before a commotion rose on the other side. Veynar braced himself for another fight, then sagged in relief when he saw that it was Gavrin, accompanied by nearly a dozen of Caelen's best warriors. They came through the gate and spread out along the path, surrounding the two younger hunters.

Gavrin took in their state with a glance. "The Head Sister found us. We heard the buildings falling from the Rest, but it was a long time before we got organized. We're missing a lot of warriors."

Veynar didn't have to imagine. He'd seen too many of them crushed with his own eyes.

Gavrin glanced at the mansion behind Veynar. "What happened?"

"I found her."

Gavrin's gaze traveled again to Cori and nodded. "Survivors?"

"None."

Gavrin crossed his arms, impressed. "Well done."

The Keeper ordered half the warriors to take control of the

house. He ordered another pair to escort Cori back to Caelen's Rest.

"I'm not leaving her behind," Veynar said.

Cori saved Gavrin from the argument. "I'm in good hands. You don't need to worry."

Without further word, she pulled away from Veynar and limped toward the others. They offered their support, which she gratefully accepted.

Once she was beyond hearing, Veynar asked, "What about me?"

"The Head Sister wanted to see you."

Veynar gestured for Gavrin to lead the way, but now that Cori was out of sight, his body lost the last of its motivation for staying upright. The darkness he'd held so long at bay rushed in and swallowed him whole, and he finally fell into the rest he so desperately desired.

CHAPTER 28
BETWEEN FRIENDS AND FAMILY

No weapon cuts deeper than the truth.

— FROM *THE SAYINGS OF CAELEN*

When Veynar awoke, it was with the feeling that a tremendous amount of time had passed. He was on perhaps the longest couch he'd ever laid on, its velvet cushioning more comfortable than any bed in Caelen's Rest. He slept without covers but wasn't cold thanks to the fires roaring in the hearth. Diffuse light streamed in through the windows, and when his focus returned he saw that the snow was falling harder now, thick heavy flakes that would swallow sound and silence the city.

He was once again in the Head Sister's study, and his first thought was if it wouldn't be better if he simply asked for a key. Then the events of the past few days broke into his thoughts, and the beginnings of a smile were wiped from his face.

"How long was I out?" he asked.

Gavrin stirred. He'd taken up position in the same chair he'd used on his last visit, and Veynar wondered what purpose he served there. Was he to protect Veynar from unwanted visitors, or was he the guard keeping the prisoner locked up? The Keeper's stony expression gave nothing away.

"A full day and night. It's morning now."

Longer than he'd expected, then, but not so long as it could have been. If Eryndel had her way, he'd have never seen another sunrise. "What have I missed?"

Gavrin tilted his head toward the window. "The storm's kept everything quieter than it would have been otherwise, but a lot has happened. The Head Sister organized rescue crews to comb through the fallen buildings, and I've heard tell of a few lucky souls that survived, but it's been below freezing since the festival, so anyone who's still missing is more than likely dead."

The Keeper scratched at the stubble growing on his chin. "According to the Head Sister, you're a hero. You saved her life, for one, but you've single-handedly changed the course of Brenwick's future. If any of Daevor's clan remain, they've buried themselves in a hole so deep we'll never find them. The Head Sister has also been crushing House Elowen before the King. They tried to claim they didn't know what was happening, but there was too much evidence. Both the warehouse where Malric was killed and the one you destroyed the final night of the Harvest Festival were owned by Elowen. And of course, it's hard to prove innocence when you're harboring assassins and allowing your house to be used to torture a member of one of Brenwick's closest allies."

Gavrin sighed, as though even talking about the events made him sick. "When they couldn't claim innocence, they tried to claim it was for Brenwick's good. That Brennor would drain the city coffers dry in the never-ending pursuit of expansion. Alas, the plea fell on deaf ears. Turns out, killing hundreds of the people you're claiming to protect doesn't win you many friends."

"What did they think was going to happen?"

Gavrin grunted. "You'd have to ask them. The Head Sister suspects they were simply opportunistic. They helped Daevor with the expectation that once the House of Brennor was weakened, they'd be able to step in and take a firmer hand in the guidance of the city. They provided the powder to Daevor, some new invention they created in the mountains to help them mine, but it's possible they never knew the full extent of what Daevor planned. If not for you, it might have worked."

The Keeper stretched. "I think that's all that matters in terms of the city. The Head Sister runs in and out of this room a hundred times a day, busier than a squirrel preparing for winter, but truthfully, I think she likes it. The House of Brennor is hurting after the assassinations, but their position in the city has never been stronger. I think she's optimistic. They have a lot of promising Sisters-in-training. Thanks to your efforts, and with a few years of hard labor, I think they'll be a powerful force for good. She has a vision, and she's determined to see it through."

Veynar noticed the subject Gavrin so carefully avoided, and his heart beat faster, fearing the worst. "What about Cori?"

The Keeper grimaced, the first real expression to cross his face since Veynar had woken up. "We think she'll recover, but it's difficult to know. Like you, she passed out not long after we showed up, and she hasn't yet woken."

The news cut deep, though after what she'd been through, it was unfair to expect anything else. She'd suffered the most.

He should have been overjoyed, but he wasn't. He had freed Cori and stopped the assassins, and those were good deeds, but there was still a hole in his chest, an emptiness his success didn't fill. Veynar put his hand over his heart. He was proud enough of what he'd done. The emptiness had a different feel, more of a question left unanswered. One about Lirael.

He frowned.

Before he could interrogate it further, the door to the hallway opened next to Gavrin and the Head Sister entered. The strain of the long days was evident on her face, but her eyes shone with purpose. Gavrin claimed that years of hard labor awaited the House of Brennor, but as Veynar looked into those eyes, he knew Brennor would emerge stronger than before. She'd settle for nothing less.

The Head Sister stopped when she saw that he was awake, and a smile spread across her face. "Our young hero! How are you feeling today?"

Veynar sat up and stretched. Considering how hurt and exhausted he'd been after assaulting the Elowen mansion, he was remarkably well. The worst of his wounds had been healed, and the minor ones cleaned and wrapped. "Very well, thank you."

Gavrin nodded. "We owe a great debt of thanks to the Head Sister. She personally supervised a great deal of your healing, oftentimes directing the healers while fielding questions from across the city."

Veynar bowed deeply. "I hardly deserve such honor, ma'am, but I thank you for it."

The Head Sister waved his thanks away. "There's no need for such formality here. We're all friends, and we've all been through a lot. Please relax."

She went to her desk and opened one of the drawers. Inside were notes, which she counted carefully. Once done, she turned to Veynar and handed the notes to him. "As promised."

Gavrin's eyes went wide. "Veynar?"

He glanced over at Gavrin, then took the notes, folded them, and put them in his pocket. As he did, he noticed that the gems were still there. He bowed to the Head Sister in thanks.

The Keeper wouldn't be ignored. "You did this for *money*?"

The Head Sister frowned. "What does it matter? After the explosions, I told him that if he killed off the Daevor clan, I would pay him. One should be rewarded for their efforts, and as we've seen with the evidence that's come to light, it ensured that justice was served."

Gavrin stood, nearly shaking. "Caelen's warriors do not kill for money!" He nearly spat the last word. "Have you learned nothing?"

Veynar cast his eyes to the floor. The money felt dirty in his pocket, but Gavrin kept forgetting he wasn't Caelen's anymore. He was going to need to find his own way in the world, and hopefully Cori would be by his side. To start fresh with the two of them would require what the Head Sister offered. And besides, he'd saved the city from further harm, hadn't he? Why shouldn't they offer recompense?

He risked a glance at Gavrin and wished he hadn't. The Keeper's face was red, and he had a look on his face like Veynar had somehow betrayed him.

The Head Sister shook her head. "Don't be so hard on him. He deserves our respect, not our condemnation. Considering all he's been through, it's the least I can offer."

Veynar frowned, something tickling the back of his mind. There was something in her voice, as though she believed the money was for more than just the death of Daevor's followers. He had that same feeling he'd had just before the explosions in the squares, that he was missing something important.

He blinked, and his whole world tilted.

"What's wrong?" The Head Sister asked.

"I'm sorry, Head Sister. I'm just trying to make it all make sense. Why did Daevor come after Lirael?"

"You know why. They believed Lirael had a remnant of Daevor. They'd asked Avelin to steal it for them."

"But how did they know that? You said earlier that you'd intercepted Avelin's letter."

The sudden silence in the room was deafening. He heard only the wood crackling in the fire. The Head Sister's breathing was uneven, and that was all he needed to know what was true. The last pieces fell into place. He was thinking faster now, Atheron's remnant better integrated with his mind than before. He spoke, voice barely above a whisper, but filled with confidence. "You're the one who had my sister killed."

Gavrin's hand went to his sword, but his hurried glances told Veynar he didn't know who he was supposed to protect and who he was supposed to attack.

The Head Sister stood taller. "I'm sorry, Veynar, but I did. She took part in the theft of one of this House's most treasured possessions. She broke her oath, and as her master, she left me no choice."

Veynar supposed that was true enough. "You lied to me."

The Head Sister crossed her arms. "Grow up. People lie all the time, and it's hardly the evil you think it is. For what it's worth, I told you enough of the truth about why. My Sister was searching for the remnant when you appeared. She would have killed you too except Gavrin appeared. In the moment, she decided the illusion was the best way forward, and I agreed. Given the tension in the city, I couldn't afford to deal with problems from Caelen's Rest. It was also necessary to squash the rumors that would have grown here."

"And it turned out to be convenient when I started hunting the Daevor for you."

The Head Sister shrugged. "I won't deny it, but I did nothing wrong. I admired Lirael, Veynar, and ordering her death was the hardest order I've had to give in years. But look what has come from it. The House of Brennor will build something wonderful here." Her excitement waned. "I'm only sorry the cost in lives was so high."

He didn't sense a lie from her. She spoke true and acted as she'd believed necessary.

And she'd ordered Lirael's death.

Gavrin tensed. "Veynar, she was within her rights."

Veynar's rage was gelid, freezing ice that pumped through his veins, the full integration of Atheron with his spirit and emotions.

Gavrin slowly positioned himself so he was between the Head Sister and Veynar. "I can only guess how you must feel, but this isn't the way. Brenwick needs her now, and if she dies, this city might very well fall into chaos. I know you don't want that. I know you still want to protect this city, the same as you always have."

The Daevor called the technique "stepping" for it allowed a trained assassin to step from one place to another, without the bother of all the travel in-between. Those just learning the technique were limited to a handful of paces and required a clear view of their destination. More advanced aeleth could step without sight, often hundreds of paces away. If he gave Atheron enough time with the gems, and he had space and time to practice, it was possible he'd reach such a level. It was a powerful technique. But for now, he knew enough.

Veynar stepped and appeared behind the Head Sister. There was nothing Gavrin could do. A short sword appeared in his hand, and he thrust it into her back, between the ribs, and slid it straight into her heart. As she fell, he took a normal step backwards and raised his hands and allowed the blade to vanish, praying to Caelen that Gavrin didn't cut him down where he stood.

"What have you done?" Gavrin shouted.

Veynar left his hands raised. "I avenged Lirael's death."

"You're a cursed fool! Do you have any idea what will happen?"

"No, and I don't care. She ordered Lirael's death and lied and manipulated us. Perhaps her intent was noble. It's not for me to say. I only act as my conscious demands."

Gavrin raised his sword. "Yours or Atheron's? Who are you now?"

He'd never considered the possibility, but he didn't have to. The decision had been his own.

And a good one at that. Never trust a leader who cloaks herself in lies.

Gavrin took a step forward, but Veynar didn't move. "I'll never fight you, Keeper." He glanced back at the windows. "Besides, there's another task that's more important. You have to call for aid. You have to let the Sisters know I killed her. Otherwise, more trouble will fall upon the clan, and they need none."

"But..." His face twisted in horror. "You can't. They'll sentence you to death."

Veynar offered a bitter smile, because Gavrin had already forgotten the sword pointed at his heart. He was too good a man, and Veynar loved him for it. "It's the only way. I'm not one of Caelen's, and you can tell them whatever version of the truth you wish. It matters not to me."

Still, Gavrin hesitated, and Veynar took pity on him.

"Help!" Veynar shouted. "The Head Sister's been attacked!"

He walked over to the window, and the Keeper did nothing to stop him. He bowed deeply, pouring all the respect he could muster into the gesture. "Gavrin, be well."

Footsteps pounded down the hallway. Veynar held his bow as long as he dared, then rose. The garden outside was below, covered in snow. He closed his eyes, stepped, and shivered as the cold washed over him. He waved to the window that Gavrin looked down from, then walked away.

CHAPTER 29
FIRST STEPS

May the journey ahead be long and filled with friends and feasting.

— CAELEN'S (REPORTED) LAST WORDS TO HIS CLAN BEFORE TRANSFORMING INTO REMNANTS.

Veynar quickly learned that money solved problems he never would have known how to solve on his own. The hunt for him began the moment he walked away from the House of Brennor. The temptation to return to the sanctuary was strong, but he feared that if he did, the Sisters would find a way to keep an eye on him. Better to assume the risk of hiding elsewhere.

He made his way to the poorer parts of the city and offered a fair portion of his money in exchange for shelter and secrecy. It was an older couple that lived more off the generosity of the Sisters than any money they had saved, and so Veynar's notes were more than welcome. They provided him ample food and a room in the attic long abandoned. It suited him well. He regained his strength, practiced the techniques picked up from Daevor's remnants, and read all the papers the old man could find.

Speculation ran rampant, and Veynar learned things about himself that he never knew, from his hatred of the Sisters to his longstanding feud with House Elowen. The hunt for him was ongoing, but they suspected he had fled toward the Broken Lands, a guess put forward by the High Keeper. She speculated that he would run to one of the mercenary groups that helped patrol the border, where a checkered past would matter little.

Another chunk of Veynar's money was given to the old couple to purchase him new clothes, and they came back with everything he'd need to survive a winter in the wild.

He didn't care much about his future. All he knew was that he didn't want to stay here.

As soon as it felt safe to wander the streets again, Veynar left the house, parting with even more of the money than he'd intended. He was equipped with food and sturdy boots. The only thing he needed yet was a bow, as it was the one piece of equipment he hadn't trusted the couple to find for him.

He drifted through the streets of Brenwick like a ghost. His senses had sharpened even further as he'd healed and his body had fully incorporated the knowledge Atheron shared. Between the cold and the dark, the streets were already quiet, and he found it a simple matter to avoid the wandering patrols.

Veynar considered stopping by the park and the climbing tree, but judged it too risky. The surviving Sisters probably didn't know about it, but his clan did, and if he'd been in their position, he'd have people watching it. Besides, his last memory of it crowded out those he'd rather hold on to. He continued on.

The clan had moved their Watch in, which meant Maeryn was still expecting him to visit. She was right to expect it. He couldn't leave without knowing. Even with the closer watch, he found it to be little trouble to sneak past the men and women he'd once served with. He cast a veil that allowed him to slip past the Watch on one of the main trails, his footsteps blending in with all the others that had traveled to and from Brenwick since the snow had fallen. One guard looked in his direction from a distance and scratched her head, as though sure she'd seen something, but the moment passed and she and her partner continued on. Veynar kept the veil up and close as he made his way deeper into Caelen's Rest.

Barrels were already loaded onto the carts as the clan prepared to make its way back toward the Broken Lands. They returned greatly reduced, a loss they could scarcely afford. The Harvest Festival should have been a time of renewal, but instead they'd walked into a devastation that would echo for generations. They deserved better, but there was nothing he could do to help them, except leave them behind.

He slipped between the houses until he reached his destination. Like most of the younger warriors upon returning to Caelen's Rest, Cori had to move back in with the rest of her family. Not next year, he thought darkly. Everyone would have a home of their own next year.

Though who knew if they would even return?

Better the relentless assault of the Graevath than the betrayal of the very people they were supposed to protect.

Two guards stood outside the door of Cori's family's house, but Veynar made his way to the back and peered through Cori's window. She was sitting in the dark, staring at the ceiling, eyes wide open. Veynar tapped the glass gently with one finger, and Cori's head snapped toward the window. He revealed himself, then held his finger to his lips. She nodded, and he stepped into her room.

She sat up in her bed, surprised at his sudden appearance, but she didn't rush to him like he had hoped she would. She looked as though she were balanced on the edge of a precipice, still deciding which way to fall.

Her eyes lacked the fire they'd once had; her spirit dimmed. The cuts across her body had faded to angry scars, but he again reflected that he had no idea what wounds lurked beneath the surface. All he knew was that if she gave him the chance, he'd spend the rest of his life trying to help heal them.

He'd thought long and hard about what he wanted to say to her, but now that he was before her, the words wouldn't come.

"You learned some new tricks," she said.

He scratched the back of his neck. "I have. It's been quite a journey."

She didn't seem interested in hearing about it.

He swallowed the lump in his throat. "I—I think I'm going to leave. I'm not sure what I'm going to do, but I was hoping maybe that you would come with me. I have enough money to help us start a new life wherever you would want. You could apprentice to an artisan, and I'm sure I'd find something to do."

She fixed him with a stare, and it sent a shiver down his spine. It wasn't lifeless, exactly, but it lacked the spark he'd come to treasure from her. Her gaze shifted, so that she was looking out the window. "You know, I never thought about what happened to you in the Broken Lands the way the others did."

Veynar frowned.

"Malric was always ready to fight for you, I think mostly because he didn't like what your actions said about him. He always said it was just a case of nerves, but I think he knew the truth. We all did. Some people just aren't meant for the Watch.

They thought you a coward, but I saw someone who didn't value life so cheaply as the rest. I loved that about you."

Her words cut like a dagger, carving the heart from his chest.

She stood and took a tentative step toward him. "I don't know the man who is capable of doing what happened in that house. And I certainly don't know the man who could claim the act with pride."

Veynar staggered.

He'd suspected. Had sensed the wall she'd thrown up as he'd escorted her out of the mansion. Had hoped it had only been the circumstances, not something more permanent. But to hear it from her lips threatened to break him.

She reached out and took his hand. Her fingers were cold, but he knew she'd pull away if he tried to wrap her hand in his own. She squeezed. "I'm leaving the clan, too. Some of us aren't meant for the Watch. Once, I thought I would go with you. I'd dreamed that I might. But I'm sorry. I won't."

Her hand was trembling, as though she were afraid of him, and that broke him as hard as the day he found his sister dead. He gently squeezed her hand, lifted it slowly to his lips so as not to frighten her further, and kissed it, barely brushing his lips against her fingertips. "I wish it were different. All I could think of the whole time you were gone was bringing you back. All I wanted was to spend my days with you, no matter what it cost."

Tears trickled down her cheeks, but still she didn't embrace him. "Thank you for coming for me. I owe you my life, and I won't forget that."

But she still wouldn't come with him, the unspoken truth a weight around his neck, choking the air out of him.

"I still love you," he said.

She closed her eyes and nodded quickly, wiping her tears

away. "I know, and trust me, that means more than you can guess."

She said nothing more.

The room was suddenly too small. He needed to leave. Brenwick, the Rest, even Cori. He needed to put all of it behind. He let her fingers drop, then turned and stepped out of the room and out of her life.

He took a deep, shuddering breath of freezing cold air.

It hurt.

But only for a moment. Cold reason embraced him, and he saw and thought as clearly as he ever had.

"Thanks," he whispered.

You're welcome.

Veynar shoved his hands into the pockets of his cloak. He left Caelen's Rest alone, leaving only footprints in the snow behind.

Also by Ryan Kirk

Testaments of the Forsaken

A Day for Dead Saints

The Legend of Adani

Born of Light and Shadow

From Shadow to Flame

The Ascension of Light

Children of Light and Shadow

Legacy of Light and Shadow

A War of Light and Shadow

Waterstone

The Rise of Shadow

The Shadows Beyond

The Last Sword of the West

Last Sword in the West

Eyes of the Hidden World

A Sword Named Vengeance

Wraith's Revenge

Frontier's End

Song of the Sagani

Legend of the Sword in the West

Nightblade

Nightblade

World's Edge

The Wind and the Void

Blades of the Fallen

Nightblade's Vengeance

Nightblade's Honor

Nightblade's End

Saga of the Broken Gods

Band of Broken Gods

Fall of Forgotten Gods

Rise of the Resurrected God

Oblivion's Gate

The Gate Beyond Oblivion

The Gates of Memory

The Gate to Redemption

Relentless

Relentless Souls

Heart of Defiance

Their Spirit Unbroken

The Sentinels Saga (with Taylor Crook)

Path of the Eternal Sun

A Path Divided

A Path Reforged

Primal

Primal Dawn

Primal Darkness

Primal Destiny

Song of the Fallen Swords

These Fallen Swords

Night of Sword and Shield

Song of Rising Shadow

The Silence Between the Songs

Elegy of the Fallen Swords

Standalone Novels

The Last Fang of God

Blades of Shadow: A Nightblade Story

Of Blood and Broken Dreams

About the Author

Ryan Kirk is the award-winning and internationally bestselling author of over thirty fantasy novels spanning nearly a dozen worlds. He lives in Minnesota with his family, where he enjoys long, meandering walks outside even when the snow is high enough to cover his legs. When he isn't glued to his keyboard, he's usually in the woods, either on foot or on bike.

 facebook.com/waterstonemedia
 instagram.com/authorryankirk
 bookbub.com/authors/ryan-kirk

A small press bound by the belief that every voice matters.

Sign up for our newsletter to learn about new releases and more.
https://oliver-heberbooks.com/subscribe/

Follow us on social media:

facebook.com/oliverheberbooks
instagram.com/oliverheberbooks
amazon.com/oliverheberbooks
youtube.com/@OliverHeberBooksPublisher

www.ingramcontent.com/pod-product-compliance
Lightning Source LLC
LaVergne TN
LVHW041905070526
838199LV00051BA/2500